Praise for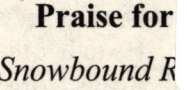

Snowbound R

CARLA KELLY

'I have run out of complimentary words for
Carla Kelly. Just don't miss her stories. They are
always stirring, heartfelt, and memorable.'
—*Amazon* review
on *A Naval Surgeon to Fight For*

JOANNA JOHNSON

'Joanna Johnson's lively writing flows across the
page with pace at times yet sensitively lingers at
moments of tenderness and sensuality drawing the
reader in.'
—*Goodreads* review
on *The Return of Her Long-Lost Husband*

SAMANTHA HASTINGS

'Hastings does a fabulous job of creating a fun,
entertaining and swoony Regency romance that
has pockets of intrigue and danger.'
—*Goodreads* review
on *Wedded to His Enemy Debutante*

Carla Kelly started writing Regency romances because of her interest in the Napoleonic Wars, and she enjoys writing about warfare at sea and the ordinary people of the British Isles rather than lords and ladies. In her spare time she reads British crime and history. Carla lives in Idaho and is a former seasonal park ranger and double RITA® Award and Spur Award winner. She has five children and five grandchildren.

Joanna Johnson lives in a little village with her husband and too many books. After completing an English degree at university she went on to work in publishing, although she always wished she was working on her own books rather than other people's. This dream came true in 2018, when she signed her first contract with Mills & Boon, and she hasn't looked back, spending her time getting lost in mainly Regency history and wishing it was acceptable to write a manuscript using a quill.

Samantha Hastings met her husband in a turkey sandwich queue. They live in Salt Lake City, Utah, where she spends most of her time reading, having tea parties and chasing her kids. She has degrees from Brigham Young University, the University of North Texas and the University of Reading. She's the author of *The Last Word*, *The Invention of Sophie Carter*, *A Royal Christmas Quandary*, *The Girl with the Golden Eyes*, *Jane Austen Trivia*, *The Duchess Contract*, *Secret of the Sonnets* and *A Novel Disguise*. She also writes cosy murder mysteries under the name Samantha Larsen. Learn more at her website, SamanthaHastings.com, and connect with her on social media: X @HastingSamantha, Instagram @SamanthaHastingsAuthor and Facebook @SamanthaHastingsAuthor.

SNOWBOUND REGENCY CHRISTMAS

Carla Kelly,
Joanna Johnson
and
Samantha Hastings

MILLS & BOON

First published in Great Britain 2025
by Mills & Boon, an imprint of HarperCollins*Publishers* Ltd,
1 London Bridge Street, London, SE1 9GF

www.harpercollins.co.uk

HarperCollins*Publishers*, Macken House, 39/40 Mayor Street Upper,
Dublin 1, D01 C9W8, Ireland

Snowbound Regency Christmas
© 2025 Harlequin Enterprises ULC

A Christmas Houseguest © 2025 Carla Kelly
Their Yuletide Reunion © 2025 Joanna Johnson
The Christmas Husband Charade © 2025 Samantha Hastings

ISBN: 978-0-263-34541-4

11/25

MIX
Paper | Supporting
responsible forestry
FSC™ C007454

This book contains FSC™ certified paper
and other controlled sources to ensure responsible forest management.

For more information visit www.harpercollins.co.uk/green.

Printed and Bound in the UK using 100% Renewable Electricity
at CPI Group (UK) Ltd, Croydon, CR0 4YY

CONTENTS

A CHRISTMAS HOUSEGUEST

Carla Kelly

Dedicated to parents everywhere who seem like islands of calm in a chaotic world. We, their children, learned later that they were only picking their way through life, hoping for the best, the same as we are.

Chapter One

Not long before Christmas 1811

An orphan of many years, Sailing Master Andrew Hadfield, Royal Navy, never expected much mail. From his earliest days at sea, he expected nothing except official directives as his career advanced. A warranted officer, he waited for such a letter now from the Navy Board, assigning him to another ship, once he was cleared to depart from hospital.

Safely ashore at Stonehouse Hospital in Devonport, he was several months into recovery from two hungry years captive of the French in a Spanish prison overlooking the Bay of Biscay. The bosun's mate died soon after their arrival at the naval hospital, and Captain Tate had been released from the officers' ward in another block. Four remained.

Before he left, Captain Tate promised to invite Andrew to spend Christmas with his family in Kent. 'I owe you my life, Master Hadfield,' he told Andrew as his son helped him from the ward.

He did. Captain Tate had been too weak to survive under his own power after they tied a rope made of every rag they wore, and shinnied naked down the outer wall of their prison. Two of their number fell to their deaths. When the makeshift rope ran out, Andrew grabbed the captain and jumped into the ocean.

It had been the effort of Andrew's life to swim toward an alert Fast Dispatch Vessel sailing for England. Exhausted by even the skinny weight of Captain Tate on his back, Andrew barely survived. The FDV hauled them aboard and sailed back to the blockade to transfer them, the captain deeming them in too desperate a situation for even the short dash to Portsmouth.

Reeking and filthy, the escapees suffered further as buckets of sea water were poured on them on the blockader's deck. Andrew took cold comfort in knowing any who died of *that* shock would be buried at sea, and not dumped in the prison's hog pen.

Captain Tate must have forgotten about the invitation once he left Stonehouse; no letter came. No matter. Andrew prepared to spend Christmas in the ward, assisting the tough-as-nails matron. That Navy Board letter would come soon, announcing his next ship.

As he ate and rested, Andy Hadfield discovered another healing property of Stonehouse Hospital: The constant stress of his naval calling rested more lightly upon him there. Because of his special gift with nautical mathematics, he had become a sailing master. From the captain down, every tar knew Andrew's value, and with value came unending stress.

As a master, he was responsible for a ship's trim, the weight balance from bow to stern and optimizing of sails to keep a ship afloat and dangerous to the enemy. Every lieutenant on a frigate outranked him, but all deferred to his quarterdeck command in battle. Sailing masters knew their killing trade.

Last night's gathering after the evening meal gave him food for thought. The bosun was a wise man, and everyone listened when he spoke. 'Lads, I've been thinking: Christmas is nearly upon us. Just for fun, if you could ask for any present, what would you like?'

First there was good-natured laughter from men who never received gifts, and who had probably been at sea for all Christmases since King Louis lost his head and Napoleon set Europe ablaze with his ambition.

Silence, then a foretopman spoke. 'My gift to myself? Passage to America. I'll become a Yankee.'

Hoots and laughter followed. The cook wished for a sponge cake with gooey icing, which brought enthusiastic applause. The carpenter's mate wanted his tools back, left behind when their frigate sank and they had no choice but to swim to Spain and surrender.

'What would you make?' someone asked. The carpenter nudged the foretopman. 'I'll build you a nice cabin in America!'

They looked at him. Andrew tried to shrug off their attention. 'It's nothing,' he attempted to answer, but the others were having none of it. 'Confess, Master Hadfield,' the bosun bellowed in his official loud voice.

'Very well, you miscreants,' Andrew said, which

brought smiles. 'I have no family.' He took a deep breath. 'Just once, I want someone pretty to see me off from the dock before a voyage. Oh, and be there when I returned.'

Trust the bosun. 'Master, they're not pretty, but any number of terrified midshipmen would be happy to see you off, provided they could stay behind!'

'I have frightened some,' Andrew admitted, when the good-natured laughter died. 'Some—I call them successful—probably never put a feather in the hold without making sure the weight won't affect the ship's speed.'

'Good for them,' the bosun said, then yawned. ''Tis late, lads. Here's one more Christmas gift to think on— what gift would you like to *give*?'

Then it was time for more food—they could never get full—and final rounds from the overworked surgeon. The matron made her last round; quiet reigned.

Andrew thought of the bosun's question. Last week, a wife had arrived at the hospital, letter in hand. 'Marshall? Marshall?'

The other surviving foretopman gasped. He held out his left arm, the right severed at the wrist during that first year in prison. Now he had a hook. 'My love, you came! I wrote and you finally came.'

Andrew watched as she ran to her husband's bedside, and gathered him in a tight embrace. When they could speak, the words tumbled out. Marshall's letter sent to their Bristol address had gone astray. 'We moved. Willie and I returned to my father's farm.' She waved the much-travelled letter. 'This arrived two days ago. Let's go home, Marshall.'

'Amy, I have a hook,' he sobbed. 'I am useless!'

Andrew remembered the wife's gentle words. 'Silly. There's work on the farm.'

Andrew knew he would never forget what happened next. She pressed her forehead against her husband's. 'Dearest, I gave you my whole heart, as you gave me yours. We have enough.'

That's what I would give, Andrew thought, as he settled himself for sleep. *My Christmas gift would be my whole heart to someone.*

Chapter Two

Next morning at his usual spot in the mess hall for ambulatories, Andrew found a page torn from what looked like a recent edition of the *Naval Chronicle*, that dry-as-toast journal of fleet actions and promotions. He put too much sugar in his porridge, stirred and read.

'Well, I'll be…'

'Bad news?' the matron asked, as she buttered toast for a one-armed man.

'No.' He laughed and held it out. 'Mrs Mason, it seems that I am a hero.' He looked around at his fellow shipmates and prisoners, engaged in conversation and eating, always eating, even as he did. 'Read it.'

She did. He knew she was a no-nonsense nurse. She had seen everything, except perhaps such an article. She stared at him. 'You, Master?'

'Me, which shows you how little the chap who wrote this knows about prisoners.' He tapped the article when she handed it back. 'We were in that bloody hell on earth together. No heroes. Just us.'

To his further surprise, in mere minutes, the medical

director of Stonehouse himself turned up, fairly bursting with enthusiasm. As Andrew tried to sprinkle more sugar on his porridge, Chief Surgeon Holyoke grabbed his arm, spraying sugar across the table. 'Master Hadfield, look!' He held the current *Naval Chronicle* in its entirety. 'Read.'

Andrew put down his now-empty spoon and held out his scrap of the article. 'This came my way. Our little swim off the Spanish coast has made us famous.'

'More than that,' the chief said, and turned his attention to the matron. 'Mrs Mason, our sailing master here has been called a hero for swimming with Captain Tate on his back.'

Andrew picked up his spoon and dug in for more sugar, embarrassed at the attention. He was not an acclaim-seeker. 'Any of us would have done it,' he murmured, wanting the conversation over. 'I happened to be clos-est to him.'

The surgeon was having none of that. He waved his arm around the table, where Andrew's fellow escapees were seated and watching this little to-do with interest. 'The Royal Navy has declared your sailing master a hero for carrying Captain Tate on his back through stormy seas to the blockade. What say you?'

Lord help me, Andrew thought, as his partners in terror and incarceration cheered.

'See there?' the chief said. His expression sobered and he tried another tack. 'The more this dismal war grinds on, the more we need our heroes.'

'I'm no hero,' Andy protested, but softly this time, because his protestation was going nowhere. 'I did my duty. We all did.'

Chief Surgeon Holyoke then gave him more to stew about. 'Very well, sir, I won't tease you.' He chuckled. 'But I have to say that all the wounded officers in Block Two are reading their *Chronicle*s. The word is out. You might find yourself the center of attention.'

Oh, Lord no. So much for his plans to rest in hospital until he got that letter from the Navy Board. Holyoke himself had hinted only yesterday that since he was more sound of mind and limb, he could take leave for a week or so.

But go where? He had been an orphan since thirteen, workhouse escapee and the personal property of the Royal Navy because Napoleon's never-ending war was, well, never-ending. Even the idea of leave was foreign to Andrew Hadfield, who hadn't been long off a ship in years, except to be captured.

He mulled the matter around, walking up and down the ward, sitting beside other sailors worse off than any of his men now, who were in various stages of recovery. It was clear that Stonehouse needed the bed he would vacate. He paid a visit to the chief surgeon, finding Holyoke in his office behind mounds of paper. Andrew smiled at the sight, which earned him a glare from the surgeon, and then a sigh.

'Do you know, Master Hadfield, there are days I miss the chaos of life aboard ship?'

'I do not doubt you, sir,' Andrew said. He didn't care for paperwork, either. As nasty, terror-filled and boring beyond belief his prison days had been, he never once missed the tedium of his daily entry in the ship's log. For some reason known only to God or Neptune, a ship's sailing master kept the official log, not the captain. Andrew had yet to meet a master who relished that exacting task.

'What is on your mind, Master?'

'Sir, you mentioned I could leave for a week or so,' he said. 'How do I get approval?'

The chief pushed aside some of the paper. 'I must declare you fit enough to stagger about, and have your signature to the effect that I have not lost my mind in so doing.'

Right there in the admin block, Holyoke listened to his heart and lungs, prodded a little here and there and signed a paper testifying that Andrew Hadfield, sailing master, thirty-seven years old and possessed of all his parts, was sound enough to inflict himself upon the world again.

It came with a caution. 'Do not exert yourself, Master,' the chief said, his expression serious. 'Your entire ordeal might recall itself to your mind in ways you have not anticipated.'

'That sounds ominous and cautionary.'

'It should. I mean it.'

But where was he going? He had no family. He mentioned his dilemma at dinner, and his fellow crewmen had all manner of ribald and hilarious suggestions, none of which appealed. He finally decided on the most prosaic of destinations: nearby Plymouth and more specifically, the Drake, favoured hotel of the officer class. He had two mundane tasks in Plymouth, both of which were necessary. Maybe something else would occur to him.

Two days later, Master Hadfield sprang himself from Stonehouse with a few misgivings that surfaced almost immediately, to his dismay. Burdened solely by a tattered, hand-me-down and nearly empty duffel slung over his shoulder, he discovered that walking from the Stonehouse quadrangle to the nearest hackney stand exhausted him. He considered returning to the safety of the hospital.

Andy's misgivings receded, mainly because the short ride to Plymouth restored him sufficiently. Even more positive was his visit to Carter and Brustein, where the chief accountant happily knew what to do with Andrew's official voucher for two years' back pay.

His additional request for cash in hand to refurbish himself and finance a Christmas visit somewhere also met with enthusiasm. 'With this voucher and your already-existing prize money, you're doing well, sir,' the accountant said, which Andrew suspected was high praise. Accountants were built that way. 'Name the amount, and I will send you on your merry way.'

Maddy and Son's Clothier was his next stop, to be measured for badly needed new uniforms. Arriving naked on the deck of the blockader had been followed by a borrowed nightshirt, then cast-off clothing at Stonehouse from less-fortunate warrant officers who didn't survive the hospital. He was no clothes horse, but disliked being this shabby.

Maddy's wasn't far from Carter and Brustein's, but he stopped several times to rest, sitting on a bench by the water. The wintry breeze seemed to whistle through his skull, reminding him of the chief surgeon's caution: 'Do not, I repeat, do *not* overexert yourself.'

To his relief, the clothier shop was warm. Andy spent the next hour nodding where needed as the tailor measured him for new uniforms. He asked the tailor that trousers, shirts and coats be left a little roomier, because he was still putting on weight, or hoping to, after that sojourn in a Spanish *fortaleza* where food was scarce and beatings regular.

The tailor came to attention at that news. 'You were one of those gallant men who escaped and swam to the blockade?'

'Aye, we did. Where did you…?'

The tailor waved his tape measure around, indicating the universe at large. 'Everyone knows. And one of your number carried the captain on his back?'

'Aye, one did.' That was all Andrew said about the matter. His intention now was to go to the Drake, Mrs Fillion's marvelous inn, and eat. He knew the doughty lady well enough to know that plenty of heroes passed in and out of the Drake. He wouldn't be noticed.

'Master Hadfield, where should we send your new uniforms?'

'I suppose my order will take some time?' he asked, unsure what address to leave. He knew the Drake would store whatever he had ordered from Maddy's until his return from anywhere—to be determined—even Bangkok, for that matter. 'I suppose the Drake is best. I realize that Christmas is no time to demand uniforms.'

'Master Hadfield, your order goes to the top of the

list,' Mr Maddy himself said firmly, when he totted up the bill. 'You're a hero.'

Sigh. A hero.

Andy took a careful stroll to the Drake, still embarrassed that a mere walk exhausted him. He gave Mrs Fillion the now-traditional kiss on the cheek that every mariner administered, and asked for a second-floor room. She held out the key, and being Mrs Fillion, couldn't help a saucy comment.

'Master Hadfield, if you ever marry, I will put you and your wife on the third floor at the back, the quiet floor for couples long away from each other, thanks to Boney and the blockade.'

He refused to let her embarrass him, because truth to tell, he liked Mrs Fillion. They all did. 'No woman is that brave, my dear,' he teased in turn.

'These are your best years,' she reminded him.

Then why do I feel eighty? he asked himself.

Andrew considered the matter after his dinner of beef roast, chicken, a mound of potatoes and two puddings. When Mrs Fillion circulated among the tables, he remembered the clothing he ordered and gestured to her.

'Mrs F, I have ordered new uniforms, well, new everything,' he said. 'I wonder, could I leave them in your storeroom, if I do decide to travel a bit?'

'Aye, you may. Come with me.'

He followed her into the kitchen, where he snagged two biscuits, then down steep stairs to the storeroom he remembered. He paused in the doorway, seeing trunks, books, rain slickers and boxes. The sight drew him up sharply, because he knew that many of the long-stored items could never be reclaimed by dead men.

'There's the whole history of Napoleon's wars here,' he said.

'Aye, lad. It always gives even *me* a start when I open the door.' She stood a moment, then directed him to the right. 'There's some space here. You tell me if you think it is enough. Your new hat will take up some space.'

He observed a tidy area. 'This is fine. I shouldn't need you to keep it long.'

A grimy letter, stuck half under a box on the shelf below, caught his eye—rather, the name did. He looked closer, then reached for it. He blew off the dust, remembering precisely when he had written it to a widow. 'Mrs Fillion, this is a relic from the Nile. I left it here by mistake. I know what I will do now.'

'You mean you won't stay here and eat?' She looked at the name and sighed. 'My goodness. The Battle of the Nile. Isn't that what you chaps called it?'

'Or the Battle of Aboukir Bay.' He gestured to the letter. 'You remember Sailing Master Edward Hale, don't you?'

She nodded. 'He loved to talk about his wife and their daughter, Sadie.' She touched the name, running her finger across it. 'Didn't you…? Weren't you…?'

'Aye. I was his mate at the battle. He died in my arms and I became the sailing master,' Andrew said, remembering too vividly the yard-long splinter from the quarterdeck railing that flew into Master Hale's neck, killing him instantly. Once he set his mentor down on the bloody deck and moved to the master's position, Andrew's own course had been charted.

It was a gamble, at best. Mrs Hale had long known of her husband's passing, but the forgotten letter became his purpose. 'Mrs Fillion, I've known Edward's widow and Sadie for many years. I believe I will look for her at Endicott, their last address. This is only my account of the battle but she might like it. Endicott isn't far from here, is it?'

'Nay, lad. Ten miles maybe.' Mrs Fillion started toward the open door. 'I know she wasn't a young woman, but it's been no more than…than…'

'Almost thirteen years,' he said, thinking of where his life had taken him since then. There were times in prison when a day seemed to stretch into a fortnight. Thirteen years. 'Not that long. I'll find her.'

Chapter Three

Andrew spent the rest of the evening observing the Drake's perpetual whist game. The other officers knew who he was and what he had endured. The whispers went around, but they were too kind—or too involved in whist—to question him, which suited him.

Back in his room, he put the letter in his nearly empty duffel bag. It was a small thing, something easily overlooked. He had meant to give it to Mrs Fillion to mail to the sailing master's widow, because there was no time for even a short trip of consolation to Endicott.

'Are you still there, Mary?' he asked out loud. 'I earnestly hope so.'

He lay wide awake for the longest time, remembering the battle in Aboukir Bay, falling masts, decks splintered at close range and the fearful explosion of the French *L'Orient*, close enough for his *Leander* to feel the sudden heat. He knew Aboukir Bay had been his first mention in the *Naval Chronicle*, because his captain cited his courage under the guns of *Spartiate* and *Tonnant*, and the death of Master Hale, well-known in the fleet.

He barely slept, and woke to bad weather, which went from bad to worse during breakfast, rain becoming sleet, then snow and icy roads. It may have matched his mood, thinking of the undelivered letter, but he was impatient to be off.

To his chagrin, not even the mail coach moved from Plymouth until mid-morning. Before he left the Drake, Mrs Fillion handed Andrew two slices of bread and meat, delivered with apology in her eyes. He ate the sandwich before he was halfway down the road, unable to resist food.

He made himself comfortable in the mail coach, seated in a corner with his borrowed boat cloak to keep him warm. He regarded his companion travellers with interest, mainly because one stood out.

She was a lovely English beauty, the quiet kind. Her hair, brown with red highlights, was pulled back into a bun low on her neck. She glanced at him once or twice, out of blue English eyes the hue of his own.

He knew from Mediterranean experience that women of Italy and Spain powdered themselves to get that delicate blush. This lady needed no embellishment. He admired her, happy to know that England still produced the fairest flowers.

Seated close to her and leaning against her arm was a little chap. The two of them made a pretty picture, clearly mother and son. So much for his wandering thoughts.

Or not. The next person to board was a younger woman cut from the same cloth as the first beauty. He noticed the baby bulge that even a cloak couldn't hide. When she touched the little boy's head, Andy noticed a gold band. He laughed to himself, surmising now that this was a mother and son, and Pretty Lady perhaps an older sister.

The last person to board plumped herself down beside him. She wore a winter hat that had seen a few years, like its owner. She wedged a large basket with eggs and bread between them.

No one said anything. He knew he had no leave to brazen up a conversation with women as ordinary as himself, but who appeared well-mannered. It would be a silent trip, and a short one. Endicott was eleven miles away.

So he thought, except that the journey became an ordeal, thanks to the weather. In the space of an hour, he learned how ill-prepared he was, how utterly useless.

They made adequate time, until the road turned icy. The coachman slowed down immediately. The same could not be said for a post-chaise, whose outrider, coated with ice, tried to pass the mail coach. The result was two of the post horses down and the chaise spinning around and blocking the whole road. From the look of his front leg, one horse would never rise again. The other flailed and kicked, striking the horse behind him, which took exception and bit the animal. Hysterical shrieks inside the chaise made Andy wince.

The mail coach couldn't move forward, plain and simple. It couldn't turn around, as other vehicles piled up behind. The post rider did the necessary thing. He took out a pistol.

Pretty Lady across from him closed her book, her face a study in concern. 'Bess, Papa would have a fit if he knew what was going on,' she said. 'Cover Ben's eyes and ears.'

Bess obeyed, then turned her face into her sister's shoulder, which told Andy worlds about both women, because he knew what command looked like. Pretty Lady stared at her lap as the post rider fired.

Egg Lady, seated next to him, shook her head. 'Now there's a bloke without a job.'

To his surprise, Pretty Lady acknowledged him. 'Sir, you do not see this sort of thing at sea.'

'Not horses,' he replied, pleased she didn't mind conversation with a stranger. 'Not even mermaids,' he added, which made her smile.

The other horse thrashed about, but the road was too icy to attempt raising the animal. It kicked slower and slower, resigned to its own fate, as other wagons and vehicles piled up behind the mail coach, with the post-chaise blocking the entire road in both directions.

Hours passed as carters and drivers milled about, then retreated to their own vehicles to wait. The sisters whispered among themselves, Egg Lady slept and Andrew shivered. Worse yet, Andy felt his still-shrunken stomach growling. He possessed no warmth or strength to deal with this, except he knew that he had to.

Something worse happened, something unexpected. His ordinarily rational mind, used to hardship, suddenly yanked him back to that hated prison, where he recalled one awful night. The most sadistic of their keepers left a plate of roast beef and buttered bread outside the grate where prison food was usually shoved in. They saw and smelled the food, but could not reach it. The memory became reality again, rendering Andy nearly helpless.

It became too much. His remembered trauma landed him back in prison. A wooden door in his mind swung shut, as it had two years ago. To his horror, he began to weep. 'I'm sorry,' he gasped between bouts of tears.

Escape. He had done it once before. He tried to leave the coach. Instead, he dropped to his knees and fainted.

He came around quickly enough. Egg Lady held him tight, right there on the floor of the coach. 'What has the war done to you?' she murmured, as Pretty Lady wiped his forehead. Good God, how could he be *sweating*? But he was.

'Food. Anything,' Andy managed to say. 'I've been a prisoner of the French. It's hard…can't explain…so hungry.'

'No need to explain,' Egg Lady said. She handed him half a loaf of bread. 'An egg,' Andrew urged, 'please,' appalled that he sounded like a beggar and not a sailing master, respected by captain and crew.

She dug a little well in the loaf, cracked in two raw eggs, and held it to his mouth. He swallowed the eggs and chewed on the bread until he felt rational again.

He sat back, still in Egg Lady's embrace, and spoke to Pretty Lady. 'I spent the last two years imprisoned in Spain, courtesy of the French,' he said quietly. 'Cold. No food. I thought I was done with that ordeal, but it came back now. Forgive me.'

'There's nothing to forgive,' Pretty Lady said, her eyes kind. To Andy's both relief and humiliation, she took charge. 'I will see what we can do. Stay here, Ben,' she told the boy. 'Bess, stay inside. We can't have you falling.'

Andrew heard her talking to the coachman, who stuck his head in and explained their situation. 'Air's warming a tad, sir. All it takes is a little degree or two. No snow now. We'll be moving eventually.' He shook his head at the post-chaise stalled in front of them. 'Poor horses. I treat mine better.'

Egg Lady tried to straighten up. 'Ooh, I'm not used to this. Old bones.'

'Let me help you.'

Pretty Lady was stronger than Andy would have thought. She helped him to his seat first, then guided Egg Lady back to her place. She calmly took charge.

She seemed to understand Andrew's embarrassment. 'I'm certain your trials outweigh any of ours. I can do this.'

He saw only concern on her face. 'I am Sailing Master Andrew Hadfield. I should have stayed in hospital.' That sounded stupid, but his well was dry.

'I'm Rose Harte. This is my sister, Bess Wilkins, and her Ben. Let me help you.'

'I'm so ashamed.'

'No worries, sir.'

Andy wanted the bottom to drop out of the mail coach, and the road to open and swallow him whole. Instead, he listened as the sisters conferred.

Bess whispered to her son, who seated himself next to Andy. 'Now, sir,' Bess said, 'I am going to wrap your cloak around you both. Ben is chilly. You can keep each other warm.'

Andy's arm went around Ben, who smiled at him and snuggled close. 'There you are.' She looked at her sister, standing in the coach door. 'What now, Rosie?'

'I have an idea.'

She was gone only a few minutes. When she returned, her cheeks were even rosier. If he hadn't felt so useless, Andy knew he could have enjoyed the moment. Rosie, she was.

'Here's what I did, sir,' she said to him. 'The post rider has removed both horses. He still has two, of course. I petitioned our coachman to ask the post riders with the chaise if they can take you to Endicott with them. Since this is a mail coach, our driver must make two stops before we get there. The chaise will go straight through, even with only two horses.'

He wanted to tell them he could manage, except that he knew he couldn't. 'Thank you,' he said. 'So kind.'

The wait continued. Ben was a warm little furnace, as Bess predicted. Andy's eyes were closing when the mail coachman opened the door a crack. 'Sir, that post-chaise is free now. I will ask the occupants if you can accompany them as far as Endicott, where there is a good inn.' He brightened. 'I'll tell 'um you are a sailor what kept blokes like us safe from the Frogs. We'll see.'

In minutes, their coachman returned, angry. 'The post rider agreed, but his passengers won't hear of it. "A sailor might murder us for our money," that wretched woman said!' A muscle in his jaw worked. 'They'll be gone in a few minutes, and good riddance. We will get sorted out soon. I'm sorry, sir. It's a slow ride for you, after all.'

His glum expression nearly broke Andrew's heart. 'I am sorry you had to ask.' He looked at the goodness around him. 'I'll manage. I've had some food.'

In minutes, Ben snuggled close and returned to sleep, giving off marvelous warmth. Egg Lady cracked two more eggs into a cup, stirred vigorously and gave it to Andy. Nothing ever tasted better.

He had closed his eyes when the coachman called down from his perch. 'We're next in line!'

The sisters whispered together. 'Sir, my husband will meet us at Endicott. We'll try to get you to… Where?' Bess asked.

'The local inn,' Andrew told her. 'I am trying to locate the widow of a sailing master who died at the Battle of the Nile.'

'Your world is so far away from ours, and certainly more consequential,' Pretty Lady told him. 'We owe you a debt for keeping us safe from Napoleon.'

I owe you a debt for kindness, he thought. *I had forgotten how kindness felt.*

Chapter Four

Rosie Harte waited until the navy man slept. There was no denying the exhaustion on his face. Working in Plymouth, with occasional ventures beyond the ledgers and clerks of Gooding's Maritime Naval Stores, had acquainted her with navy men of firm expression, tight lips and abundant wrinkles, especially around their eyes. This man seated across from her had the same look, except he was entirely depleted.

'Such men have stories to tell,' she whispered to Bess.

Her little sister could be a tease. 'Rosie, Mr Gooding probably did you a favour, keeping you safe inside from navy men and their yarns!'

'Aye,' Rosie replied with both feeling and affection. 'You might be right.' She sighed. 'This one sounds genuine. Prison? Imagine.'

She returned to her book, determined not to worry, as the coachman picked his careful way along a route travelled faster in better weather. She knew Papa would be waiting for her in Endicott, whether the roads were passable or not. That was Papa.

She thought about the comforts of home. Aunt Dorothea Hudgens would have a hot meal ready, accompanied with her good-natured scolding about how her precious niece was living in a dangerous town with sailors on the lookout for vulnerable females. *I am not a vulnerable female*, Rosie thought. Still, it pleased her to know that someone loved her enough to worry.

She looked at the navy man, wondering if anyone in his life worried about him. She decided no, not if his destination was an inn at Christmastime.

Her thoughts took her home. Aunt Dorothea, widowed and childless, had cared for Papa and her nieces as long as Rosie could remember. When Papa stewed over whether his oldest child should leave his prosperous farm for God-help-us Plymouth, Aunt Hudgens calmly assured him that ladies had brains, too.

Rosie had used her brains for eight years. She was single, and possessed of a modest income. Lately, though, something had entered her heart, turned around a few times like a dog before the hearth and made itself at home. That vague 'something' reminded her every time she saw Bess so happy with her husband and child, and another on the way. At twenty-seven, Rosie knew she didn't want domestic life to pass her by.

Eight years earlier, she had no qualms about taking a position as clerk at Gooding's Maritime Naval Stores in Plymouth, even though such ambition in a woman was rare. She smiled at the memory. Dear Vicar Ewing of St. Timothy's had been her teacher in his school for parish children unburdened by tutors and wealthy parents.

It had been the vicar who cajoled his sister's husband, John Gooding, to take on his numbers-minded student in his business. The job came with a comfortable room on the upper floor above the store. She never expected to be paid as well as the men, even if her skills equalled theirs. That was how the world worked.

There were other considerations. Aunt Dorothea was not getting one minute younger. Rosie knew her aunt had maintained her own house in Endicott, even though she lived at the farm. She hadn't begrudged caring for two motherless girls and keeping her brother's house. Perhaps Rosie could relieve her dear aunt of the toil and let her return home. Rosie knew she could keep house, if no suitor showed up. She was already a spinster.

Rosie looked up from her contemplation of her gloves. She could barely see the sailing master as dusk approached. Rosie couldn't recall a time when she had missed even one meal. *Does one catch up on food, after years as a prisoner?* she asked herself. Unlikely.

'Think,' he muttered. Nothing more.

Surprised, she watched him, aware she had no idea how men managed their lives on fighting ships, her nation's defenders. She thought of salt beef, yards of canvas and buckets of smelly tar that she carefully balanced with precision in Mr Gooding's ledgers. *Her* navy had been reduced to numbers in a ledger, and here was a navy man mumbling in his sleep, 'Think.'

She smiled when Bess snuggled close, much as Ben kept company with the sleeping man. She felt her sister surrender to sleep, leaving Rosie to worry about the icy road and the patient horses trained to bit and harness in all weather.

Rosie glanced at the sleeping Egg Lady. Now it was *her* job to oversee everyone's safe arrival at Endicott, since only she was awake.

So she thought. Rosie turned her attention to the sailing master, whose eyes were open now. She wondered if he could take some gentle humour. Why not? She would surely never see him again.

'See here, sir,' she whispered. 'It is *my* watch. You are at perfect leisure to sleep.'

He chuckled. Weary, threadbare and taxed to the limit, at least he could laugh. It was forward of her to quiz a stranger. He could reply or ignore her.

'That is usually my occupation,' he said, keeping his voice low. 'I spent two years watching over a skinny bunch of tars in prison. Duty dies hard.'

'Or not at all,' she replied. He didn't seem like someone who engaged in small talk.

He sighed. 'And so I think things through.'

He sounded weary. It was brazen of her, but she reached across the small space separating them and touched his ragged cloak. 'Truly, it's my turn. Sleep.'

He did. She sat there, comfortable in Bess's warmth, Bess a trusting little sister through trying times, and now a treasured wife to a good man. *Bess dear, I could envy you, if I didn't love you*, she thought.

So Rosie Harte watched over them. Not far from Endicott, she felt the road ice up again, with corresponding caution from horses and coachman, who watched over them all, and the Royal Mail in its padlocked box.

Their stops at small villages were quickly accomplished. Finally, through swirling snow, Rosie saw Endicott. She wondered if Mr Coachman would blow on his yard of tin in this silent world. He did, because his horses were tired and there were fresh ones waiting for the harness and the continuing trip taking them through other slumbering villages toward Exeter.

Everyone woke up by degrees, sailing master first, then Egg Lady, Bess and Ben.

'Mama, will Papa be here for us?'

'Aye, son,' Bess said. She nudged Rosie. 'Sis, you're a fine pillow.'

The coach swayed as the driver left his perch. He opened the door. 'Endicott, thank the Lord.' He held out his gloved hand for Egg Lady. 'Is someone here for you, goodwife?'

She pointed to an elderly gent picking his way across the frozen ground. Rosie saw her father next, getting down from the familiar gig, with her brother-in-law right behind him in his larger vehicle.

The sailing master waited for his turn to leave the coach. Rosie thought he might object to a hand down from the coachman, but he didn't. 'Still not too steady, sir?'

'Alas, no, Mr Coachman. Is there an inn?'

'Full up,' said the ostler cheerfully, as he reached for the lead horses' harnesses. 'Roads are bad in all directions. You know inns and Christmas, sir.'

'Is there somewhere I can wait?'

Poor man, you are so weary, Rosie thought.

Bess and Ben had already been handed into her husband's gig. Papa held out his hand to her. She looked at the sailing master, who leaned against the mail coach, eyes closed. The navy officers in Plymouth always appeared in control and decisive. This one was tired, he was sick, he was human and he appeared not to know what to do.

Her heart went out to him, and she did something unexpected, against her usually cautious nature. 'Papa, may we help this man? He's a Royal Navy master of some sort who escaped from a Spanish prison. May he stay with us tonight?'

She took Papa's hand and tugged him toward the coach, where the ostler was harnessing the new team. The sailing master opened his eyes at their approach and tried to brace himself in what she was certain was his usual military way. He failed utterly.

Please, Papa, please, she thought.

He didn't fail her, even as Rosie wondered why this mattered so much to her. 'Ho, lad, you're coming with us,' Papa stated firmly. 'Nothing is open in Endicott, and you look like someone who bit off more than he can chew.'

She held her breath. Master Hadfield could easily say no, and do…what? She took his arm, silently begging him not to resist. 'Papa, we're kidnapping this stubborn man and taking him home.'

Papa took his other arm. 'Sir, I never argue with my daughter when she is resolved.'

The sailing master did not resist. In fact, he surprised her, perhaps as much as she had surprised herself.

'Lead on. I've been captured before. Believe me, this is more pleasant. Aye, lead on.'

Chapter Five

Andy had no particular recollection of what followed, except that someone strong helped him onto a wagon seat of a small vehicle he remembered from his own farming boyhood. In no time he was sandwiched between the big man and Rose, who kept her arm around him.

His memory became random. He remembered a farmyard, and then an older lady spooning delicious stew into his mouth like a farmwife feeding an orphan lamb. He hoped it was the farmer who half carried him upstairs and removed his clothing, then dropped his nightshirt down his thin frame.

He remembered saying 'Two years a prisoner will do this,' and that was all. He was done. Not even gale force winds of the velocity around Cape Horn could have roused him.

And yet something did. During the night, he became aware he was muttering in faulty French, back in that prison of the mind that Stonehouse's chief surgeon had warned him against. He panicked and braced for death when the door opened. Instead, he heard a chair moved right beside his bed. In another moment, his hand was clasped in a warm and soft grip, that and nothing more.

Now it was morning. An older fellow occupied the chair, the man he vaguely remembered who had helped him out of his clothes and into bed, surely the father of Rose and Bess. He recognized the same kindness in the eyes remembered from yesterday's ordeal, when he probably made an idiot of himself.

There he was, still at the mercy of others, which should have bothered someone used to command and obedience. Right then, in that pleasant room with icy shards rapping on the window, he knew he could relinquish command. This was a tidy home. He was no prisoner.

'I am Andrew Hadfield, sailing master with the Channel Fleet and currently without a ship,' he said simply. 'You have taken in a real orphan from the storm.'

'I am Frederick Harte and this is my farm.'

Frederick Harte was no poor crofter. Andy sat up, intrigued, hearing the quiet pride. He saw heavy curtains, the sort used to keep out winter's chill. A fire crackled merrily in the hearth. A cat curled up on the armchair closest to it, opening one eye to regard him, then rolling over. Andy admired the multicolored rag rug. 'You run a taut ship,' he said. 'There was another lady, too, and a little boy who kept me warm under a blanket.'

'That was Ben, my grandson. He and I have snuggled a bit. A little furnace, is Ben.'

'He kept me from shaking to pieces,' Andy said frankly. 'Lately, I have the devil of a time getting warm.' He sighed. 'The surgeon at Stonehouse didn't want me to make this trip, but I can be hard to argue with. Ask any of my crew.'

'Spoken like a navy man! Bess Wilkins is Ben's mama and my younger daughter. Her husband's farm abuts mine. Rose is her older sister. She works in Plymouth,' Farmer Harte said and nodded to Andy. 'Come to think of it, for all that she looks so sweet, Rosie can be hard to argue with, too. She refused to take no for an answer last night.' He waved his hand around. 'So here you are.'

Where are my manners? Andy asked himself. 'You are all kindness, but surely there is room in that inn now?'

Farmer Harte waggled his finger. 'I doubt the road is passable. Here you will remain until we can get you safely to Endicott.' He then gave Andy the kind of assessment his own father—rest his soul—would have fixed on a calf that wasn't doing well. 'We will keep you here until *we* decide you are fit enough to move.'

'Mr Harte, I am yours to command.'

That brought a laugh from his host. 'Strange position for you, lad? No fears. There's no doubt you've been through ordeals we never have to endure. We're plain folk, but the food is good here.' He cocked his head toward the door. 'I hear Rosie on the stairs.' He winked. 'They squeak, so don't try to escape her!'

Andy laughed, in spite of his scruffy face needing a shave, and his hair looking worse than usual. Farmer Harte kindly arranged two pillows behind him. The bedding smelled faintly of lavender, so pleasant. He leaned back, savouring the bliss of it all.

The door opened and in came the farmer's pretty

daughter with a tray of food. She set it on the nearby table, and pulled back the curtains on a winter storm.

'I'm glad this didn't happen last night,' she said, 'else we would still be stuck on the open road.'

He knew she must be thinking: *And you would be in even worse state.* He accepted that unspoken implication calmly, as he accepted all bad news in his chaotic life. She had already seen him at his worst, or nearly so. At least he wasn't a prisoner. *I should apologize to them*, he thought and opened his mouth to speak.

She held up her hand. 'No more apologies, sir. Papa reminds me that farm life can be dull, indeed, and we like company. I doubt you have ever been a burden. You are not one now.'

She sounded like she meant it, and Andy relaxed further. '*Au contraire*. I have been, and will continue to be a burden, hiss and byword to unsuspecting midshipmen.'

The farmer laughed at that. 'None of those here. Rosie, I am surprised your aunt didn't come upstairs with you.'

'She's coming,' Rosie said. 'Aunt Dorothea will expect you to clean your plate. She is a tyrant.' It was said with good humour, which told him worlds about the Hartes.

'I will not disappoint her,' he said, then remembered Egg Lady from last night. 'If that kind woman with the eggs had added the crushed eggshells to my emergency menu last night, I'd have eaten them, too.'

Well, blast and damn, he hadn't intended to make her eyes fill. She looked away and collected herself, then moved the dishes from the table to a bed tray. 'No eggshells here, sir. Scrambled eggs, bacon and toast, with kippers on the side and Aunt Dorothea's custard with cinnamon sprinkles.'

She placed the tray on his lap and he dug in, making short work of the best meal in years. He swore he could taste each egg in the custard. To his surprise and then his delight, Rosie Harte watched him with a smile.

'You're enjoying this as much as I am,' he said.

'I am,' she replied, with no embarrassment. 'You've been starved. How do you manage?'

He was full, by God, for the first time in a long while. 'I doubt I will ever be able to linger over a meal, at least until I abandon the fear that once the meal is done, there will be no more. Thank you,' he said simply. What else could he say? Naval life in wartime had a way of occupying a man's mind completely. He didn't know how to explain this unending, grinding hardship.

His eyes leaked a little, damn them. She wiped them with her apron, which smelled of cinnamon. 'Rest.' He did as she directed.

Chapter Six

When he woke hours later, she sat beside his bed, knitting. He watched her, peace in his heart for the first time in years. He realized what she was doing, and he felt immediate kinship.

'Miss Harte, I believe you are standing the watch.'

'That is what you call it?'

'Aye. From a ship of the line to a cutter, someone is ever-watchful.'

'Then I thank *you*,' she said simply. 'In these desperate times, we have cause to thank the Royal Navy.'

She was a woman with no pretensions and no airs and graces. 'Sir, there is a portable commode in the dressing room. If you need assistance, I will call my father.'

There was no point in embarrassment. 'I can manage.'

She left him to it. After the initial dizziness of standing, he managed. His shabby uniform hung in the dressing room. He looked at it, noting that someone had brushed it and heavens, sewed on a loose button. What a household this was.

He got back in bed and relaxed completely. Even in

Stonehouse, he felt obliged to revive as quickly as possible, because those remaining alive were still his charge. He was in charge of no one here, and he liked the feeling.

After a modest interval, Rosie Harte returned. 'Come in,' he said to her knock, and she did, bearing a tray with more of the earlier custard and ale. She was followed by an older woman who bore some resemblance to Miss Harte.

She set the tray on his lap and gestured to the woman. 'This is my Aunt Dorothea Hudgens, Papa's sister. She raised me and my little sister, Bess, after our mother died. If you want to compliment the cook, here she is.'

'Thank you, Mrs Hudgens,' he said, and blew her a kiss, which made both women laugh.

'No one leaves this farm hungry,' Rosie's aunt replied. 'I am Aunt Dorothea to everyone in Endicott, you included now.'

Was that even kinder than good food? As sure as if he belonged there, Andrew felt himself folded into this family. In the face of such kindness, he knew better than to argue. 'Then I thank you, Aunt Dorothea.'

'This snack is just to tide you over. Dinner will come along soon enough,' she said, obviously pleased. 'My brother has declared that since you are a hero to the Royal Navy, you are our hero, too.'

Good God, what was this? 'Um…' was all he had the wit to say. Rosie sat beside his bed after Aunt Dorothea left, moving the tray when he finished.

'Blame my father,' she said. 'When he divested you of your uniform last night, what looked like a page from a journal fell out of your pocket. Here.' From her apron pocket, she took out the article from the *Naval Chronicle*.

'I'm no hero,' Andy insisted.

'I read it. Sounded heroic to me.'

'We were desperate.'

Was there something in his tone that caused her to rest her hand on his arm, even briefly? She gave him an inquiring look, not a look that demanded answers, but one that wanted to know more, if he felt like talking.

To his surprise, he did. At Stonehouse, he left most commentary to the bosun, who liked to talk, and perhaps impress the matron. Still, there were times he felt it might be a relief to tell someone the whole story, if only to assure himself that there was nothing heroic about it: just a day in the life of desperate men.

'Take a seat, Miss Harte.'

'Call me Rosie.'

Was it that simple? 'Very well, Rosie,' he said then, 'I am Andrew. Andy if you choose.' He put his hands behind his head. 'We had been in *la fortaleza* for eleven months. The bosun used burnt firewood on the wall to count the days, which turned into months.'

'It sounds boring,' she said. 'I mean, you probably hadn't a knitter among you.'

He laughed, relieved at her light tone. 'Miss Harte...'

'Rosie.'

He closed his eyes to remember better. 'One of the foretopmen had a nagging cough, and we were so thin. We had to do something. To do nothing meant certain death.'

'Had you planned an escape?'

'We were thinking about making a rope out of our clothing and going down and out through the hole where we...' How to say this?

'I understand perfectly,' she said. 'I assume everything dropped into the ocean.'

He stared at the ceiling. 'The walls were thick, but we knew there was a cell next to ours, probably with prisoners. We never saw them.'

He didn't mean to groan. She touched his arm. 'One night there was a fearful row. We heard it through all that stone. Screams, weeping, pleading...'

Again her hand touched him, resting longer this time. 'I can only tell this once.'

'Once, then.'

'Our door banged open and the French devils forced us into that adjoining cell. Rosie, those prisoners had attempted what *we* were planning, except there was a grate at the bottom of the hole. No one could escape into open water.'

He glanced at her and saw her eyes staring as if into the hole itself. 'The Frogs made us stand there as the tide came in and drowned those men.' He couldn't help his tears. 'They wailed and pleaded and we could do nothing.'

What a churl he was to tell this story. She wept, too, wiping her eyes with her apron, then so kindly wiping his.

'None of us spoke good French, but those fiends made us understand that would be our fate, if we tried to escape.'

As he lay there trying to collect himself, Rosie fetched the carafe of water on the bureau and poured him a drink.

She supported his head with her arm. He didn't really need her help, but he wanted it, craved it.

'But you're here. What did you do?' she asked, when she could speak.

'They left the bodies in that hole. Then one day, they opened our cell and counted out three of us. *Un, deux, trois.* I was number three.'

'Oh God,' was all she said. Her knitting lay in a heap at her feet.

'They took us to that damned and haunted cell and I knew it was over,' he said, 'except it wasn't. We were to gather the men's effects into a pile, perhaps for burning. In the doing, I found a rasping saw someone had hidden.'

He heard her sudden intake of breath. 'Keep breathing, Rosie,' he said, amused in spite of his dire tale.

'I suppose I must,' she murmured. 'You hid it somehow and took it back to your cell like a crazy man.'

'I did. It went into a gap in the stones where the mortar had eroded. There it stayed for months.'

He let her think about that, aware then that the door had opened and Farmer Harte and his sister stood there, transfixed, eyes wide. He leaned closer to Rosie. 'Missy, you had better take that tray from your aunt. It's starting to rattle.'

Without a word, she did as he said, putting it on the table—probably to grow cold, but he didn't mind. Cold or hot, he would eat it. When Rosie looked around, Aunt Dorothea was seated in her chair, and Papa in the window ledge. Andy reminded himself that he was just a sailor and not a gentleman, and patted a spot on his bed. To his surprise and delight, she sat.

'Tell us how you escaped.'

'There was one window in our cell, high up, with four iron bars. For six months, one or another of us stood on someone's shoulders and we sawed away with that little rasp.'

'Noisy,' Farmer Harte commented.

'We worked during thunderstorms, or naval barrages from the blockaders.'

'You could have been easily discovered,' Rosie said.

'To say that we were constantly on edge, expecting them to find out, simply beggars the language,' he said simply. 'Even now, I jump at unexpected noise.'

'I promise not to burp,' Farmer Harte said, which made everyone laugh.

'I will hold you to it, Papa,' Rosie teased him back. She turned her lovely eyes on Andrew. 'You must think we are callous, to laugh at your predicament.'

'Not at all,' he assured them. 'You should have heard some of our jokes. That's how people in tough situations survive.' *May you never know such fear*, he told himself, *especially you, Rosie. May you always be warm and safe.*

The story seemed easier to tell now. 'We worked nearly through the top of two of those bars, but not all. Then we started on the bottom and did the same. Almost but not all. Six months' labour.'

'Are you the most patient man in the universe?' Rosie asked. She had made herself comfortable on his bed, her back against the footrest. He could have reached out and touched her shoe, but he was no fool.

'Patient? I am now. There we were, starving and getting weaker every day.' He sighed. 'Two of our original number died. We were now eight.'

'I would pray for more storms,' Aunt Dorothea said.

'We did, those of us who still believed in anything,' he returned. 'I am among that number, although countless midshipmen and crew I instruct in ship trim, ballast and navigation would doubt it. I am exacting, ma'am, but I believe.'

It sounded silly to his ears, but as he looked at his three hosts, he knew they understood. It gave him heart to continue. 'It was late autumn, when our blockade tends to pull back to avoid the danger of winter storms blowing vessels onto a lee shore.'

Silence. Rosie's eyes were troubled. 'No fears, Rosie. We sawed and starved until we were ready.' He sniffed. 'Do I smell bread on that tray?'

Aunt Dorothea respond quickly. In a moment he had a buttered roll in his hand. She apologized that it wasn't hot from the oven, but he waved that away. 'It is divine. You can't imagine.' He ate quickly, savouring the butter, and had the strength to continue.

'That final day, we watched clouds roll in. After supper—the usual meal, warm water that a chicken ran through on stilts—Captain Tate said this was the night. We were too weak to stay much longer. It was now or never. When the lightning and thunder began, we stripped and tied our clothes together—rags, really—

and did our balancing act to cut through those remaining bits of iron bar.'

Farmer Harte nudged his sister. 'Dotty, what's the most desperate thing you ever did?'

She gave him such a glare that Andy was happy not to have it directed at him. 'I believe it was when *you* were born. I told Mama that if it was a brother, I was going to run away!'

Everyone laughed and the tension broke. 'Did you?' Andy teased.

Aunt Dorothea smiled. 'I got as far as the meadow just outside this window and turned back because—' she stopped, and buttered him another roll '—I didn't want to be hungry.'

'Wise child,' Andy said. 'We doused our light. The bosun was the strongest. When there was a long roll of thunder, he broke through the bars, knotted one end of our pathetic rope around one of the other bars, and…and told us to shinny down the rope, one at a time.'

'Was it long enough?' Rosie asked, her voice small, her eyes huge.

'No. We ended up jumping into the water before we wanted to. Oh, so cold. Captain Tate was struggling just above me, so I hung on to the rope. I put him on my back when he came closer. I leaped and started swimming.'

He remembered waves so high that he must have swallowed half of them, weighed down and weak as he was. All he could do at that moment was mentally swim again in frigid water with the old man on his back, which landed him precisely where he had been in the mail coach. Would it never end? He started to shiver, even though the room was warm.

Rosie did an extraordinary thing. She edged closer on the bed, took his face in her hands and kissed his forehead.

'Silly man,' she said, for his ears alone. 'You *are* a hero.'

Chapter Seven

Such manners! All Rosie could think of was something her brother-in-law, Peter, said in times of stress. 'Great gobs of monkey meat, what you must think of me?'

Perfect. Everyone laughed, no one louder than Master Hadfield. 'Now you must tell me Happy Christmas,' he said, which made no sense, but set them off again.

'This is hardly funny,' she said feebly, then dragged them back to the story. 'How did the navy find you in the water?'

'Luck. The bosun was strongest and he swam toward the blockade while the rest of us floundered. We were drifting south. There was a strong current near shore. A Fast Dispatch Vessel heading from the blockade to Portsmouth nearly ran him down. They dragged our sorry carcasses aboard and took us back to the nearest blockader. Luck,' he repeated.

Rosie heard amazement mingled with terror in his voice, as if still not believing he had escaped. *No wonder he weeps at night*, she told herself. Then another thought struck home. *Who will hold his hand in the inn?*

Aunt Dorothea stirred herself. 'I should warm your dinner.'

'No need, ma'am. Really.'

She didn't argue, although Rosie knew she wanted to. Aunt Dorothea always maintained her own taut ship. She set the tray on his lap and the sailing master wasted not a second in downing the meal.

'It's better warm,' Aunt Dorothea tried once more.

'You can't imagine how good this is.'

'No, I cannot,' she said. 'I will leave you to it. Rosie, bring the tray downstairs when our hero is done.' She patted her breast. 'My heart cannot take more excitement! Come, brother, let us find that bottle of rum I hide in the flour bin.'

Rosie laughed as Master Hadfield rolled his eyes. After the door closed, she picked up her knitting and sat in her chair again. She hoped she wasn't babbling, but she felt the need to comment. Even better: a massive change of subject. 'Barring terrible years in prison, I can't imagine this is how you usually spend Christmas,' she began.

He surprised her. 'I have never "spent Christmas," as you say,' he told her. 'My father was a poor farmer in Hampshire, eking out a living on a few acres. Nothing like this farm. A good Christmas meant a portion of beef.' She could tell he wasn't ready to sleep. 'Things grew worse after my mother died.'

She almost—but didn't—ask how things could be worse. She waited for Andrew to continue, almost dreading what he would say, yet wanting to know more.

'After my father died, I was sent to the workhouse. I ran

away to the Royal Navy and have been at sea ever since. No Christmas for me, except rum on the twenty-fifth.'

He didn't sound sorry for himself. As she knitted and glanced at him now and then, his eyelids grew heavy and he slept, his expression peaceful. She watched the sleeping man, his hands open and relaxed, and not bunched into fists from last night's ordeal. This wasn't the same man on the mail coach. 'Good,' she said softly.

Rosie took the tray to the kitchen at the same time Papa came inside, blowing on his gloveless hands. His eyes brightened to see her, making her certain Papa intended this Christmas visit to encourage her to remain here.

Papa had his own news. 'It's not precisely balmy outside, but I think the road to Endicott is safe enough.'

'Not yet, Papa,' Rosie said quickly. 'Master Hadfield needs to rest another day.' *I don't want him gone now* was what she didn't say.

Papa had no argument. In fact, he surprised her. 'I wasn't planning to uproot him yet.'

'Didn't the ostler tell us last night that the inn was full?' Rosie asked. 'Where will he stay?'

'Tell you what, Rosie. I'll pick up my flour from the miller, so Dotty will make us all manner of Christmas delights. I can inquire about a room at the inn.'

I hope you don't find one, Rosie thought. 'I suppose you must.'

She should have kept her eyes on her knitting. It touched her heart, even surprised her, to see Papa regarding her with tenderness. *I am cherished*, she thought simply.

'Daughter, do you have that chronicle thing in your pocket?'

'I do.' She pulled it out and handed it to him.

'I plan to stop at the public house on my way home and share this around,' he told her. 'I can't think of a time when anything exciting happened in Endicott, at least not since Farmer Goodwin's wife ran away with his brother.'

'Papa!'

Aunt Dorothea, strait-laced, proper aunt, laughed with him, to Rosie's amazement. She shook her head. 'Sometimes I wonder about you two,' Rosie said, then added something from her heart. 'Maybe I should stay here and organize you both.'

'I wish you would,' Papa told her.

There was no overlooking Aunt Dorothea's wistful expression, or the way she kissed her brother's cheek and said, 'Fred, do look in on my house when you are in the village.'

'As always,' he said cheerfully. 'I'll only be in town long enough to spread around the news about a hero staying at my farm.'

After he left, Rosie watched her aunt gaze into nothing, and scolded herself for never fully appreciating Dorothea's decision to leave her own home and move to the farm to raise two girls. She had been in Dorothea's house on Chandler Street several times, admiring the furnishings and air of comfort. Her late uncle had been a solicitor who died of a wasting disease that left his physician helpless. As her aunt gazed out the window, Rosie knew she was seeing herself on Chandler Street again.

'You want to be on Chandler Street, don't you?' Rosie asked softly, not wanting to wreck whatever memory her selfless aunt enjoyed, thinking of earlier times.

'I cannot deny it. Horace has been gone so long. Why am I still attached to brick and mortar on a pretty street?'

Her aunt had never spoken like that, talking to her woman to woman, and not aunt to niece. 'Because you have good memories,' Rosie said. She kissed her aunt. 'You would like to live there again.'

'Your papa needs me here.'

'Not if I decide to return home.' There, she had said it.

'That is true,' Aunt Dorothea said. 'I think you are old and practical enough to keep your father from folly.' They laughed together.

The afternoon dragged. Rosie wondered how much good cheer Papa was downing in the pub. Restless, she tiptoed upstairs and peeked in Andrew's room. To her relief, the sailing master slept peacefully. It touched her heart to see that his fingers were now curled around his thumbs, something she had noticed when her little nephew slept with no cares. She watched the even rise and fall of his chest, and found herself breathing along with him.

'Aunt Dotty, I think Master Hadfield is surely fit enough to eat dinner downstairs with us,' she announced as she returned to the kitchen.

'I was going to suggest the same thing,' her aunt said. 'Do you know, I think he is a charming man.' She laughed. 'I recall a time when Vicar Ewing admonished the young ladies in the parish to beware of navy men.'

'I remember,' Rosie said. She leaned closer. 'I was too young to understand what he meant.'

Her aunt gave her a long look. 'The vicar might have been half in jest, you know.'

'Perhaps. Somehow I have managed to survive eight years in naughty Plymouth without a regret.'

'Hmm. I wonder, was that good or bad?'

'Aunt Dorothea!'

'Just a thought, dearest. Here is a knife. Peel me some apples.'

Chapter Eight

Papa came home none the worse for wear, even if he did smell of ale and his eyes were brighter than usual. Rosie thought back to those hard years after Mama died and he stopped smiling. She felt like laughing now, settling into the kitchen, wrapping dough around the last of the sliced apples for the apple turnovers Aunt Dorothea planned for pudding.

Along with the fragrance of ale and the chill of the outdoors, Papa brought in a battered letter. 'This was in the gig,' he said, placing it on the kitchen table. 'It must belong to our slumbering guest.'

'It looks a little worse for wear,' Aunt Dorothea said. 'You could take it upstairs, Rosie. No. Leave it. Master Hadfield should eat down here tonight. Fred, would you check on him? Dinner will be ready soon.'

Papa returned minutes later, his expression lively. 'What did I find but a caged animal pacing up and down, wondering where his trousers are!'

Aunt Dorothea laughed, which made Papa stare because she might smile now and then, but this hearty laugh was a new development. 'Silly me! I washed them and sewed on two buttons. They're in the washing room. Take them upstairs, Fred.'

Papa retrieved them, stopping on the way upstairs to say, 'He claims he is going fair crazy with the smell of hot apples!'

Aunt Dorothea pointed to the ceiling with her turning fork. 'Cooking for Master Hadfield is greatly satisfying. The man will eat anything.'

The man came downstairs when Rosie was setting the table in the breakfast room off the kitchen, where they took all their meals, the actual dining room having been turned into Aunt Dorothea's private parlor. Rosie heard him talking to Fred in the kitchen, and hurried with her task, wanting to see him, to assess him and assure herself that he was going to thrive here better than in a room in Endicott. Why it mattered, she couldn't have explained to a jury.

To her delight, he joined her in the breakfast room, carrying the plates. 'I told Aunt Dorothea that I am a useful sort. Plates for you, Rosie.' He watched her. 'Ah, so the knife and spoon go on that side?'

'Silly man. You know they do. I suspect you have dined with admirals.'

'One or two.' He took a deep breath of kitchen fragrances. 'I swear I could put on a stone or two, just breathing here.'

'I doubt you will be so fortunate in town,' she warned.

He straightened one plate so the painted rose lined up with the edge of the table. 'Fred—I am to call him Fred—

said the innkeep told him that all the rooms were occupied until after Boxing Day. I never thought Endicott would be so busy. He told me I am welcome here.'

'You are,' she said, even as she felt her face grow warm. Aunt Dorothea saved her by bringing in a roast of beef with more ceremony than usual.

Dinner was a delight, a prosaic meal to them, but everything to the sailing master, who ate steadily and with great appreciation. When Aunt Dorothea brought in the apple turnovers and set them down in front of him, they couldn't help watching him down that first one, and then a second.

'We used to dream about food,' he said finally, which made Rosie swallow down her emotion.

'Wh-what in particular did you dream about?'

He gestured at the remains of the food on the table. 'Nothing this fancy. All I really, truly wanted was porridge drenched, positively buried, in sugar and cream.' He smiled at his own recollection. 'Here I am, and I am grateful.'

Rosie knew better than to look at her father. She had known him to get weepy over a new lamb struggling to its feet for the first time.

'I nearly forgot.' Fred left the table and returned moments later with the letter. 'You must have left this in the gig.'

'I did.' Andrew set it next to his empty plate. 'This is why I came to Endicott.'

'You, sir, will be our after-dinner entertainment then, because we want to know why,' Papa said. 'Let us hear it in the sitting room, where I can put my feet up and unbutton the top button on my trousers when no one is watching. Let the plates soak, ladies. This we want to hear.'

Papa motioned Andrew to the most comfortable chair. He sank into it with a sigh, the letter on his lap. 'I won't bore you with the details of what some are calling the Battle of the Nile,' he began, then told them about the massive explosion aboard the Frenchies' *L'Orient,* which damaged his frigate, the *Leander.* 'My sailing master died on the deck, and I took over,' he said. He held up the letter. 'I wrote a letter to Master Hale's widow, hoping to deliver it in person. She and their daughter, Sadie, have always been so kind to me. I have known them for years.'

He tapped it. 'A simple letter, but we limped into Plymouth for drydock work, and were sent immediately to Chatham instead. I should have left the letter with Mrs Fillion, but I forgot. I only found the letter a few days ago, at Mrs Fillion's hotel.'

'Who is she?' Aunt Dorothea asked. 'Oh, I shouldn't pry into your affairs.'

Andrew smiled. 'Nothing like that. Mrs Fillion owns the Drake, a hotel in Plymouth where many of us stay.'

'I know the Drake,' Rosie said. 'Everyone does in Plymouth. It's famous for its Royal Navy clientele, including Lord Nelson.'

'Rest his soul,' Andrew said. Rosie watched his expressive face grow serious, even sad. 'We can leave our possessions there, until our return to Plymouth and the Drake.' He shook his head. 'Some never return to claim them.' He ran his hand over the letter, then held it up. 'I left this letter in the storeroom by mistake, and the address was rubbed away by a box on it. I am in Endicott to find Mary Hale. Do you know her?'

They didn't, to Andy's obvious disappointment. Papa cleared his throat. 'What was your sailing master's name?

'Edward Hale. He taught me everything I know. His knowledge was extraordinary. I was most fortunate to be a pupil.' He smiled what Rosie called a reminiscing smile, something she had seen often enough on Papa's face as he remembered his own love, Nancy. 'He had one flaw. He was fond of losing at cards.'

Papa understood. 'I suspect you want to know how Mrs Hale has fared through the years.'

'Precisely. What if she needs my help?' He spread out his hands. 'But you have not heard of Edward or Mary Hale?'

'Alas, no,' Papa said. 'All the same there might be someone in Endicott who knows.'

He folded his hands across his ample belly, made more ample by his sister's turnovers. 'Sir…'

'Andrew. Even Andy, remember?'

'Andy then. We are not formal. Are you up to a short walk?'

'Aye, and I need one. Any day now, Mrs Fillion will be getting a letter from the Navy Board for me.'

'And?' Papa prompted.

'I will be invited, nay commanded, to appear on thus and such day to be assigned another ship. I must be more physically sound. I need to walk.'

It was Rosie's turn to look away, not wanting him gone.

Strange, that. She hoped no one noticed, but Papa was watching. 'Rosie, I propose that you walk our Christmas guest to Endicott. He can inquire in the pub and you know the village. Someone might remember her.'

'Certainly, Papa. I promise not to march our sailing master in a quick step.'

'The last thing I need,' Andrew said, his tone light and teasing.

'Very good,' Papa said. 'I have farm matters to handle here with my son-in-law, and Dotty, I know you want to bake your Christmas biscuits and other unimaginable treats, now that you have adequate flour.'

'Indeed I do,' Aunt Dorothea stated firmly. 'Check with the magistrate, Rosie. He claims acquaintance with everyone in Endicott, probably from the time when William the Conqueror waded ashore.'

'I shall.' A glance at their houseguest showed a smiling man. 'Yes, we will walk tomorrow.'

Chapter Nine

Andrew knew someone came into his room in the early hours, that time when his prison dreams became more vivid. The worst was the first time he stared into the piss hole to watch fellow Englishmen pleading for someone to pull them out. Even worse was to be compelled to watch as the water rose and drowned them. And here he was, begging for mercy. Thank God for Rosie's gentle hand on his arm.

Over breakfast, he could tell from her tired eyes that his late-night disturbances were keeping her from sleep. 'I am so sorry.'

'No need for apology,' she told him, then soothed his heart. 'There is so little we landlubbers can do to comprehend even a fraction of your burden. You are saving us from a tyrant. That is sufficient for me.' She surprised him then, and perhaps herself. 'No, it is not sufficient! I... I... worry for you.' She hesitated, then continued, 'I truly do.'

The day was surprisingly balmy for December in Devon. Endicott was less than a half mile away, looking not at all like the wintry village with icy streets which formed his first view. 'It's not precisely the Mediterranean, but I am pleasantly surprised,' he told Rosie as they walked along slowly.

He probably hadn't fooled her when he announced that he would keep a slow pace because she was short. He had already watched her bustling about the kitchen to recognize a woman of great energy. *He* needed the slow pace.

He hadn't fooled her at all. Partway there, when he wanted so badly to rest, she stopped and pointed down at a smooth path. 'Rough ground,' she lied. 'Let me take your arm, please.'

He offered it gladly, and she steadied him.

They stopped twice more, once on her pretense that she had a pebble in her shoe. The other time when she stopped, he said, 'Rosie Harte, you are walking slowly, taking my arm and complaining of pebbles, but I am on to you. You are no deceiver.'

She gave him a wide-eyed, innocent look, then laughed. 'Andrew Hadfield, there is no harm in taking care of you, and so I shall.'

What could he say to that?

Endicott wasn't much of a village, but he admired Christmas wreaths on doors, and even some of the places of business. Rosie directed him toward the public house. 'I will be across the street in Notions and Sundries. When you finish in here, you can save me from embroidery thread.'

'I take it you are not a seamstress,' he teased.

'Ledgers and numbers are my forte. I know double

entry and bottom lines. I do knit, but not well. Give me numbers any day.'

A husband of the seafaring type would never have to worry about you, Rose Harte, he thought with admiration as he entered the pub. *You can manage money and probably people.*

He knew no one, but the occupants of the pub all seemed to know him. Someone let out a huzzah, and others joined in. He looked behind him, wondering who of importance stood there, and they laughed.

'Nay lad, 'tis you,' a drinker said. 'Farmer Harte told us your story, and now we want to hear it from the hero himself.'

Someone spotted him a tankard of hot buttered rum. A bowl of stew miraculously appeared. He downed both as he told them the whole story. In this second telling, he felt something inside him let go.

'Now I am here, looking for the widow of my sailing master at the Battle of the Nile,' he concluded, knowing he needed to find Rosie before she died of boredom in Notions and Sundries. 'Do any of you know Mary Hale? She is the widow of Edward Hale, and I know she lived here.'

He looked around at men shaking their heads. 'Sounds familiar,' someone said. 'Can't place it,' said another. 'Recently?' chimed in a third.

No one knew. *Blast and damn*, he thought, as he stepped outside. At least the sun was shining, even if he wanted to chew nails and spit them out. He turned his face to the sun, remembering the warmth of tropical climates, enjoying the moment.

He looked across the street at a fast-moving woman with a determined look on her face. He could tell Rosie knew something. 'I thought I was going to have to wade into that pub and drag you out,' she said, breathless.

He took her arm. 'What did you learn?'

She took a deep breath and managed a smile, the sly kind that made him wonder about women in general and this one in particular. 'I learned that I will never embroider, knit well or crochet, but I already knew that. The man I eventually marry—poor fellow—had better be able to afford a dressmaker.'

'I am certain he will,' Andrew said, mentally going over his accounts ledger at Carter and Brustein's. He spotted an empty bench. 'Over here.'

'Well?' he asked when they sat. 'I came up short in the public house.'

'I, on the other hand, discovered that the best way to find out about women is in a notions shop.' She grasped his hand. 'I learned that Mary Hale lived on Canterbury Street. When her funds ran out, she was taken to the workhouse.'

He shook his head, weighed down with such awful news. 'Master Hale knew everything in the world about sailing, but he was a babe in the woods over money. Is the workhouse here?'

'No. It's in Ashburton, on the way to Exeter.'

'May we go now? I am ready.'

'Tomorrow. There is more bad news.'

She turned tear-filled eyes to him, and he was a no-hoping goner. *I am the world's most easily duped man,* he thought. *I am worse than Master Hale*. It took every ounce of discipline he possessed not to wrap her tight in his arms. 'What in the world…?' would have to do.

'You don't know him, but Vicar Ewing has the living of St. Timothy's Parish.'

That's nice, he thought, wondering how this could possibly matter as much as a widow living hand to mouth. 'And?'

'The lady behind the notions counter said that Sir William Keeting is turning him out and replacing him with his nephew,' she said. Bless her heart, she took pity on his blank look. 'Sir William, a baronet, controls the living of the parish. You can't imagine how important Vicar Ewing is to us.' She sat a little straighter. 'He taught a parish school for pupils such as I. Most of us here have little money and no titles, and so the vicar educated us.' Her shoulders drooped. 'Yes, his gout flares now and then, but he is our dear cleric.'

He knew this mattered to Rosie, even as he yearned to snatch Mrs Hale from a workhouse. Rosie looked at him as if he could say the word and solve the dilemma. 'I am outgunned and outclassed in this matter,' he told her, his air of capability a myth at the moment. 'Can anyone help Vicar Ewing?'

'Perhaps not,' she said, after a moment's silence. 'But I will listen to him and cry with him. This way, Andrew.'

The vicarage was comfortable and timeless looking, built to withstand the wind and rain that often plagued Devon. 'Rough ground,' Andrew said as they approached the house, and took her hand. The path was clearly smooth, but she did not quibble.

The vicar opened the door himself, his face serious, until he took a good look at Rosie Harte and ushered them in. Introductions went around. 'Master Hadfield, stories are circulating about your escape from a prison in Spain in the middle of a raging gun battle,' Vicar Ewing said, amusing Andrew how fast a modest tale of skinny men escaping a prison could turn into a battle with Boney himself.

Vicar Ewing hobbled over to a chair and gingerly propped his leg onto a footstool. 'There now, my dear Rosie,' he said. 'It is improving.'

Thankfully, Rosie wasn't one to chat when disaster loomed. She cut right to the source, like Alexander the Great's bold action with a knotted rope at Gordium. 'Vicar, the ladies in Notions told me you are being turned out by Sir William Keeting.'

'Dear Rosie, you know Sir William can bestow the living of this parish on anyone he chooses. He controls it.'

'Yes, but…'

'It's his right, child,' the vicar said gently. 'He has chosen to give it to his nephew Milton Keeting, who currently assists in a parish beyond Exeter.'

'That's not fair, sir,' Rosie said. 'You were our teacher, and…and…your sermons kept me awake.'

'Well, most of them,' Rosie said, when the vicar laughed. Andrew saw her lurking smile, and blessed them both for cheering up each other. 'I mean, I really remember the Beatitudes.'

'"Blessed are the peacemakers," dear child,' Vicar Ewing reminded her.

'What will you do? Where will you go?'

'I do not know.' Andrew heard all the uncertainty. 'I will have a small stipend, but beyond that…' He shook his head.

'I will write to the Archbishop of Canterbury,' Rosie declared. Andrew knew better than to laugh. He could tell she meant it.

'Please do,' Vicar Ewing said. 'In the meantime, come to Christmas Eve services as usual, Miss… But it is Mrs Hadfield now, eh?'

Rosie stared at him. So did Andrew. Then they stared at each other. 'Oh, no, sir, he is not… I mean, he is a very nice man, but he is a hero in the Royal Navy and trying to find a widow and…' She stopped. Andrew did everything in his power not to laugh, because she was adorably hilarious.

'I am babbling,' she said with some dignity. 'Circumstances have made Master Hadfield our Christmas guest.'

'You are a lucky guest, Master Hadfield,' the vicar said.

He was calm, unflappable, and yet Andrew saw someone with a knowledge of human nature. And the Keetings, people he didn't know and didn't want to, were turning him out? Folly.

'I *am* lucky,' Andrew said. 'This sounds like an unexpected Christmas for all of us. Mary Hale would have been one of your parishioners, I assume. Her late husband was my mentor in the sailing business. We learned she is in the workhouse in Ashburton.'

'I have visited her there. She is keeping house for the workhouse guardian, his wife and four unpleasant children. Nasty little beasts.'

'What can we do, sir?' Andrew asked.

'Get her out somehow.'

'What can we do for *you*, vicar?' Rosie asked.

'Alas, not much. Vicar Milton Keeting and his wife are already in town, staying with Milton's father, who is Sir William's younger brother.' He smiled then. 'You know him, Rosie, the younger brother who soiled his hands with trade and is now far wealthier than the baronet.' He rubbed his hands together. 'We do enjoy a bit of scandal now and then in Endicott.'

That declaration was followed by a sigh, and a glance at the mantelpiece clock. 'Time for me to prepare for evensong, my dears. I will also gird my loins. I have been informed that Mrs Keeting is coming here during evensong to measure for curtains. I suggest you hurry home, dear Rosie and Master Hadfield.'

Rosie nodded. Dusk was on them when they left the vicarage. 'Rough ground,' she whispered, and put her hand in his. 'Andrew, this is not the Christmas I bargained on.'

'Neither did I,' he said, 'but what do I actually know of Christmas? I had initially planned to stay at the Drake, eat, read and wait for new uniforms.'

Her voice was soft, and he leaned closer as they walked slowly. 'I was hoping for a Christmas with time to gather ivy for a wreath, and drape holly on unsuspecting nooks and crannies in the house, and sing carols and eat too much.'

'You can still do that. I'll be happy enough to locate Mrs Hale, and prepare myself for that letter from the Navy Board.'

He stood still with the foolish notion that he might be falling in love with Rosie Harte. Surely not. No, no, not when the Navy Board could summon him any day. After all those years at peril on sea, he knew better. He had committed himself to duty until the end of an endless war. Only an idiot would fall in love.

Chapter Ten

Aunt Dorothea had prepared a dinner of roast duck, mounds of potatoes so fluffy and buttery that Rosie swore she saw tears in Andrew's eyes. There were also green beans strung, dried and reconstituted. But where was her aunt?

'Where is she, Papa?'

'Lately, she has been going to her house on Chandler Street once a week,' he said. 'She prepares dinner for me before she leaves. All these years…she misses her home.'

I should be here so she can return to her home permanently, Rosie thought. She looked down at her hands, one so recently in Andrew's firm grip because the ground was fictionally uneven. *I do not know where I should be.*

Since no one was moving the conversational ball, she picked up the sorry thing, telling her father of Vicar Ewing's fate, which only turned Papa more reflective than usual. It seemed that the vulture of bad news was flapping all around the table.

'I should have warned you about that,' Papa murmured. 'I heard more in the public house yesterday to explain that wretched turn of events.' He leaned forward, his elbow just missing the potatoes. 'Sir William is deep in debt. His younger brother is in trade and is now richer than Croesus, whoever that chap is. It seems that Reverend Milton Keeting, Sir William's son, cannot keep his grubby hands off parish funds. To avoid a scandal—according to the stalwarts in the pub—Milton is taking over St. Timothy's. In exchange for this atrocity coming our way, his uncle will pay off Sir William's debts and smooth things over for Milton.'

'So I heard,' Andrew declared. 'I'm exhausted by all this local intrigue.'

'It gets better. Milton and his wife are already at Keeting Manor.'

'Yes,' Rosie said. She stirred around uneaten potatoes and gravy. 'Vicar Ewing said they were coming over to the vicarage to measure for new curtains.'

'She must have recovered then,' Papa told them.

'From what?' Andrew asked.

'The exhaustion of strong hysterics! Apparently she and Milton were trapped in a post-chaise in that mess of ice and snow that stalled you. I have it from Dotty, who heard it from the housekeeper at Keeting Manor, that someone tried to foist a poor sailor off on them in their post-chaise, because he needed help.'

'It was our mail coach,' Andrew said. 'I was that poor sailor.'

Rosie saw the sadness in his eyes. 'Rough ground,' she whispered to him, wanting to take his hand. Papa looked at them both, a question in his eyes. 'Papa, she told our coachman that she feared they would be murdered.'

Papa laughed, but it was mirthless. 'Dotty heard it from the housekeeper that she is only now recovering from, er, emotional distress.'

'I remember Milton,' Rosie said. 'He was a slimy lad who made fun of us because we could not afford a private tutor. It appears he has not improved.'

'That, dear child, is how the world works,' Papa replied. He glanced at Andrew. 'Has this been your experience, too, Master Hadfield?'

'Aye and more's the pity. Why is it that the worst people seem to suffer no consequences?'

To Rosie's dismay, the conversation turned Andrew quiet. After dinner, he begged off from playing whist. 'It's been a long day,' he said. 'I don't know what will happen tomorrow when I go to the workhouse in Ashburton.'

'I am coming, too,' Rosie told him.

'Should you?'

'Yes,' she said, sad he should think he must bear the weight of their sorry world. Maybe that was the price of leadership. 'Yes,' she said firmly.

He smiled at that, and she took heart. 'We'll take the gig to Ashburton. I will handle the reins. Something tells me that a lifelong sailor probably doesn't know one end of a horse from the other.'

'Correct. It's been too many years since I sat on my father's old nag and sawed at the reins,' Andrew said. 'You will be my coachman, and I promise not to murder you.'

The droll way he said it made her laugh. She touched

his arm. 'What you must think of us?' she asked, as she followed him to the foot of the stairs.

'You can't imagine, dear lady.'

Why 'dear lady' should keep her awake half the night, Rosie didn't understand. To make her positively grumpy, the bed was cold. She thrashed about, thinking of Papa wanting her to return home, and Aunt Dorothea yearning to retire to Chandler Street, after all her years of loving service to her brother and nieces. There was Vicar Ewing, turned out of his parish where people needed him. What would happen to his parish school?

She tried not to think about Master Hadfield, except that was what finally sent her into slumber, dreaming how nice it would be to cuddle with him on a cold night. That dream had entertained her off and on all year, if she were honest with herself. This was the first time the cuddling man had a name and face. *Rough ground*, she told herself.

He woke after midnight, talking out loud, then pleading. She hurried to him, sitting by his bed, holding his hand until he returned to sleep, comforted. She couldn't help herself. *Who will do this when you return to the perils of battle and the sea? Will anyone care as much as I?*

Morning brought Papa's pronouncement that they were taking his son-in-law's larger gig to Ashburton, because he was coming, too. He obviously expected no argument, but he was prepared with one and presented it, anyway. 'See here, Master Hadfield, with your nautical command and my local clout, we can find this woman and extract her from a workhouse. I have an idea.'

'Which is…' Rosie prompted.

'I'm thinking about it, daughter. Some sort of genteel employment?'

'I'll never argue the matter,' Andrew said. 'My area of expertise does not extend to horses, as your daughter pointed out, and what do I know of shire life?'

'You will never be a country gentleman,' Rosie teased, which brought a genuine smile to her houseguest.

'Never.'

He sounded so decisive this morning, and not the weary man who begged off on whist and went to bed early. His eyes looked as tired as hers, but she already knew he possessed a reservoir of strength she could only imagine. *I do believe the workhouse is in for a real battle,* she thought, basing her supposition on something she couldn't define.

She put on her warmest cloak and let the sailing master hand her into the gig. The three of them sat rump to rump on the slightly wider seat. 'Your cloak smells of brine, sir,' she teased as Papa spoke to his horses and they started to Ashburton.

'Nice odour, eh?'

'I wouldn't have thought so only a few days ago,' she said, thinking of no objection as his arm circled her waist. After all, the man had to stay on the seat, didn't he?

Ashburton came soon enough. 'Do you know where the workhouse is, Papa?'

'I do. Your brother-in-law and I each acquired a field labourer from there.'

'I didn't know, Papa. What happened to Pete's after harvest?'

'Pete hired him permanently, and he had the good sense to marry the goose girl.'

'Bravo,' Andrew said. 'What about your workhouse labourer, sir?'

'He wanted to go to New Hampshire, America, so I paid his way. I get a letter every year.'

'Papa, you are a philanthropist,' she teased.

Her joking ended when they turned onto Warwick Road, and she saw a dismal pile of grey stones ahead. 'So grim,' she said, much subdued.

Papa patted her knee. 'This is why I sent a workhouse man to New Hampshire. I didn't want a good man damned by his hedgerow birth to be punished for his poverty in *this* place.'

Rosie kissed his cheek, grateful beyond measure for such a father. She glanced at Andrew sitting on her other side. Could there be two such excellent men in one gig?

She didn't think the bleakness outside could be duplicated and worsened inside, but it was, with dirty walls and not much furniture. 'Rough ground,' she whispered when they entered the building. She said it quietly enough so Andrew could not hear.

Amazing man, to have such acute hearing. She felt his gloved hand in hers and she took heart.

Papa knew where to go, which relieved her. A workhouse was no place to wander. Her heart broke at the sight of children with lowered eyes and uncombed hair, sitting in silence, waiting for…something. Three bony women dressed in grey sacking huddled together, the middle one weeping.

Papa stopped in front of a wary-eyed man sitting at a high desk, the kind of perch where everyone had to look up. Rosie saw it as another way to humiliate people who, from the looks of them, had been fed a steady diet of humble pie.

'I must speak to the guardian,' Papa said, in a voice Rosie wasn't familiar with.

'I will see if he is in.'

'He is in,' the man holding her hand said. It was also a voice she was unfamiliar with, a voice of absolute command, even beyond Papa's. It was the voice of someone who knew suffering even more extreme than this. Still, he held her hand. She squeezed his.

'Who may I say is—'

'Sailing Master Hadfield and Frederick Harte from Endicott. We are not patient people.'

Rosie felt prickles up and down her back. No wonder France and Spain were learning how implacable and relentless the Royal Navy was. As they stood in the dismal corridor, Rosie committed herself. Even if she never saw him again after Christmas, she wanted the man still holding her hand to know something important. She stood on tiptoe, one eye on her father, who watched the sad little ones, and leaned close. 'You may think you are not a hero, Andrew, but you are. Don't quibble.'

He smiled at her words, a boyish grin that threw off years of war. 'You're a hero, too, Miss Rose Harte. I may have a presumptuous little plan for Mrs Hale, once we spring her from this midden. That is, if others are agreeable.'

The guardian stomped into the corridor, his luncheon napkin tucked in his collar, his eyes blazing, clearly not a man to be disturbed at meals. Rosie knew in her heart of hearts that the guardian didn't stand a chance. He just didn't know it yet.

Chapter Eleven

Andrew eyed the guardian. 'Mrs Mary Hale is an inmate at this institution. Aye or nay?'

'What right do you—'

'Aye or nay?' Andrew snapped, already tired of this man.

'Aye.'

Challenge me and regret it, Andrew thought. 'She is the widow of my late, excellent sailing master, Edward Hale, who died at the Battle of the Nile thirteen years ago. I want Mary Hale immediately remanded to my care.'

'You have no right.'

'I have every right.' He narrowed his eyes, and the guardian took a step back. 'She is destitute. I am relieving England of the obligation to care for her.'

He turned, looked deep into Rosie's lovely eyes and took a bold chance. He raised her gloved hand to his cheek. 'Right, my dear? We need a housekeeper, and I want her to be Mrs Hale. I owe her husband a debt, one I can repay, at least in part, by offering his widow more pleasant surroundings than this dung heap.'

He knew Rosie wouldn't fail him. She hadn't failed him in the mail coach when she saw him at his worst. She hadn't failed him during lonely nights, when she held his hand. In daytime she sat beside him with her knitting, which was more soothing, more normal, than he could ever explain.

She didn't fail him now. 'We do need a housekeeper, my love,' she told him. 'You have told me much about Mrs Hale. She will be welcome in our home.'

Oh my goodness, Rosie, he thought, as she leaned against his shoulder, requiring his arm to go around her.

He returned his gaze to the guardian. The man's eyes bulged like a mackerel's. *Now for the final menace of a fleet action*, he thought. 'If you choose not to relinquish her, I can and will take the matter directly to the Navy Board,' Andrew said, committing a perjury he thought wasn't out of line, considering his life for the past few years. 'My ship sails in mere days and you are wasting my time. Well, sir? Are we done?'

To his relief, he saw defeat written all over the guardian's fat face. 'She is in the kitchen next door, *my* house.'

'We will remove her from it now.'

'But…but…she is my cook and housekeeper!' the guardian sputtered.

Andrew looked around the corridor. 'I see any number of women who will probably be happy to assume those roles. They can devour scraps from your table. Good day.' Oh, why not? 'I'll give a good report of you to the prime minister.'

'The prime minister?' Fred asked when they were outside again and the air was breathable. 'I had no idea you are a confidante of Spencer Perceval.'

'Neither does Perceval.'

Andrew felt Rosie's shoulders shake, so he tightened his grip. 'Don't you dare look at me,' she managed to say as they headed toward a smaller house of grey stones. 'If I start to laugh and find myself unable to stop, it will be your fault entirely.'

'You're already scolding me like that imaginary wife of mine would. Horrors,' he said with a straight face, which only made her stuff her hand against her mouth to keep from laughing.

'You two are a menace to law and order,' Frederick said, which made Andrew's shoulder start to shake, too.

All mirth ended as they stood in front of the guardian's house. 'Let's make quick work of this,' Andrew said. 'If the guardian thinks about what just happened, we might be in trouble.'

Fred nodded. 'Let's find the servants' entrance.'

'Lead on, sir.'

Down the back steps they went, frightening a kitten huddled there and looking no more prosperous than any of the inmates of the Ashburton Workhouse. Without a word, Rosie scooped it up. 'You're coming with me,' she said. 'No argument.' The little morsel cuddled closer.

Andrew didn't bother to knock. In moments they stood in the kitchen, and there was Mary Hale, turning in fright to look at them and dropping the spoon in the pot.

'Mrs Hale' was all he said.

Her response would have ripped his heart apart, if

Rosie hadn't put her hand on his back as Widow Hale sobbed and flung herself into his arms. Both her skin and her hair were greyer than he remembered, telling him more than words about her life in recent years.

'How? What?' was all she could manage.

Frederick Harte kindly helped her sit down. She tried to get up, saying something about the stew burning. 'Let it burn,' he said, even as Rosie moved the pot off the stove.

Andrew condensed his prison escape down to the needfuls, concluding with 'I recently learned you had fallen on hard times. You're coming with us. This is Frederick Harte and his daughter Rosie, who live near Endicott. How quickly can you pack?'

Rosie took over then, helping Mary to her feet. 'I'll assist you. Now,' she added, then glanced at Andrew. 'See there, sir? I'm learning how to move things along smartly, as I believe you nautical types say.'

'Smartly, indeed,' he told her, secretly delighted.

Mary looked from him to Rosie, and turned into the lady he remembered, as no-nonsense as her late husband. 'This way, my dear,' she told Rosie. 'I won't take a minute.'

It barely took that. There was hardly time for Fred Harte to clap him on the back and declare 'Remind me never to cross you! Are all navy men so fierce?'

'Aye, in the performance of duty,' Andrew said, his eyes on the door where his two favourite women in the world had vanished. 'Fred, I have an idea for Mary Hale. I know I am presuming, but tell me what you think.'

When he finished, Fred Harte gave him another clap on

the back, this one threatening his wind. 'Sorry, lad,' the farmer said when he staggered under the friendly blow. 'I forget you're still recuperating.' He leaned in closer. 'I was thinking along these lines, too.'

Andrew was spared a reply when not one but three people appeared. Mary carried a small bundle and moved fast, tugging a young girl along. 'There is a butler-looking fellow headed this way. Let's go,' Rosie said.

'Um, Mrs Hale,' Andrew started, looking at the little girl clinging like a burr to Mary's skirt.

'Matilda Madigan is my granddaughter,' Mary said, her voice calm. 'You remember my Sadie, don't you?'

Who wouldn't remember Sadie? She was a jolly, practical child. He knew she had married a foretopman. 'Certainly, I do. But...'

'Typhus took Sadie.' The widow brushed away tears. 'Her Thomas died in a prison on the Spanish coast. We don't know the details.'

Oh, God. Andrew closed his eyes and took an involuntary step backward. Could Sadie's husband have been in that cell next to theirs? He opened his eyes when Rosie took his hand in a firm grip. 'Come now,' she said softly. 'Come now.'

That was all he needed. He eyed Mary Hale's small bundle. 'You didn't have time to...'

Mary was equal to the moment. 'Edward's last, incomplete log and my Bible,' she said. 'One dress. Get us out of here.'

Fred got them out of there. Rosie threw her cloak around Mary's thin shoulders. The servants' door opened and the butler-looking fellow stood there, perhaps—the more fool he—ready to stop them. Oh, Lord, he was easy meat. Andrew knew he had not forgotten how to do his determined face, the one that even intimidated captains who thought they knew better about a ship's trim during a fleet action. He raised his forefinger and that was enough. The man stopped in his tracks.

'Get in the back with Rosie,' Fred ordered, as he pulled the little girl up beside him, and Mary Hale followed her, nimble and determined.

Andrew saw a flash of black stockings and trim legs as Rosie climbed aboard to sit with him in the bed of the gig. He wrapped his hand-me-down boat cloak around both of them and pulled her close as Fred chirruped to his horse and they left the workhouse behind.

'Nothing like a boat cloak to keep you warm, even a shabby one,' he said. There was no question where his arm belonged—around Rosie's shoulders. To his utter delight, she burrowed in close, her head on his chest.

'She shared a room with two other maids, crammed into one bed,' she told him, her voice low and full of emotion. 'Matilda slept on the floor. I wouldn't treat a dog like that. Oh. This kitten! Why did I do that?'

He laughed when she held out the kitten. 'Because you're a kind soul,' he assured her. 'Hang on. Your father is not going to waste a minute getting us back to his farm.'

Sitting in the back of a gig, close to a woman he more than admired, was a prime moment to move along whatever this was. He knew it, but damn if he wasn't comfortable and warm and asleep in minutes. His last coherent thought was Rosie's low-voiced 'Silly man. You're a terror to workhouses.' He gave up a losing battle and slept.

Chapter Twelve

Rosie Harte knew she was a careful woman, discreet and cautious because she had been raised that way by a careful aunt and a discerning father. Her love of numbers had translated into modest but steady employment as a clerk in a nautical supply firm. She lived quietly and carefully in Plymouth, a town full of Royal Navy men, residing in the home of her employer.

She was careful with her money, giving her savings to Papa for safekeeping. Women could not bank.

Sitting beside a sleeping man, his arm loose around her, told her worlds about herself, because she knew she wanted more from life than a job and a nest egg, two things few women possessed, and might envy.

For many months, she had felt the urge for more, as she heard from friends her age who were now wives and mothers. Through her employer, she met officers and men of business, sharing tea with one, and good books with others. It was pleasant and gratifying, but little else. Her heart wasn't engaged.

Not until she had helped Andrew Hadfield through

a terrible time on the mail coach, held his hand during nightmares as his mind relived prison and starvation, and now served as his pillow in the back of a gig, had she truly understood love between man and woman. She breathed in the brine of his cloak and the odour that seemed to be his alone—Papa smelled like grain—and knew she wanted him, not as a casual acquaintance, but as husband, lover and father of her children.

And yet, and yet. He was in momentary expectation of a letter that would send him back to sea in this age of constant war. She knew she should forget him. He had made no declaration to her. There might be some tears on her part, but he would eventually be forgotten.

Easy to say, impossible to believe. She wanted to cling to him and tell him that he was the only man she would ever want, need or nurture. Other friends laughed when she shyly asked how they knew that the man they married was the one. 'Silly Rosie, you'll know when it happens.'

That was never good enough for someone of her logical mind. How did one *know*? she wanted to ask, but knew they would only laugh all the more. Now she knew, which only made matters worse. She loved a man engaged in a dangerous occupation who would be gone for weeks, months, years at a time. Every rumour of every fleet action at sea would set her life on edge. How did the wives of seamen survive such uncertainty? She had no idea if she was equal to such a life.

She had come home to celebrate Christmas, with carolling and gifts, wassail and pleasant evenings with friends, all because of the birth of God's child in Bethlehem. She knew her Bible. Babies were born all the time, but Christ was a special baby, born to save the world. That was what vicars and priests taught their parishioners. Sadly, war, kings beheaded and Napoleon conquering Europe had soured more cynical souls than hers, until even the ageless tale of a royal baby born to save them all seemed faintly ridiculous. These were trying times. How could anyone believe anything?

She looked at the man leaning against her, vulnerable at this moment, but trusting her enough to lay aside his caution and sleep. He had been masterful in the workhouse, championing a helpless woman. Now he rested in her arms as peaceful as a child, all because he trusted her. Maybe he even loved her. Would there even be time to find out? She doubted it supremely. All the same, he slept, and she rested her head against his. Maybe that was enough, in these hard times, even if it didn't feel like Christmas.

Andrew slept through most of the ride home, convincing Rosie as nothing else could, how draining had been his ordeal in prison. He heard nothing of the conversation going on in the driver's seat of the gig between two people getting to know each other. Amused now, Rosie listened as Mrs Hale explained to her father how she had been unable to survive on Sailing Master Hale's pension.

'Sir, my husband was an excellent man, but he had no card sense and loved to gamble,' Mary Hale said. She lowered her voice, perhaps so Andrew Hadfield could not hear, but Rosie learned about prize money, and how quickly her husband ran through it, when in port.

When her father asked the rescued lady what her future plans might include, Mrs Hale proudly declared that she was an excellent cook. Maybe someone needed a cook. True, there was Matilda to raise, but her granddaughter was eight, and old enough to be useful.

'Hire her, Fred,' she heard from the man beside her, who must have been listening with his eyes closed. He spoke softly, only to her. 'I have no leave to intrude upon your family business, but it's a grand idea.'

He whispered this, his lips practically against her ear, which caused all manner of upset and confusion in her body. And she was supposed to *think*?

'I also have a question for you, Rosie,' he asked, as her father helped Mrs Hale from the gig, in their farmyard.

Ask me to marry you, she thought, even as she knew that was irrational. 'Ask away,' she said hopefully.

'Is this how people spend Christmas?'

She could titter and tease, but that wasn't her. 'Master Hadfield, I have *never* seen a Christmas like this one,' she assured him. 'There should be hunts for holly and ivy to make a wreath, and carolling with St. Timothy's none-too-good choir, presents, and roast duck. That is a bare minimum, and we have done none of it.'

He helped her from the gig and found himself in the embrace of Mary Hale and shy Matilda. 'Christmas should include a timely rescue of two ladies in distress,' he added, which made them all laugh. 'What a nice tradition. Mary Hale, when I think what I owe your husband,' he added, then couldn't continue.

'Whatever you think you owe,' she said softly, 'I mark

it paid in full for your kindness to Matilda and me today.' She turned to Fred Harte. 'All of you… I had begun to doubt that there was any goodness in the world.'

'There's a lot, and more,' Papa said. He kissed Rosie's hand with a loud smack. 'Let's see what sort of surprise we can give to my sister, Dotty, eh, Rosie?'

Aunt Dorothea stood close to her brother as he introduced Mrs Hale and Matilda Madigan, who let go of Mary's dress, clearly sensing this was a better place than the one they had quitted so unceremoniously. Papa was in charge and in his element. 'Dotty, please take these lovely ladies upstairs to that pretty room with the rose wallpaper.'

'Nothing that fancy,' Mary Hale said in mild protest.

'You're our guests,' Dorothea said simply. 'Come, my dears. Rosie can get dinner on the table.'

Yes, keep me busy, Rosie thought, as she set down the bewildered kitten, smoothed its fur, then quickly produced a saucer of milk. The gentle lapping soothed her heart. *I don't want to think about sailing masters.*

Dinner was a delight. Matilda ate quickly, clearly unfamiliar with such abundance. Mary Hale took her time, savouring each bite. When she looked around for more crisped potatoes, Rosie filled her plate. She glanced at Andrew, who watched his mentor's widow, tenderness in his eyes. Since Rosie sat beside him, it was a simple matter to pat his hand.

Papa was not a man to waste words or opportunity. Dinner over, he rested his elbows on the table, focusing his full attention on his sister. 'Dotty, give me your opinion. I know it's sudden, but when I think of all the years…'

His sister looked up from her own thoughtful contemplation of Mary Hale, who buttered a slice of bread for Matilda. 'What do you have in mind, brother?' Dorothea asked, her eyes drawn back to the defenseless pair.

'Provided Mrs Hale agrees, I believe I will send you home to Chandler Street, and hire Mrs Hale to be cook and housekeeper here.'

Mary gasped, her eyes wide and worried. She looked from brother to sister. Her shoulders that had started to relax, tensed once more. As if by some unvoiced warning, she reached for Matilda.

Rosie held her breath, watching the two women. To her unspeakable delight, Dorothea stood up, walked around the table and placed her hands on the widow's shoulders. 'I think it is a lovely idea, Fred,' she told her brother. 'Mrs Hale, please accept. For years I have happily and willingly lived here to help those I love.' She looked into a distance Rosie knew, because she had shared it. 'I have a lovely house. I want to be there again. You and Matilda will be comfortable here, with no worries. Please say aye.'

Mrs Hale turned her attention to Andrew. 'Master Hadfield, what say you? I know you feel responsible for us.'

'I am. Say aye, Mary. You will never regret it. I must admit this thought had crossed my mind, too.' He looked at her father. 'Eh, Fred?'

'Aye, then,' the widow said promptly. 'Matilda, we have a home.' She cried, but Rosie knew joyful tears.

'Done and done then,' the farmer said. 'Dotty, Christmas is nearly upon us. If you will spend the next few days showing Mrs Hale her duties, you will be in your own home—' he paused, and Rosie almost saw the passage of years in his eyes '—after this Christmas.'

'Dear, dear brother,' Aunt Dorothea murmured. 'I *do* need this Christmas here.'

Rosie knew Papa had his maudlin limits. 'Bess, Peter and little Ben a farm over would murder me in my sleep if I turned you out sooner, Dotty. Imagine the lumps of coal in my stocking!'

Chapter Thirteen

Andrew knew he would spend a restless night, the probability of Sadie's husband drowning, possibly in the cell next to his, high on his mind. He had no basis of fact in the matter, but the ordeal magnified itself as it had on the mail coach. Would it never end?

Bless Rosie Harte. She sat beside his bed, and when he could not be consoled, she told him to move over and held him until he slept. When he woke later, she was gone. He lay in bed, oddly conflicted. Was this truly how people spent Christmas? He almost longed for a ship again, and soon.

Something changed in the morning. He came to breakfast thoughtful and worried, trying to decide if he wanted the Navy Board to hurry up with that dratted notice, or toss it into a pigeonhole on someone's desk to languish until peace broke out.

Rosie Harte had other ideas. Looking surprisingly chipper for someone he knew he had kept awake too many hours, calming his midnight anguish, she announced to them all over bacon and eggs—Matilda just stared at the bacon—that it was time to remember Christmas.

'I promised Master Hadfield Christmas,' she said. 'Pass the toast, please.'

'Dear daughter, what do you propose?' Fred asked, his eyes merry.

'That Matilda, Master Hadfield and I find some holly and ivy, and make a wreath for the sitting room. What say you?'

So he found himself with a basket on his arm, and in the company of two charming females, one who skipped ahead, and whirled about as the mood grabbed her, and the other walking more sedately beside him.

Good Lord, was he too shy to speak? What an idiot. To his relief, Rosie took over the conversation. 'Did you notice Matilda's new dress?'

Of course he did not. He was a man. 'Oh?'

Bless her heart, Rosie overlooked his stupidity. 'Aunt Dorothea never could bring herself to discard *my* outgrown dresses. They were all in a trunk in her room. Mary Hale has assured me she is good at alterations but this one fitted Matilda without anything needing to be done.'

Say something sensible, he commanded himself. *Force yourself.* 'Uh, did I notice this morning that Mrs Hale had on a better dress than sackcloth-and-ashes workhouse clothing?'

Oh, Rosie. She looked at him as if he were a genius. 'Bravo, Master Hadfield,' she teased. 'You noticed!'

It was a lucky guess. 'Certainly,' he lied.

'Aunt Dorothea has more housedresses of her own. Granted, Mrs Hale is too thin, but my aunt had a sash that worked this morning, with alterations to come. You noticed. Good man.'

He decided to confess. 'Rosie, I didn't notice anything. I just didn't want you to think me a drooling fool. Now you know.'

What did this darling woman do, but murmur 'Rough ground,' and put her hand in his. 'Don't tell me stretchers again, Andrew Hadfield,' she said. 'I know you didn't notice.'

'Wise is woman,' he told her, gleeful to notice how she pinked up at his comment. When she turned the full force of her beautiful eyes on him, his heart performed its own impossible feat and melted. *With my blue eyes and yours*, he thought impulsively, *our children will have blue eyes, too*. What was he *thinking*?

Rosie moved on with her plans, granting him a reprieve from sensible statements. 'My aunt will spend the next few days acquainting Mary with her duties, and Matilda, too, who is now in charge of my kitten.' She squeezed his hand. 'You cannot imagine how pleased Aunt Dorothea is to return to her own house soon. Mary couldn't have given anyone a kinder Christmas gift.'

He nodded, on sure ground now. 'Mary took me aside before breakfast and said the same thing to me.' He took her hand and looped it through his arm, so he could feel her body closer. 'You cannot fathom *my* relief to see the widow of my sailing master in a good home where she and sweet Sadie's child will be safe. If this is Christmas, I want more of it.'

'It's Christmas,' she assured him, 'but I have never seen one so strange, either.'

Matilda proved to be adept at scouting out holly and ivy. His basket was filled too soon to suit him. He wanted to walk and walk. He stopped, surprised at his sudden realization. 'Rose, do you realize that I haven't had to stop and rest?' he asked. 'I'm not even tired.'

'I wondered if you would notice.'

'I'm fit for duty.'

A shadow crossed her face. She turned away. When she spoke, her voice was neutral. 'Yes. The navy will want you soon.'

They had wandered to the outskirts of Endicott, Rose quiet now, with Matilda walking beside her, wary again, and not the cheerful child who had skipped and whirled. He wondered why, until Rose stopped and knelt beside her.

'Matilda, you have nothing to fear in Endicott,' she said, her voice steady. 'No one means you harm here.'

'No more workhouse?'

'Never. Let us go down Chandler Street and I will show you Aunt Dorothea's house.'

They stopped before a pleasant structure of light-colored stone, with white shutters. Everything was orderly and soothing. 'Because you and your mother have come to help us, my aunt can return here.'

To Andrew's relief, the wary look left Matilda's face, replaced by the wonder of it all. '*We* did that?'

'Yes. You and your grandmother are a Christmas blessing to someone I love, and who raised me. You are our Christmas heroes.'

Andrew pushed his own turmoil—probably kicking and screaming—into the back of his mind as he saw goodness, even in this time of war and uncertainty. He nodded, and touched Matilda's head. 'Believe her,' he said, not minding that his voice had some command to it.

She nodded. 'Aye, sir.'

They continued down the street, until they stood in front of St. Timothy's, soon to have a new vicar, once the older man was cast overboard like so much flotsam. As the unfairness of it struck him, Andy felt his face harden. *No, no*, he told himself. *Let Matilda see only peace right now*. He calmed himself. This was not the moment to look like a sailing master directing a ship toward a fleet action.

He couldn't help glancing at Rose for reassurance. As he watched, she started to smile. *You have an idea*, he thought, relieved. 'What?' he asked, startled at how well he already knew her. You would think the matter was engineered.

Glory be, she understood him. 'Let's pay a visit to Vicar Ewing. I expect he is feeling low. You might be able to help him.'

He hoped she had a good idea; he didn't. Andrew felt the full weight of despair that he thought only came to the Royal Navy and the British Army, fighting to wear down a relentless foe bent on destruction. What a fool he was; everyone faced challenges. No one was immune, even if Vicar Ewing's trials were pale, compared to his.

She led them to the vicarage and told Matilda to knock. The vicar opened the door, his serious expression changing in an instant. 'Come in.' He looked down the street. 'I was expecting…'

He didn't need to tell them who. Andrew knew he was looking at someone girding himself for bad news. This was a man expecting eviction.

He led them to a pleasant sitting room with its view of the church, a sturdy building that had weathered several centuries of joy and sadness, no doubt. Introductions and explanations went around.

'Rose, your aunt will be returning to Chandler Street? I call that a blessing.'

'It is.' Rosie put her hand in the vicar's hand. 'She has been so kind to me, and now it is her time for her long-overdue reward.' She leaned forward. 'I only wish your own fate was different.'

Andrew watched as the vicar waved away her concerns. 'The Church of England has approved everything regarding my successor, and I will have a pension.'

'Where will you go?'

'I have no idea, but I am to leave tomorrow.' He sighed and watched Matilda pet the old dog on the hearth.

'This is too soon,' Rose said. 'Surely you can be here for Christmas.'

'Alas, no.' He looked at Matilda and lowered his voice. 'There is this as well. As I was acquainting him with his duties here, the new vicar told me there will be no more parish school.'

'No!'

'He sees no point in educating the poor above their station in life.' He glanced at Andrew. 'Hard times everywhere, eh, Master Hadfield?'

Andrew watched Rosie struggle for composure, and put his hand over hers. It was a forward gesture; he didn't care.

She mastered her emotion, and said in an offhand way, 'Master Hadfield, since he must go, you might be interested to know that our dear vicar is so good at comforting the sick. I wonder where he could do that again?'

He could have slapped his forehead at his own density. Rose did have a plan. What a woman. He knew what to do. 'Vicar, I have a solution to your dilemma.' He gave Rose the benefit of his own gratitude and raised her hand to his lips. 'She reminded me just now.'

Andrew had everyone's attention, even the dog's. He waited a moment for this idea to slink away, but it did not. 'I spent two months recently in Stonehouse Naval and Marine Hospital. We were treated well, but there was something lacking, at least in the block where I recuperated.' He smiled, more sure of himself. 'Even the chief surgeon noted it. Let me lay this before you.'

He looked at the vicar and saw all the goodness being evicted, so a worthless cleric's uncle could pay his brother and nephew out of ruin. 'Come with me to Stonehouse. I know Block Four needs someone with the time to comfort fearful tars and Marines. Someone to sit with them by day—' he glanced at Rose '—and comfort them by night. What say you? I know there is assigned housing in Stonehouse, or in the block behind it. Furnished rooms, even.'

Reverend Ewing stared at him, and Andy's heart sank. *Please, please*, he thought, wondering if he was praying, something he hadn't done in far too long.

To his immense gratitude, the reverend's expression mellowed. Andrew felt Rosie's hand on his arm and he covered it with his own. 'Please consider it, sir,' he said, overjoyed when Rose added, 'Please.'

'I will.' It was simply said, then, 'I mean, I will do more than consider it. I will do it. Tell me when.'

'As soon as I receive my orders from the Navy Board, I will let you know. We'll go together.' He glanced at Rose. 'If you are evicted, no matter. I have bumbled about at Fred's farmhouse, and there is room for another until my letter comes. Right, Rosie?'

'Right,' came her quiet reply. 'Oh, yes. When I think of all that you have done for me…'

They left a content and satisfied man, sitting at peace in his soon-to-be vacated vicarage. 'I'll write to the chief surgeon at Stonehouse immediately,' Andrew told Rosie as they started back to the farm. 'Rose, it was your idea and it's brilliant.'

'You'd have thought of it,' she allowed. 'I just gave you a nudge. You're the hero.'

She did something wonderful then that he knew would comfort him for years to come at sea, even if he never saw her again. She rummaged in the basket of holly and ivy. What was she looking for?

'Ah.' She took out a misshapen holly sprig and stood tall to hold it over his head. 'I know mistletoe when I see it, Master Hadfield.'

It wasn't mistletoe; surely she knew that. No fool, he pulled her shockingly close and kissed her. As wonderful as her lips felt, he positively basked in the way her arms circled him. She clasped her hands together in the middle of his back. He couldn't have escaped her grasp if he tried, and he did not try. He was no expert at kissing. Neither was she. They figured it out with amazing speed.

Thank goodness Matilda had skipped ahead, wrapped in her own world, which gave them a small moment to be wrapped in theirs. 'Mine is a dangerous occupation,' he told her. 'I don't know what else to say.'

He did know. He wanted to tell her he loved her. He wanted to marry her. He wanted to father her children. He wanted her to always meet him at the dock. Come to think of it, that was all he wanted in the first place, someone to see him off on a voyage. Now that he had met this woman, he knew he wanted more. He wanted someone to see him home from sea, as well. He wanted someone to share his home and bed. That much wooing probably needed more time than he had, thanks to Napoleon.

It could wait because it had to. He looked into her eyes. 'Rose Harte, you're a delight,' he said simply. 'Let's go home.'

She nodded. He crooked out his arm and hers slid naturally through it. He was still smiling until he came inside the farmhouse. Fred Harte, too serious, met him at the door with a letter. 'I wanted to tear it up, Andy,' the farmer said. 'But that would probably land me in prison forever.'

He took the letter. The insignia on the envelope told him what was inside. He opened it, read and felt suddenly hollow. 'The Navy Board orders me to report to Plymouth no later than Christmas Eve. My new ship, the *Albemarle,* will sail the day after Christmas. I must leave tomorrow.'

His heart broke into a thousand pieces. When Rosie cried out, it broke a thousand times more.

Chapter Fourteen

I can do this, I can do this, Rosie thought as she smiled through the afternoon, making things as easy as she could for the man she loved, a man governed by duty, who was leaving in the morning via post-chaise. She knew he would not declare himself now.

Papa was surprisingly grim at the news. 'Andy, we will miss you.'

'I will miss you, too,' her man said. 'All of you.'

Papa insisted on delivering the sailing master's note to Reverend Ewing himself, informing the cleric that if he was serious about Stonehouse, a post-chaise would meet him in the morning at the vicarage. He came back scowling, plopping himself into a chair in the kitchen, where Rosie folded the same napkin over and over.

'Daughter, those awful Keetings were already in residence! Reverend Ewing is trying to pack. I told him to be here by nightfall. I hope he doesn't mind the little chamber off the sitting room.'

Dinner tasted like weeds and ashes, which faintly surprised Rosie. She ignored it, pleased to see Mary Hale so animated. *You will fit in well here*, Rosie thought, happy to see her far removed from the desperate-eyed escapee from the workhouse. *I wish I could smile. Andy is leaving.*

Would this evening never end? Curled up in her favourite chair in the sitting room, she knitted and listened to Andrew explain life on the blockade of the French and Spanish coasts. She heard the eagerness in his voice, and knew where he really wanted to be, despite the danger.

A farmer dropped off Reverend Ewing and his dog, just as Papa was taking little glances at his timepiece, something he always did before he stretched and announced that it was time for bed.

'I could not stay there,' the cleric said, by way of apology. 'I trust there is room for my dog in Stonehouse.'

'The convalescents will love him,' Andrew said.

'I am not surprised you could not stay there another minute,' Fred said. 'We have long known how worthless all of Keeting's offspring are, up to and including our new and unwanted vicar. Now the brother who indulged in trade has paid off Sir William's debts, and his son will be vicar forever.'

Papa set them laughing next. He declared that perhaps he would begin attending church with the Methodists. 'They are probably rascals, but I hear they sing well! Beg pardon, Vicar.'

'Not vicar anymore, Mr Harte. Call me Reverend Ewing.'

'If I must.' Papa leaned back in his old rump-sprung chair. 'I know you too well to think you would have said anything mean to the usurper of your living. *I* would have.'

'Well, I had a moment…' Reverend Ewing replied. 'I asked the Keetings if they knew that the Royal Navy hero who has been charming all Endicott was the same fellow they refused to rescue from the mail coach in their post-chaise that evening Rosie came home.'

'I am no hero,' Andy said firmly.

'Stuff and nonsense,' the farmer said, unperturbed. 'I watched you rescue our kind Mary Hale here from the workhouse. Now you have found fitting employment for Reverend Ewing, someone we will miss.' He leaned closer in that conspiratorial way that Rosie remembered from precious moments in her childhood, when he gave her all his attention. 'I stopped at the pub on the way home. What did I learn but three of the young labourers have left to join the navy. Face it, Andy, you are Endicott's hero.'

'I give up. I surrender,' the sailing master said. 'Good night to all you rascals!'

Rosie wanted to escape upstairs to her bedchamber for a good cry, but lingered as Andrew thanked her father for his kindness. 'I suppose I will never know an ordinary Christmas, but this has certainly been one to remember. Reverend, we'll leave early.'

'You are welcome here anytime,' Papa said. 'Isn't he, Rosie?'

All she could do was nod and smile. She left the room when the others gathered around the sailing master to wish him well on future voyages. To her dismay, she realized she was beyond tears, which would have been a cleansing relief. It was time to resign from clerking at Gooding's Maritime Naval Stores and return home. She never wanted to see the ocean again.

Her troubled heart raised another objection. What if, after some fleet action or other disturbance, he needed someone to comfort him? 'Who will hold your hand then?' she asked the silence.

Rose waited all night, listening for Andy to mumble or cry out. To her dismay, she heard nothing. Lying in bed, she gathered her scattered thoughts. Only days ago, all she wanted was silence, which meant he was on the mend and didn't need her. But after her stupid mistletoe and their kiss in the meadow, she wanted an excuse to go to him at night, as she had before. There was no excuse, and she could not do it.

Not that she didn't want to get into bed with this man she knew—knew!—she loved; she did. Blame Aunt Dorothea, who, years ago, gently explained the rules of courtship and marriage, none of which seemed to apply in this time of war and turmoil. Rosie stayed in her bed, wide awake, regretting every moment of her indecision. Some instinct told her that Master Andrew Hadfield would never come to her bed. Another instinct assured her that he wanted her precisely as much as she wanted him. In her practical mind, *heartache* was a word fit only for bad novels. But what else was this feeling except heartache? Her heart ached because she knew he would not make the move. He had spoken several times about his trade, and the misery it extended to other innocents—Mary Hale and Matilda Madigan, for example.

'Drat your hide, you're too good a man, Andy,' she whispered into the dark. 'You think you are sparing me from a sad life. Did you ever think that my life is going to be a barren desert without you?'

She closed her eyes as dawn came, only to be shaken awake what seemed like minutes later by…by Mary Hale?

'Wake up, Miss Harte! You've overslept and Master Hadfield and Reverend Ewing are about to leave!'

Rosie sat up, shook her head to clear the fog and leaped out of bed. 'Why didn't my aunt…?'

'She didn't know what to do,' Mary said as they hurried down the stairs. 'My dear, she doesn't understand what it is to love a navy man, and I know you love Master Hadfield.'

Rose ran past the mirror in the hall, determined not to look at it because she knew her hair was a fright and her flannel nightgown so old that Methuselah's wife probably wore it.

She dashed past Aunt Dorothea in the entry way, not even slowing down for the gravel of the driveway. The chaise was already moving.

'Stop!'

She knew that voice of command. She had heard it only the day before yesterday in the workhouse. The post-chaise rider did precisely that as Andy flung open the door. He grabbed her and held her close, speaking softly as only a sailing master could, at rare times. 'I'll be back.'

'When?'

'I don't know. Kiss me quick. Tomorrow is Christmas

Eve. I'll stay at the Drake tonight, and we sail the day after Christmas.' He held her off for moment. 'I will be back,' he said, then kissed her with all the energy of his heart, mind, body and soul. She knew it.

Rosie stood there, hardly feeling the cold gravel biting into her bare feet. The man she adored put his hand on her head like a benediction, then left her.

Mary Hale and Aunt Dorothea shepherded her into the house.

'I love him,' she said simply. 'I truly do.'

Dorothea and Mary Hale sat close to her, part of that great sisterhood who knew what it was to love a man. Suddenly, she didn't want them there. Both had actually known the physical love of husbands, and she had nothing. She sobbed out that horrible fact, then regretted making them sad for their own losses. 'I can't say anything right. Forgive me.'

When she dared look, she saw two women she knew she could never hate. Dorothea took her hand. 'My dearest darling, my little brother knew before any of us.'

'*Papa?*' she asked in disbelief. 'Surely not.'

'He's in the cattle byre. Go talk to him. Um, here are your dressing gown and slippers, you wild woman.' Aunt Dorothea kissed her cheek. 'He has something to tell you.'

Rosie grabbed her robe and picked her way to the byre, where Papa contemplated one of his placid cows chewing her cud.

'Papa, what do you have to tell me?' she demanded.

As she stared at the indecision on his face, she understood a great truth. This man she admired and who always did the right thing, was probably picking his way through life the same as she was. She knew uncertainty, and she saw it on his face, too.

'Two things. That first morning, I told Andy Hadfield a real whopper.'

'Papa?'

'I told him that the inn was full up and he would have to stay with us.' He sighed and looked at the cow.

'He did tell me you said that, Papa. It was a lie?' She tried to collect her thoughts. 'You…you barely knew him then, Papa. Why would you do that?'

She watched his eyes and saw sudden longing. She took his hand and held it to her cheek.

'It's this way, dear one,' he said. 'That first night when you insisted he should stay, there was something in the way you looked at him.'

She remembered her concern for a man utterly wasted. What else? 'What…what could you possibly have seen?'

Papa took a deep breath. 'There was something in your eyes that reminded me of a time when your mother—God rest her—looked at me that way.'

'Oh, Papa.'

'There is this, also, which you need to know. The next day, he and I were chatting, and I asked him what he wanted for Christmas, since he was staying with us.' He smiled at the memory. 'I had to coax it out of him. I prodded a bit.' He took her hand. 'He told me all he wanted was just once for a pretty lady to see him off at the dock. Just once.'

He patted her hand as she cried, then gave her his

handkerchief. 'Give it a good blow, Rosie dear, then go pack.' He took out his timepiece. 'There will be a post-chaise here in about thirty minutes. I arranged it yesterday, after that unwanted letter from the Navy Board arrived. I know! I know! I am not impulsive. Well, except when I am.'

'I don't know where to go, what dock…' She calmed herself and remembered. 'He just told me he would be at the Drake tonight. Tomorrow is Christmas Eve, and he sails on the twenty-sixth. My goodness. I must pack.'

She hurried to the door of the byre, then stopped. 'Papa, I haven't even wrapped your present. There should be stockings over the fireplace. The carolers are coming by this evening. There's no wassail.'

'I doubt the carolers will sound any better than they ever do,' he said, and she heard all the good humour. 'Go on now, if you want to lose your virtue in a Plymouth hotel.'

'Papa, you are trying me… If I have to, I'll propose to him.'

He grinned. 'Your mother did that, God rest her.'

'*Mama?* I didn't know that! Papa, I love you.'

Chapter Fifteen

Papa must have given the post-chaise riders extra money to urge them to race the distance to Plymouth at a spanking pace. Rosie stared out the window at the usual December gloom, with grey skies and rain, snow or sleet threatening.

She remembered the Navy Board letter stating that the *Albemarle* was sailing on the tide the day after Christmas. She had time.

In Plymouth, she directed the post-chaise rider to take her to the Drake. She already knew she would have to write a letter of resignation to Mr Gooding and thank him for her years of employment. After all, if Mama could propose to Papa all those years ago, she could propose to Andrew, too.

They stopped at the Drake, with its magnificent view of the harbour, where she saw warships waiting, with lighters and dinghies piled with nautical supplies, many from Goodings, sailing toward them to load victuals, extra rope, tar and cannonballs for the ships for war. She knew the docks themselves could not accommodate all the frigates, and some were too large to dock in shallower water. Somewhere out there was the *Albemarle*. The post rider interrupted her contemplation to hand over her satchel and wish her Happy Christmas.

She had never been inside the Drake. She doubted ladies of good reputation ever walked up to any hotel desk by themselves, as she was doing. A woman with wildly curly red hair stood at the desk, speaking to a man wearing that imposing fore-and-aft hat, his boat cloak turned back to display one gold epaulet. It was all so splendid. Rosie had never felt so out of place in her life.

When the woman handed the captain a key, she turned her attention to Rose. 'How may I help you, my dear?'

'I am Rose Harte, and I am looking for Sailing Master Hadfield. Do you…?'

'Thank God!' the woman exclaimed. The woman came around the desk. 'I am Mrs Fillion.'

'Pleased to know you. Andrew mentioned you,' Rose said, wondering at the woman's excitement. 'I know he is leaving the day after tomorrow and…'

Mrs Fillion grabbed her cloak. 'Master Hadfield came here earlier today to register, but his captain met him on the way out. The orders were changed. The *Albemarle* is leaving with the tide this afternoon. Hurry!'

Rose dropped her satchel, picked up her skirts and ran with Mrs Fillion through that tangle of alleys, nooks and crannies that made up the Barbican. 'He told me you might come here, but he wasn't certain,' Mrs Fillion gasped as they ran.

'I love him,' Rose said, wondering at her total lack of

decorum. Was that what happened when a woman loved a navy man? She would have to ask Mary Hale about that later.

Out of breath, they came to the dock. 'Where, where, where…?' Mrs Fillion muttered, clutching her side as she tried to breathe. 'Thank God, there it is, and docked. Lord bless us. We all love Master Hadfield. Did you know he is a hero?'

'Yes, I heard something about it,' Rosie said. 'How will he know I am here?'

'He's been alone all these years. It got about among his mates that all he ever wanted was for a pretty girl to see him off on a voyage. They say he always watches with the other men.'

That breaks my heart, Rosie thought. *Dear, dear man.* 'What should I do? Where should I stand?'

'Wait right here,' her escort said. 'I will wait in the Mermaid's Tears over there and watch. I won't have you walking through the Barbican back to the Drake by yourself. Cheers, dear.'

Rose stood in front of the *Albemarle*, not a large ship, not like the really big ones anchored further offshore. She was already familiar with the prisoner hulks closer to the jetty, where French prisoners suffered. She had seen this harbour view many times in summer, when several of Mr Gooding's employees, her among them, watched ships come and go.

She waited patiently, supremely unsure of herself. Their one kiss had been memorable, but he had never spoken his mind to her. Whatever happened, it was already a Christmas to remember.

There he stood, hands on the rail, his smile filling the entire universe, her universe. He doffed his hat and bowed to her.

To her embarrassment, she heard a great cheer rise up from the deck of the *Albemarle* as Sailing Master Hadfield, her hero and evidently theirs, as well, hurried down the gangplank, grabbing her just as she hoped he would. As he kissed her, the cheer spread to adjacent ships.

'We are making a scene,' she said when she could speak.

'Aye, we are,' he agreed. 'You *would* choose this morning to oversleep, dear lady.' What did he do but make it worse, nuzzling her neck and whispering, 'Good God, that flannel nightgown…'

'Oh, hush. I was awake all night, waiting to hold your hand,' she explained. 'Did you really sleep all night?'

'Aye, for the first time since I shimmied naked down that rope. I owe it to you.'

Oh my but that next kiss was a barn burner. The observers cheered again. She held him off. 'You are my hero and don't you dare deny it. I love you.'

'Not the wisest thing you ever did.'

'It is,' she assured him. 'Must I propose to *you*? I will, you know.'

'No need,' he said, his voice close to her ear so she could hear him above the commotion. 'I love you. Please marry me, Rosie Harte.'

'Aye,' she said promptly, which made him gather her

scandalously close. 'It's like this—the *Albemarle* has been in dry dock over steering issues. We are making a shake-down cruise only as far as Portsmouth. Here's what you need to do.' Lord have mercy, could he *get* any closer? 'Pray that I will find some defect that will mean a few more weeks in dry dock. Steering and trim are my domain aboard ship and I am a master of it.'

She laughed, her hand to her mouth. 'Do you think you will find something wrong?'

'I am positive,' he said. 'I will get a special license in Portsmouth and marry you the moment we dock back here in, oh, let us say four days.'

She nodded, even as the practical side of her wanted more information. 'Master Hadfield, will there *really* be anything wrong with the *Albemarle*?'

'You will never tease that out of me.'

It was still daylight, but Andrew's new boat cloak was all encompassing. 'Even if I touch you here and here?' she whispered, amazing herself. 'Maybe even here?'

'Miss Harte, you are a menace to mortal man,' he said, as his breathing became more rapid. 'No, not even there, there or there.'

'I am a menace and you are my hero.'

He kissed her once more, then stood at attention at the bosun's whistle, signifying the captain was moving up the gangplank now. 'We're sailing with the tide. Mrs Fillion will find you a quiet berth on the third floor. Keep that berth warm.'

'Andy....'

'When I get back, we'll house hunt, well, later. Kiss me quick and wish me Happy Christmas.'

She did, and held his hand all the way to the gangplank, where the bosun took out his timepiece and winked at her future husband. Andrew looked toward the stern of the vessel and frowned. 'Uh-oh. I see something that will need adjusting when we return in a few days. I'd better tell Captain Matthews.'

'Andrew, you're the menace.'

He whispered in her ear, 'I remember something even more important. Hush now.' He gathered her close again. 'Dearest, I give you my whole heart, as you give me yours.'

Epilogue

January 1, 1812

Dear Father-in-law,

In future, please let me call you Father, for so you are to me. I married your lovely daughter yesterday in Stonehouse's chapel by special license, with Reverend Ewing officiating. We were both disappointed that the weather didn't allow travel. Rest assured that Rosie Hadfield took the unfortunate news like a navy wife. Sometimes times and tides work in our favour, and other times, no. This applies to ice and snow equally. (Call me vain, but my new uniform and lid were both ready, so I was no embarrassment.)

Our shakedown cruise to Portsmouth was long enough for me to notice a little flaw in the stern by the rudder. We will be in dry dock for another week, and then I am off to the blockade. My life is not my own, until war ceases. Pray it will be soon.

Before I leave, we will occupy some hours house-hunting here in Plymouth. Rosie shook her head at my suggestion that we also look in nearby Torbay, a pleasant place where ships also dock. Such a darling she is! She said Torbay would be too far away, since she plans to meet my ship any time of the day or night. 'I will be at the dock,' is all she said. She means it.

Dear sir, I know this wasn't the life you wanted for your child, a life of worry because Napoleon continues to rage across Europe. Recent scuttlebutt suggests he might be looking east to Russia next for conquest. We shall see if that dampens his ardour for more warfare, if such is the case.

In the meantime, we of the Royal Navy maintain our vigilance in keeping our shores free from war's strife. We will always stand the watch. This is my pledge to you and to my dear wife and children, if we are so blessed.

I confess to remaining unsure of how to spend Christmas as normal people do, but I do know this: maybe it makes me a regrettable heathen, but it didn't feel like Christmas until I put a ring on Rosie's finger. What a gift for both of us.

My best to you and your housekeeper, Mary Hale. I trust Matilda is dusting everything in sight, and Mary is feeding you well. I know Mary likes you because she told me so before I left your farm. Give

your sister, Dorothea, a good report from Rose that
she is blooming and keeping me loving company.

With love from both of us,
Andy and Rose Hadfield

* * * * *

THEIR YULETIDE REUNION

Joanna Johnson

For all who would like to stumble across
their own Duncan beneath the mistletoe

Chapter One

Fresh snow soaked the hems of Jane Stockwell's skirts and cloak as she walked slowly back to Great-Aunt Deborah's now quiet house. Every front door she passed was crowned with a holly wreath, candles glowing in windows and great boughs of frosted greenery wrapped around railings, but no such festive cheer warmed her heavy heart. There was nobody left now to share a cup of mulled wine with or join at the piano for carols, and as she drew closer to the grand house she'd once called home she felt her raw throat contract.

She'd been barely eighteen when her father's unwise investments had thrown his family into dire financial straits and her life as she'd known it had changed for ever. Keeping all five Stockwell children at home had proven impossibly expensive, and so Jane had been duly dispatched the fifty or so miles from Bristol to Wilton to throw herself on the charity of her wealthy, long-widowed great-aunt.

With only a disappointing and perpetually absent son of her own, Deborah had accepted her nephew's youngest daughter as her companion and, although it had taken a while for the decided old lady and shy girl to come to understand each other, their relationship had developed into a deep affection nothing could shake. If it hadn't been for her great-aunt's kindness in taking her in, Jane had no idea how her family would have survived, and after their closeness for the past six years she could hardly believe the indomitable Deborah Franklin was gone.

The freezing December wind tugged at the black veil concealing her face and she straightened it without breaking her weary stride. At least at the funeral she'd had a legitimate reason to wear the dark lace she never left home without, although there had been only a handful of mourners there to whisper among themselves about Miss Stockwell's choice to always hide her face. The snow had been falling thick and fast for the best part of a week and the blocked roads meant the town was cut off from the rest of the world, no carriages able to get in or out and the residents trapped in a prison of sparkling white. Great-Aunt Deborah had deserved a far grander send-off than the poor weather and her son's apathy had allowed, and the thought made Jane's already dangerously moist eyes prick again as she reached the impressive front door of Maybury Place.

It was warm in the house as she stepped inside and pushed the door closed behind her. A maid appeared to take her sodden cloak and, despite the weight sitting on her chest, Jane was touched to notice that the other woman had pinned a black ribbon to her apron to mark the unhappy day.

'Some more cards came for you while you were out,

ma'am. I've put them on the desk in the parlour. I've stoked up the fire in there and sent down to the kitchen for some tea. You must be wanting some after the chill of the churchyard.'

'Thank you, Ellen.'

Jane tried to smile, although of course the maid wouldn't have been able to see it through the veil even if she'd succeeded. She'd take it off in a moment but only once she was sure she had the tears that still wanted to escape under strict control. 'I'm sorry you're having to do the work of three people. I'd hoped my cousin Franklin would have allowed all the staff to stay on when he takes over the house, but sadly that wasn't to be.'

'I understand. Mr Franklin must do as he will.'

Ellen would never presume to express what she thought of the new master's determination to eradicate all traces of the previous owner he'd thought so little of, although there was a suggestion of a downward turn about her mouth. 'I don't suppose you know when he might come, ma'am?'

'I do, in fact.' Jane's jaw tightened. 'He intends to take possession just after Christmas. He told me only a few hours ago, as we stood beside his mother's grave. He's been gracious enough to allow me to spend the rest of this week and Christmas Day here, but I must be gone before he arrives on the twenty-seventh.'

The maid's careful discretion suffered a momentary slip. 'Forgive me, ma'am, but surely you won't stay here for Christmas? In this great house, all alone?'

Ellen's dismay echoed Jane's own, but all she could do was shrug. 'I don't have much choice. The snow has made the roads too dangerous for me to travel back to my family in Bristol. I'll pass a quiet Christmas in this house… the last one I ever will…and then…'

She broke off. The idea of spending even one more day at Maybury Place without her great-aunt was almost more than she could bear, but what else could she do? She had nowhere else to go, although even if the snow didn't melt she didn't trust her second-cousin not to throw her out onto the street regardless.

He'd only bothered to make a single fleeting visit after being told that Deborah was dying and even that had been to inspect the property he was so eager to inherit rather than to provide comfort, his poorly concealed impatience for his own mother's demise something Jane would never forgive. It was that casual cruelty that had made it necessary for her to make the decision that had spoiled all her hopes of future joy, her fear of what would surely have happened to Deborah if she'd been left alone to her son's care meaning Jane had been left with only one choice…

'Excuse me. I think I'll go to read those cards.'

She turned for the sanctuary of the parlour, determined to reach it before her composure fled completely. All inside was as the maid had said: a hearty fire leapt in the grate, its orange ribbons reflecting off the teapot waiting for her on the table beside the sofa where she sat most evenings, although now, of course, she'd have to do so alone.

A pile of condolence letters and cards sat neatly on the mantelpiece but she didn't pick them up as she moved closer to the fireplace. Instead, the large mirror hanging on the wall above it showed her veiled figure approach the glass and hesitate before reaching up to unpin the bonnet from her head.

As always, it came as both a relief and a trial to remove the mask of stuffy lace, and she saw her reflection show the same as she pulled the bonnet off entirely and met her own gaze.

She still had the thick chestnut hair she'd often been complimented on and wide-spaced blue-green eyes Great-Aunt Deborah had always said were kind. She could claim a straight nose, a slightly pointed chin and an endearing scattering of freckles—in sum, a countenance she'd had no reason to despair of before fate had intervened.

Jane sighed.

Slightly tilting her chin, she inspected the left side of her face for what must have been the thousandth time. She knew every inch of the scarring splashed across it by now, so there was no reason for her to turn her head to follow its progress into her hairline other than to torture herself more than her grief already did. The carriage accident three years ago had left her with a permanent reminder of the agony she'd felt as broken glass had rained down on her, slicing through her skin and only missing her eye by the scantest hair's breadth. A ridge of pink bisected her eyebrow, curving down to join the raised welts on her cheek, each scar like an angry island set adrift upon unmarked flesh. They no longer caused any pain but they would never disappear, just as she would never forget the stares that had followed her before she'd taken to wearing a veil every time she set foot outdoors.

Setting her bonnet down on the mantelpiece, she care-

fully traced a fingertip over the worst of the red streaks
coursing across her cheek. It was hardly surprising that
children had been wary of her, but she might have expected adults to better attempt to cover their horror. It
had made her feel ashamed to see the pity in their eyes,
pity that had sometimes bordered on disgust, and she had
long since reconciled herself to the fact that no gentleman would ever again look on her with desire. No man
would want a wife who couldn't show her face, she knew
without any trace of doubt, and so to remain with Great-
Aunt Deborah had been her only path…although now
even that single door left open to her had been slammed
irreversibly shut.

Her heart felt as though it was folding in on itself,
trying to curl up as small as possible to hold the least
amount of pain.

*No Auntie and certainly no prospect of a husband.
There's nothing to be done but to go back home and try
to pick up the pieces of my life there—if such a sad, empty
thing can be called a life.*

At the very back of her mind, in a shadowy corner
she always tried to avoid recognising, something stirred.

She didn't want to allow it. The memories held in that
out-of-the-way place wouldn't make her feel any less
wretched, but they took advantage of her sadness and
pressed forwards while she was too weak to hold them
in check.

Once upon a time she'd had a chance at happiness and
had to let it slip away, she acknowledged with dull reluctance as she stepped back from the glass. Someone had

wanted to marry her, and it was her greatest regret that she'd had to say *no* instead of the *yes* she'd yearned to shout from the rooftops. She hadn't seen him since the day he'd left Wilton a few weeks before her accident, taking her shattered heart with him, but even if he'd returned she was certain he wouldn't want her now. She'd been whole and unscarred when he'd left and now she would never be either of those things again, not much of a prize for a man who could have taken his pick of any of Wiltshire's single ladies.

Lieutenant Duncan Fitzjames had been good-looking, clever and kind and doubtless still was, and it would have come as no surprise to learn he'd secured a wife almost immediately after duty and circumstance had forced her to turn him down.

'That was at Christmastime, too,' she murmured aloud to the empty room. 'Between the loss of him and Auntie, I don't think I'll feel merry at this time of year ever again.'

Her great-aunt wouldn't have wanted her to bow to self-pity. *One mustn't wallow*, she almost heard Deborah saying, the thought bringing a brittle smile to her lips. The old lady had possessed spirit, although of course it was far easier to show fortitude when one wasn't facing the bleak expectation of a lifetime without love.

As much as she had tried to forget about Duncan, her recollections of him had never faded, his anguished face the last time she'd seen him indelibly imprinted on her mind, and she'd lost count of the number of times she'd wondered where he would be now. If things had been different, she would have been his wife, settled and happy and perhaps raising a family of her own—but instead she was none of those things, only a sad, quiet shadow of the person she'd been before his abortive proposal and the accident had joined forces to knock her off her feet, and she hadn't known real peace since.

The front doorbell clanged.

For a moment she stood very still, dismayed as the chime echoed down the hall. Who on earth would come calling on the day of the funeral? The few of Deborah's acquaintances that had managed to brave the snow had already paid their respects at the church, Jane receiving their condolences through a numb haze while Cousin Franklin stood by, indifferent and detached. There was no reason for anyone to come to the house, and her dismay deepened at the notion of having to play hostess while her innards felt as though they had been hollowed out.

She waited. Ellen would answer the summons; a few days before, it would have been a different maid who opened the door, but of course Cousin Franklin had wanted most of his mother's servants dismissed. As it was now he who was in charge, Jane hadn't been able to argue, although as the ringing echo died away without prompting any response she had to wonder whether he had made a mistake.

Another few seconds elapsed with no sign of move-ment out in the corridor. Ellen must have been either too busy to answer or hadn't heard the bell, and with only a brief pause to gather herself, Jane retrieved her bonnet from its perch on the mantel.

The absolute last thing she wanted at that moment was

to speak to anyone, but her conscience wouldn't allow her to ignore whoever stood outside in the cold. The low winter sun was beginning to set and the temperature dropping along with it, and she knew that Great-Aunt Deborah would never have entertained the idea of letting a guest freeze.

With practised speed, she pulled on the bonnet and veil. Usually, when visitors came she would wear a wide-hemmed cap and sit at a careful angle to conceal the injured side of her face, but as time was of the essence her black lace would have to do. The full veil would hide the redness of her eyes as well as the scarring that made people stare, and as she had no idea who could possibly be intruding on her at such an awful time, she was glad of as much protection as she could get.

With deep unwillingness, she left the parlour and hurried into the hall. Still no servant appeared; the only other person present was her unwanted caller, a dark shape just visible through the stained-glass panels of the front door. Whoever was waiting for her was tall, their large silhouette backlit by the dying sun, and despite the far more important things crowding her mind, she was struck by a vague and niggling thought that she'd seen it somewhere before.

Duncan's heart felt far too loud beneath his shirt as he watched a blurry figure approach the green-painted door. *What am I doing here? This is a mistake.*
The fact that he knew it was a servant who was coming to open it didn't make any difference to the stranglehold

that apprehension currently had on his throat. There was mercifully little chance he'd catch sight of Miss Stockwell, hidden away as she must be in her private grief, and yet every nerve was still wound tight to find himself on her doorstep once more. Three years ago he'd left Maybury Place with no intention of ever entering it again and even standing outside brought him closer to the house—and the painful memories it stirred—than he liked.

With grim determination, he tried to rein himself in. He would hand over the note his mother had sent him to deliver, pass on his own condolences to whichever maid appeared in the doorway and then leave at once. If he lingered too long there might be a possibility of snatching a glimpse of Jane, and as he had no intention of seeing her during his brief visit to Wilton it would be best if he made himself scarce.

The indistinct shape of the servant reached the door and he forced his cold face to surrender its grimace.

Just because he had no *intention* of seeing her, however, didn't mean he didn't *want* to. In truth, there was nothing he wanted more, the image of her smile still as fresh in his mind as if he'd last seen it only yesterday rather than years before, but the gut-wrenching disappointment of their final meeting cast a pall that couldn't be erased. She had turned down his offer of marriage without telling him why, and just because some time had elapsed since then didn't mean anything had changed—apart, perhaps, from the unblemished beauty of Jane's heart-shaped face.

The usual surge of compassion and concern he always

felt when thinking of what had befallen her was cut off by the inward swing of the door.

There was a pause that lasted for around half a second. He *just* managed to gather an impression of a figure swathed head to toe in black as it flashed in front of him, but then it vanished as quickly as it had appeared, the door abruptly shutting again with a resounding bang.

Duncan blinked, his mother's note still in his gloved hand.

Why did that servant just slam the door in my face?

Confused, he hesitated to ring the bell again. Through the stained-glass panels, he could make out the person was still there, standing apparently frozen to the spot, and it was another few moments before he heard the handle turn.

The door opened much more slowly than it had the first time. The black-clad woman revealed herself with uncertainty he could sense even through her veil, and for one agonising beat he thought his heart had stopped.

He didn't need to see her face to know it wasn't a maid who stood before him. The way she held herself was instantly recognisable, her back straight and shoulders high and square, and the slim sweep of her waist in her mourning gown was one he'd have known even in the darkest night. She'd let him place his hands there years ago, during the time he'd thought they were destined to be happy together, and nothing would ever steal away the knowledge of that secret curve.

'Jane?'

Her name fell from his lips as easily as breathing,

something it seemed he'd almost forgotten how to do. He hadn't expected to see her, and to find her suddenly in front of him was disorienting, the years falling away in the blink of an eye.

'Duncan.'

Her voice was low and unsteady, although to him it was still the sweetest he'd ever heard. 'I'm sorry. Please forgive me for closing the door. I was just… What are you doing here?'

Duncan was aware she'd spoken although her questions barely registered. His attention was on other things, her nearness rendering it impossible to think.

For days, weeks, months he had ached to be close to her again, all the while knowing it would be a mistake, and now that he could have reached out and touched her it was difficult to control the urge.

'I came to see my mother for Christmas,' he managed, with at least some semblance of control. 'I arrived just this morning, although I had to walk much of the way from Salisbury as no carriage could get through the snow.'

Jane nodded, or he assumed the jerk of her head was meant as such. He couldn't see her expression through the gauzy mask, only a shadowy outline of her features, and his stomach clenched as he recalled the reason why.

It had been a carriage accident, his mother had said in her letter a short while afterwards, one he'd received while preparing to take his broken heart back to sea. Mrs Fitzjames was unaware of the connection between her son and her neighbour's companion and had relayed the news without any notion of the horror with which it would be received. It had seemed such a shame to his mother that a pretty girl was now so scarred that she'd resorted to wearing a veil to hide herself from prying eyes, although Duncan's reaction had been far more visceral. He had wanted to return to Wilton at once and challenge anyone who dared make Jane feel ashamed, adamant that nothing could ever detract from her perfection—but of course he had not acted on that desire. She had made it very clear that any understanding between them was at an end and he'd had to accept it, even if the thought of her unhappy and in pain was like a pebble in his shoe that pricked him with every step.

He looked down at her, unable to tell if she was looking back. There was no way to guess what she was thinking or whether she was pleased to see him after so long a time, and his uncertainty allowed other questions to follow in its wake.

Would she still smell the same if he buried his nose in her hair? he wondered. Would she still melt into his arms if he kissed her, the way she'd used to before everything had fallen apart? He wanted to know all these things and more, and yet her veil stood between them as more than a mere wisp of lace. She hid her face from him and her feelings too, both things she had once allowed him to appreciate so intimately, and although everything in him longed to look into her eyes once more, he knew better than to ask.

'My mother wanted me to deliver this,' he said hoarsely, holding up the note as if to prove his presence on her doorstep wasn't his idea. 'She's extremely sorry she wasn't at the funeral. She's currently recovering from a bout of influenza, otherwise she would certainly have been there. I know she and your great-aunt had been friends for a long time.'

Jane took the note from him. Her hand was bare, he saw, her fingers just as dainty as he remembered, and he wasn't sure if the tremor in them was due to the cold air or something else.

She didn't unfold the paper, although she did incline her head again in another ambiguous nod. 'Please assure her I wasn't offended. To tell the truth, I was so in a world of my own I hardly noticed who was in attendance and who wasn't.'

'That's understandable.'

Duncan shifted slightly, aware he ought to say something more. Jane's countenance might be hidden but the quake in her voice was telling and the knowledge that she was hurting was like a knife between his ribs. It was as though the time apart had been nothing at all, all the years and miles between them vanishing—for him, at least—into a meaningless void.

Even during their separation, no other woman had managed to challenge the hold she had on him. His fellow officers had tried repeatedly to introduce him to young ladies they encountered between voyages, each determined to win a smile from the grave lieutenant who had left his heart behind in England, but none had succeeded. He'd only wanted a wife if that wife was Jane, and as that was an impossibility he'd seen no point in being anything other than distantly civil to the pretty misses dangled under his nose. His love had been given and could not be taken back, and he knew it would be cruel to make anyone else Mrs Fitzjames when his affections already belonged elsewhere. Every woman deserved to be her husband's first choice and that wasn't a promise he could make, resolved instead to remain alone after Jane's rejection rather than settle for someone who would surely want more than he could give.

His throat felt constricted, as if he'd tied his cravat too tightly. 'Please accept my deepest sympathies for your loss. I know you held Mrs Franklin in the highest regard.'

'Yes. I did.'

Jane's black-sleeved arms moved to wrap around herself. Probably she was freezing, standing in the open doorway, but she spoke again before he could suggest she go back inside.

'So,' she went on, with the definite air of one trying to change the subject. 'You're to have a pleasant Christmas with your mother, just the two of you. How agreeable.'

Duncan took the hint. 'It's not quite just the two of us. My three nieces are staying with my mother while my sister and her husband are away for his health. With them in the house, the atmosphere is…lively.'

The black bonnet tilted slightly. 'You have three nieces now?'

'Georgiana was blessed with twins. If *blessed* is indeed the right word for one who looks so continually harassed.'

A breath of wry amusement came from behind the lace, the hint of a laugh reminding him of how comfortable they'd used to be together.

'And you? What are your plans for Christmas?'

Jane seemed to hug herself more tightly. 'I shall stay here until the snow clears enough for me to return to Bristol,' she said quietly. 'My cousin Franklin has kindly allowed me until the day after Boxing Day to gather my effects, after which he will come to take possession of the house and everything in it.'

'Everything? Your great-aunt didn't make any provision for you?'

The bonnet shook from side to side. 'She couldn't. A condition of her late husband's will. She was allowed to enjoy everything the estate had to offer during her lifetime, but nothing ever truly belonged to her. It was always my great-uncle's intention that their son would inherit everything, right down to the last silver fork.'

'I see.' Duncan just managed to stop himself from frowning. He didn't have the advantage of a veil to hide his expression and he imagined she wouldn't want to see his poor opinion of the Franklin men reflected in his eyes.

She had lived there for six years, devoting herself to Deborah, and this was how she was to be treated? He knew John Franklin was unpleasant—everyone in Wilton was aware of his greedy, self-interested nature—but to think of him turfing Jane out of what had been her home was beyond the pale. Deborah had been at her son's mercy and now it seemed Jane was too, and although he tried to remind himself that her welfare was no longer any of his business, it was still a hard pill to choke down.

'So, you intend to stay here alone until Franklin comes?'

'Yes. I'll have no trouble bearing the solitude.' She spoke decisively and yet somehow, he suspected she was trying to convince herself as well as him. 'The time to myself will be useful. I can finish packing and of course I shall help the servants to ready the house. I'll be so busy I doubt I'll even notice it's Christmas at all. It's what Auntie would have wanted.'

He wasn't sure he believed her. Deborah had been fiercely protective of her great-niece and would surely have been horrified by the bleak picture Jane had just painted. The old lady would have wanted Jane's happiness, not for her to be lonely and abandoned at Christmas of all times, but yet again he had to remind himself of his place.

She didn't want him, he told himself as he watched her rub the cold black silk of her arms. Any connection they'd once shared had died on the day she had turned him away and he had no right to intrude, even if seeing her again made him want to catch her up and kiss away the sorrow she was trying so hard to keep from her voice.

He cleared his dry throat. 'You've had a difficult day. I won't detain you any longer when I imagine you must want to be alone.'

He half wanted her to ask him to stay, and he couldn't deny a pang of disappointment when instead she nodded. 'Thank you. And thank you for bringing the note.'

'You're welcome. With my mother ill and most of her servants busy wrangling my nieces, I think I may have to fill the role of postmaster for some time yet.'

Jane stepped back, retreating closer to the open door.

The house behind her was perfectly still and silent as a tomb, no movement stirring anywhere other than the slight ripple of her veil in the December breeze.

There was a pause. By the subtle upward angle of her head, he thought she must have been looking into his face, and not for the first time he wished he could do the same to her.

'You look very well, Duncan,' she said softly, the words almost lost amid her swathe of black lace. 'It's a pleasure to see it…and you.'

Duncan swallowed painfully. Did she mean that? She sounded so sad and tired but pretending not to be and it caught him in the vulnerable place seeing her again had torn open like an unhealed wound. Every feeling he'd had for her three years ago rose up, trying to burst their banks, and turning away with a hurried bow took almost all the strength he had left.

I shouldn't do this again, he thought severely as he made himself walk back down the path he'd never intended to revisit, determined not to look over his shoulder. *I think it's best that I stay away from her for the short time I'm here. Anything else will just make things worse— for me, if not for her.*

Chapter Two

Mrs Fitzjames looked up from her invalid's bowl of blandly nourishing porridge, towards where her son was seated opposite her across the breakfast table. 'I've decided to ask Miss Stockwell to come here for Christmas,' she informed him. 'From what you told me yesterday, it seems she'll have a lonely time otherwise. It's the least I can do, given how long Deborah and I were friends. Will you please call to tell her once you've finished eating?'

Duncan choked on his coffee. 'What? You want to invite—?'

'Miss Stockwell. Yes. It's only charitable, and besides, you may need the help.'

Blotting spilled coffee from his lap with his napkin, he stared at his mother. 'Help? With what?'

'Looking after the children.' Mrs Fitzjames pushed aside her bowl with an unenthusiastic glance at its contents. 'I'm still too exhausted to run around after them and their nurse has recently been ill herself. The poor creature is only just returned to her post and can hardly keep up with them. My servants are busy with the extra work Christmas brings, so I'm afraid any additional entertaining must fall to you…and perhaps, if she's willing, Miss Stockwell.'

She gazed at him expectantly, but Duncan didn't speak.

He didn't trust himself to. If he opened his mouth, his mother would hear the horror in his voice, and that would prompt questions he didn't want to answer.

There was no way on earth he could go back to Maybury Place to see Jane again, he thought with absolute certainty. He hadn't meant to encounter her *once* during his brief visit, let alone spend an entire week in her presence, a thought so wildly tempting he didn't dare consider it.

One encounter had been enough to bring the full might of his weakness for her roaring up from the depths to which he had pushed it, and if he let himself go to her a second time there was no guarantee he wouldn't make a fool of himself. He hadn't slept all night for thinking of her, her sad, black-draped figure ceaselessly invading his mind, and eating was out of the question, the coffee he'd just spluttered over the tablecloth the only thing he'd managed to force down since he'd found himself face to face—or at least, face to veil—with the woman he still considered the love of his life.

'She's grieving,' he muttered, concentrating on his stained napkin rather than his mother. 'Doubtless she would much rather be alone than here with us.'

'You could be right. On the other hand, a distraction might be just what she wants. Do you have any idea what she's likely to prefer?'

Duncan stiffened slightly. 'Why would I know that?'

Mrs Fitzjames spread her hands. 'I thought I recalled the two of you were friends during the time you spent here previously. What was it—two years ago?'

'Three.'

'Oh, yes. I remember now.'

Duncan twisted the napkin between his fingers, immediately regretting correcting her so quickly. There was something in her tone he didn't quite like; it was a little too knowing, and if there was one thing he wanted to avoid it was his mother getting ideas about things he had no desire to discuss.

'You have no objection to my asking Miss Stockwell, then? Other than suspecting she might not accept?'

Very carefully, Duncan poured himself another cup of coffee, buying a moment in which to think.

Of course he had objections, he thought distractedly. He had almost nothing else! To have Jane in the same house as him, sitting in the same rooms and breathing the same air, would be torture he didn't know if he could withstand. For a full week he'd have to see her without touching, hear her speak without being able to kiss her petal-soft lips, forcing himself to keep his distance while wanting to get closer with every beat of his heart. It was a hopeless situation every instinct told him he had to avoid…and yet something inside him held back.

She's so unhappy.

His stomach clenched. As much as he wanted to spare himself the suffering he'd have to endure if she came to stay with them, abandoning her to a Christmas of lonely grief was far worse. Even now, long years since she had rejected his proposal and unwittingly sentenced him to a life spent alone, he still valued her wellbeing above his own, and to cut her off to spare his unrequited feelings wasn't something he could bring himself to do.

He realised he was frowning and stopped quickly before his mother could notice. It would be selfish for him *not* to ask Jane to join them…but would it also be selfish if he wanted her to accept, which some masochistic but undeniable part of him certainly did? He was torn: there was no good outcome whichever way he turned; no way in which he could entirely stop the past from following him into the present, and as he was doomed, no matter what he did, he supposed he ought to do what was right.

'I've no objection, Mother. This is your house. Who you invite into it is entirely up to you.'

'Excellent.' Mrs Fitzjames nodded briskly, still pale beneath her cap but a little of her usual animation returned. 'If you've finished spilling coffee all over my tablecloth, perhaps you'd be good enough to call on Miss Stockwell.'

'Of course.' Duncan tried to smile, although he feared his face was too rigid for it to be particularly convincing. 'Being your errand boy was something I enjoyed so much the first time. Why not again?'

A criss-cross trail of footprints followed Jane as she walked another lap of Maybury Place's snow-covered garden. Her feet were beginning to get damp but she hardly noticed, too distracted to pay attention to anything so trivial.

His hair's longer now. There are a couple more lines

*on his forehead, and he didn't look quite so careworn
last time we met.*

A wet branch brushed her bare cheek, making her
shiver. She wasn't wearing a veil in the privacy of the
garden and under other circumstances she might have
enjoyed feeling the cold air on her skin. Today, however,
she had far more important things to think about: every
tiny detail of Duncan's appearance was seared into her
brain, flickering through it as she walked, and although
the first flush of shock had subsided, that didn't mean
her mind was at ease as it replayed the moment of finding him standing on her doorstep once again.

He was as handsome as ever, she'd noted the first instant she'd realised it was him on the other side of the
door, her mute amazement mingling with an instinctive
thrill. No other man had such broad shoulders or intelligent brown eyes, or a mouth that was so expressive
even when closed. The years had only changed him the
smallest degree—which was more than she could say
for herself.

A familiar sense of shame curdled within her. What
must he have thought when she'd opened the door with her
face enveloped in black lace? He must have known why
she was veiled—probably his mother had mentioned it,
she and Great-Aunt Deborah having been such friends—
and she shrank from the knowledge that he would have
wondered what lay beneath. Her ruined countenance was
no longer the one he'd professed such admiration for, or
even loved, before she'd been forced to turn him away...

'Don't think about that,' she rebuked herself harshly,

her voice as sharp as the icicles that hung from the windowsills, but it was already too late.

She could still remember every moment of their first meeting—one far more magical and filled with hope than their last—and although it made her mouth twist with pain, she couldn't help but recall how butterflies had erupted in her stomach when he had smiled at her from across his mother's parlour. He'd asked to be introduced and she had been delighted to spend the rest of the card party at the same table as the dashing lieutenant, her heart beating so quickly she'd half expected to faint. Duncan had been so interested in everything she'd had to say, asking questions and making her laugh until she was sure she'd never encountered a more charming man in her life, an opinion that had deepened over the next six months into a love she'd fully expected to take to her grave.

'But I couldn't marry him.' This time her voice was quieter, much of its strength lost to unhappiness and regret. 'I couldn't leave Auntie all alone. She was already so unwell, and if I'd gone to Southampton with Duncan instead of staying here to ensure she was looked after, Cousin Franklin would have deliberately let her fade away.'

Her numb hands curled into fists, anger suddenly licking at her like an open flame.

Franklin hadn't even tried to hide his disdain that day she'd met him, quite by chance, as she'd returned from walking in the park. Deborah had been having one of the bad spells that so often plagued her and so opted to stay at home, and her son's reaction upon being told of his mother's current discomfort had sickened Jane to her core.

'Ill, but still persevering, I see. I can't help but think your company must be the only thing keeping her alive.'

'Thank you, sir.'

'It's hardly a compliment. I can't say I approve of the older generations insisting on lingering over their fortunes while others are waiting to inherit. There's something so undignified about making themselves a constant nuisance when they ought to stand aside.'

'By stand aside...you can't mean die? You wouldn't wish for your own mother...?'

'It's the way of the world, Jane. She's had a good life. It's about time I had my turn, rather than this continuous throwing away of money on doctors that only keep her clinging on. I've half a mind to put a stop to her seeing them altogether.'

The memory of that fateful conversation was no less revolting even after the passing of three years and still it made her lip curl as she trudged across the frozen grass. What kind of man openly confessed his desire for the death of his mother, just so he could possess her wealth? In that moment the scales had fallen from her eyes: she couldn't leave Deborah undefended, not once she'd realised the depth of Franklin's contempt and neglectful intentions. After everything her great-aunt had done for her, taking her in when her family had been in distress, there was no way she could have abandoned Auntie to such malice, although the price for her devotion had turned out to be higher than she ever could have known.

Jane's face crumpled. Of all her regrets, not being able to tell Duncan the real reason she had rejected him was the biggest. Great-Aunt Deborah would have been horrified to learn Jane had refused him on her account, but it had been the only thing to do. The old lady would have suffered otherwise, her own son caring for nothing but the inheritance he valued far more than his ailing mother, and although it had crushed Jane's heart into dust to let Duncan slip away without a proper explanation, she'd refused to take the selfish path.

He's probably glad I let him go. I can't imagine any man wanting to be tied to me now.

The thought was devastating and yet she couldn't deny its accuracy. Duncan must have celebrated his good fortune in escaping now he had seen her again, relieved to have been spared a wife he could take so little pride in. He was free to choose another woman with whom he wouldn't be ashamed to be seen, and although his solitary presence at his mother's house for Christmas suggested he hadn't yet wed, Jane was sure he couldn't be alone for long.

She stumbled slightly, blaming the snow but knowing it was really despair that made each step an effort. After three years apart, Duncan was unexpectedly within arm's reach, yet as untouchable as if he'd still been at sea. The desire to see him again was suffocatingly strong…but wouldn't she just be hurting herself if she sought him out, causing herself even more grief on top of what Deborah's death had already heaped upon her like a heavy mound of earth?

She only realised she was crying when the tears made her cheeks feel cold. The house loomed over her as she trailed across the garden, now a forlorn, empty shell of the home it had been when her great-aunt was alive, and all of a sudden the idea of going back inside it filled her with dread.

Now they'd begun, it seemed the tears didn't want to stop. They made her throat ache, the freezing air joining forces with them to make it difficult to breathe, and it was only the sound of boots crunching through the snow behind her that helped to stem the flow.

Hurriedly wiping her face with the flat of her palm, she turned around. 'Yes, Ellen? Was there something—'

The rest of her sentence died in her mouth.

'My apologies. I didn't mean to startle you.'

Duncan held up a steadying hand. He stood hardly any distance away, clearly concerned by the way she had flinched back on seeing him, her reflexive pleasure at recognising her unexpected visitor veering immediately into dismay.

Jane stayed very still, horror pinning her to the spot. Her face was bare and her head uncovered and there was nothing she could do to stop him from seeing the full extent of her scars, her disfigurement laid out before him, stark red against white. She saw his eyes flicker over the network of raised skin and felt a vivid wave of shame wash over her, the back of her neck growing warm despite the icy ground.

So. Now he knows.

Mortified heat flared in her cheeks. She wanted to

cover herself but she seemed to have lost the use of her hands, only able to stare in silent torment as Duncan bowed.

'Forgive me for calling unannounced. Your maid let me in and as she seemed busy, I took the liberty of going to look for you myself. I hope I'm not intruding.'

He straightened up again, his dark hair gleaming as he moved in the pale sunshine. His eyes met hers: after that first lightning-fast glance at her scars his gaze didn't waver again, although Jane knew he had already seen too much. His expression was carefully controlled, whatever he was thinking well concealed behind his usual good manners, but she was no fool. He'd be feeling the same combination of pity and distaste as everyone else who had caught a glimpse of her since the accident and her heart sank that any sweet past memory of her he might still have carried would now be soured by the present's unpalatable truth.

'Not at all,' she managed faintly. 'Will you come in-side?'

Privately, she prayed he'd refuse, but she wasn't to be granted any reprieve.

'Only if it's convenient. There's something my mother would like me to ask you.'

'Of course. Let's go in.'

She gestured for him to walk ahead of her. She had no idea what Mrs Fitzjames could want to ask her and even less real interest. Duncan's presence and the feeling of oppression that soaked into her as she entered the great gloomy house were overwhelming, grief and embarrassment obliterating everything else. It was an odd feeling, caught between delight at seeing Duncan again and wishing he would leave, and she wasn't sure which side would triumph as she followed him into the parlour and waved him towards a chair.

'Would you like some tea?'

'No, thank you. I won't stay for long.'

She sat in her usual place on the sofa, glad to be able to angle herself away from him. Her heavily frilled cap lay on the table next to her and she itched to put it on, only the thought of drawing more attention to her face stopping her from snatching it up.

Duncan settled himself in his seat. He looked slightly ill at ease but was clearly trying to hide it; the sole giveaway was in the way he constantly spun the brim of his hat through his fingers as he shifted in his chair and, straightening her skirts, Jane risked another glance at him out of the corner of her eye.

I recall us sharing that armchair, a dangerous little voice piped up in the back of her mind. *He'd wait until Auntie went to bed and then draw me onto his knee, his hands pushing into my hair as he turned my face to his—*

Her fingers locked together on her lap in a punishing squeeze.

Stop that. Thinking such things will do no good whatsoever.

She'd never thought to see him in Maybury Place's parlour again and it was difficult to keep the memories under control. At one time there would have been such tension between them she could have tasted it, their need to touch each other simmering just below a surface so exhilarat-ingly fragile it might have broken at any moment. As soon as Deborah left the room they would be pulled together as if by a magnetic force, Duncan's kisses chaste to start with, but rapidly growing in passion until they'd had to break apart to stop things from going too far.

Jane tightened the vice-like grip of her hands. She would have given anything to be able to fall into his arms again, but of course that was a wish that wouldn't come true. Duncan had seen her for what she was and any nos-talgic fondness he might have entertained for her would never again kindle into desire.

Pain had begun to grow deep inside her. It was a dull ache, building every time she moved, but she tried to push it aside.

'You mentioned your mother had a question for me.'

'Yes.' He nodded, looking away from her to examine the glossy black silk of his hat. 'She was wondering… that is, if you still had no more pressing engagements… if perhaps you would do us the honour of joining us. For Christmas.'

He shot her a swift, unreadable look, still holding his hat in front of him like a shield, and Jane felt her eyes widen.

'Spend Christmas with you?'

'And my mother and nieces,' Duncan amended hast-ily. 'I can't promise it would be a very restful time, but it might perhaps be more agreeable than the alternative.'

Jane's heart leapt against her ribs. A whole week with

the Fitzjameses? Day after day of waking to know that Duncan was never more than a few rooms away?

She took a breath. It was the most agonisingly tempting offer she'd received since he had proposed three years earlier and she felt the same powerful urge to accept as she had when he'd turned to her on one knee.

A change of scene would allow her some respite from the unceasing burden of her grief, she thought dazedly. Any distraction from her unhappiness was certainly a strong inducement to take Mrs Fitzjames up on her invitation—but she'd be lying if she pretended it was the only one, her yearning to be close to Duncan a threat she couldn't ignore.

It would be a mistake to spend more time with him. My feelings would grow stronger whereas his would not, leaving me even more sorrowful than when I arrived.

He was watching her, the dark eyes she admired so much trained on her face. He still hadn't taken another glance at her scars; they might as well have not been there at all for all the notice he took of them, his tactful kindness raising a lump in her throat.

'Thank you. It's an extremely generous offer, but I'm afraid I cannot accept.'

She paused uncomfortably. What reason should she give for her refusal? She could hardly tell him the truth of why she didn't dare return with him, and yet it would be the height of bad manners to reject his mother's generosity without an explanation.

Inspiration struck.

'I fear my appearance might unsettle the children,' she

said reluctantly, grimly satisfied that her excuse wasn't a lie. 'I wouldn't be so rude as to wear a veil in your mother's house and I worry your nieces would be frightened.'

Her hands were still grasped in her lap and she preferred to look at them rather than her guest, not wanting to see him realise that she was right.

'They would not.' Duncan's voice cut through her rising shame. 'I would explain to them,' he stated simply. 'The twins are too young to understand, but their older sister is a tender-hearted girl and would be happy to accept anyone I call a friend.'

Jane's breath caught. 'A friend?'

'Yes. If you would allow me to think of you as such.'

His gaze was so direct it made her flush. It was hard to read his expression but she knew what hers must be, all the blood in her body suddenly rushing to her face.

He would still be my friend? Even after I sent him away without really telling him why?

Her throat dry, she managed a nod. 'That would make me happier than I have been in a long while.'

'Then friends are what we shall be.' The set of his countenance changed a fraction. 'Your happiness is still something I care about…even now.'

Jane stilled, unsure she had heard him correctly. He'd muttered the second sentence, making it difficult to catch over the crackle of the fire between them, and she thought she must have been mistaken when he briskly went on.

'So. Are you resolved, then, to spend this Christmas alone?'

She hesitated, two responses teetering on her tongue.

Going with Duncan would be painful. She'd have the torment of being in his presence while knowing she had no right to expect anything but unforeseen friendship from him, unable to touch him where he had once placed her hands himself. He was out of bounds and she had to respect it, her previous rejection of his proposal and now her injuries ensuring his romantic feelings for her had long since died. There was nothing left for her to cling on to…and yet still she couldn't turn her back.

I'll be miserable anyway, she acknowledged bleakly. *Nothing will make me forget Auntie's loss, and if I'm to be sad whatever I do, perhaps I should throw caution to the wind.*

Pretending to study her fingernails again, she snatched a glance at him through her downturned eyelashes. He was so handsome, everything about him just as appealing as it had been when they'd first met, and the full extent of how much she'd missed him hit her like a runaway carriage. No other man had ever meant so much to her and never would, and in spite of everything that urged her to be careful, she knew her decision had already been made.

'No.' It was a struggle to speak, her heart pounding so hard she was certain he must be able to hear it. 'If your invitation still stands, I'd be pleased to accept.'

Caught up in the whirl of her feelings, she couldn't tell Duncan's reaction, although she was aware of a short pause before he replied.

'Good. In truth, you'd be doing me a favour. It's fallen to me to help entertain my nieces and I would very much appreciate some help.'

Slightly dazed by her own recklessness, Jane nodded. Assisting with the children would be a welcome task. It would make things less awkward if she was useful, there for a purpose rather than as a burden not of Duncan's choosing. There was still the chance the girls would be apprehensive at the sight of her but she tried not to think about it, the desire to leave Maybury Place's sad shadow—and, if she was entirely honest, to spend more time with Duncan—overcoming her fear.

'I'll go to gather a few things, then. As most of my belongings are in bags already, it shouldn't take too long.'

She stood up. Immediately, Duncan rose likewise, his usual courtesy bringing him to his feet—which also happened to bring him abruptly within a few inches of Jane's face.

She didn't mean to make a noise. She meant to turn and leave the room, but somehow instead her breath fled at finding him so close, escaping in a sound worryingly like a gasp.

There was barely a hand's span between them, something she thought she saw him realise at much the same moment she did. Three years ago, he would have bent down and kissed her if she'd stood gazing up at him like that, his arms sliding around her to draw her against the firm plane of his chest, and her insides shuddered now as she watched his pupils dilate. Doubtless it was the memory of that former passion that made his eyes darken rather than any current want, although her own wish that he would stoop down to claim her lips was every bit as strong as it had been long before.

Far too late for any veneer of dignity, she managed to find her tongue. 'Excuse me,' she mumbled. 'I won't keep you waiting.'

To her relief, Duncan stood aside. 'Take all the time you need. There's no cause to rush.'

With another mumble that she hoped he'd interpret as thanks, Jane stepped round him, heading for the door. It might well have been the case that *he* was in no hurry, but *she* certainly didn't delay as she scurried from the room.

Chapter Three

Duncan tried his best not to stare, but he knew he was fighting a losing battle.

The kitchen was a hive of activity. All around him, maids kneaded dough and stirred bubbling saucepans, the fragrance of festive spices and orange peel scenting the air, and in the candlelight the stray wisp of chestnut hair peeping from the edge of Jane's extensively frilled cap gleamed like burnished bronze. She was concentrating, her brow slightly creased as she helped his eldest niece stir the mincemeat that was to fill the pie cases they had made earlier that morning, and when she was too distracted to guard her expression she was so lovely he couldn't look away.

He shifted uncomfortably in his chair, masking the movement by jiggling the twins perched on his knees. They too were absorbed in the serious task of Christmas pie making, helping to cut the pastry stars that would sit on top with enthusiasm that far outstripped their skill. Some of the scraps of dough on the cook's huge table were distinctly oddly shaped and there was a great deal of flour scattered where it shouldn't be, but as he watched Jane's mouth curve into an unconscious smile any thought of such trivial matters faded away.

Her smile's just as sweet as it always was. How is it she doesn't realise?

She'd been anxious about meeting the children, worried they might be wary of the scars she was so determined to hide from the world, but her fears had proven unfounded. Aged just two and a half, Maria and Eliza were too young to look at her with anything other than innocent curiosity, while six-year-old Charlotte was bright enough to be warned to be polite. Aside from a few interested glances when Jane had first arrived, the girls had remained unfazed, their behaviour good enough to put many adults to shame, and the speed with which they had warmed to her had likewise warmed his heart. After only three days under his mother's roof, it was as though Jane had known his family all her life, and Duncan couldn't help but wish that could continue for the rest of it.

His insides gave a warning squeeze.

No. Don't open that door.

He tried to heed his own advice, but it was damnedly difficult when her blue-green eyes were currently so lively, a stark difference to the red-rimmed horror they'd shown in Maybury Place's garden when she'd realised he had seen her bare face. Of course he'd been shocked at the extent of the pink ridges, vivid against her pale cheek, but in the very next moment he'd known nothing had changed. She was still Jane beneath the layers of black bombazine and lace, any alteration going no deeper than her skin, and if he'd have thought she would have welcomed him telling her so he would have admitted it at once. For all her embarrassment and desire to shy away from being seen Duncan now hardly noticed her scars at all, the only thing he observed when looking at her being the woman he still loved.

Blessedly unaware she was being admired from the other side of the table, Jane scraped around the edge of the bowl.

'There. I think that's all mixed now.'

Charlotte nodded in agreement, oblivious to a floury handprint across her nose. 'I think so too. What's next?'

'We need to put the mincemeat into the pastry cases.'

Jane passed his niece two spoons. 'Scoop up a little bit with this one and push it in with the other. Yes,' she went on encouragingly as Charlotte dropped a formless blob of filling into the baking tin. 'Exactly like that. These are going to be perfect.'

All three little girls beamed with pride, even Duncan's mouth twitching as he caught Jane's eye.

Her cap hid much of the left side of her face but, even so, he thought he saw her flush at his smile. When she blushed like that, she was the prettiest thing he'd ever seen and he only just managed to catch himself in time, the instinct to slide a hand across the table towards her one he couldn't seem to shake. Once upon a time she'd have twined her fingers around his and he felt a stab of regret that such a thing wouldn't happen again, the latest in a long line of disappointments he'd suffered since she had arrived at his mother's house to cause him such unintended trouble.

He watched her discreetly tidy the mess Charlotte had made of the pies, obviously taking great pains not to hurt his niece's feelings as she repaired the sticky damage. Her kindness was unchanged; misfortune and grief hadn't sharpened her edges as they might have in someone else, her character still much the same even if the outer shell was different—and that was where the problem lay.

Every time she enters a room it's as though she's sucked all the air out of it.

He swallowed a sigh. It might have seemed overly dramatic, but it was the truth. Whenever he was in her presence, he found it hard to breathe normally: she was always either too close or too far away, making him tense when she looked at him, yet frustrated when she didn't, and the sweet notes of the rose water he knew she dabbed onto her wrists each morning might as well have been specifically designed to make him lose his wits. It made the whole house smell of her, subtle but enough to catch him every time…and yet, despite his discomfort, he knew he'd done the right thing in asking her to stay.

She might have been unwittingly driving him mad, but it was a price worth paying if it meant she'd have a merrier Christmas than she would otherwise. After that she'd return to Bristol and he to Southampton, and the knowledge that they were unlikely to meet again made his stomach feel full of sharp rocks.

His train of thought was abruptly diverted by Maria trying to slide off his knee. Eliza had also started wrig-

gling and he had to act fast to stop both twins from top-
pling onto the floor.

'You can't run about in the kitchen, girls. It isn't safe.'

There came mutinous whining at being restrained. Cutting pastry stars had been amusing for a few minutes but
now his youngest nieces were clearly getting restless and
it came as something of a relief when their nurse appeared
at the kitchen door.

'Please forgive the interruption, sir,' she called, strain-
ing her voice to be heard above the clamour of the kitchen.
'It's the time Miss Eliza and Miss Maria usually have
their nap.'

Carefully, Duncan got to his feet, juggling a twin in
each arm. He thought he caught Jane slide him an admiring glance at his grappling skills and had to stop himself from looking too pleased as he carried them to the
safety of the door.

'Here. A delivery for you.'

He set them down just inside the corridor. Immediately, each twin claimed one of their nurse's hands and she
smiled down at them, although he saw her face was pale.

'I'm sorry I had to take this morning off to see the doc-
tor, sir,' she said apologetically. 'My chest is still weak
from the influenza, but all the same it isn't right that you
and Miss Stockwell should have to do so much while I
recover.'

'Don't apologise, Miss Vine. It's important you regain
your health.'

The nurse bobbed respectfully and led the girls away,

their slippered feet pattering on the stone floor, and Duncan turned back to the kitchen.

Charlotte had progressed to placing the stars on top of the filled pies. Jane was giving her free rein to arrange them, her face slightly averted from the door. She'd angled herself away as soon as the nurse appeared, Duncan had noticed, in the same instinctive movement she still made whenever he approached her from the left-hand side, and he felt a pinch of dismay that she still thought she needed to hide.

As if anyone would dare say a word against her in this house. I'd certainly make them regret it if they did.

He sat down at the table again as Charlotte placed the final star. She studied them for a moment, assessing her work, and then brushed her hands together with the air of a job well done.

'Good. They're finished. So, what shall we do now?'

Jane laughed, the sound more welcome than she ever could have guessed. 'You certainly don't waste time. What would you *like* to do?'

'Well…' Charlotte considered for a moment. 'Last year, some boys in our town went sledging. Mama said I was too young to go, but now that I'm six I think I should be allowed. Will you take me? Please?'

Jane smiled at the imploring little face. 'I don't know. You'd have to ask your uncle what he thinks.'

For the first time in a while she lifted her eyes to his, his heart—as always—giving a leap at finding himself the focus of her attention. It was tempting to revel in it, but with his niece now peering at him likewise he had to resist.

'I suppose we can go. You'd need to wrap up warm, though,' he said firmly as Charlotte leapt up from her chair, 'and promise you won't break any bones. If I returned you to your mama in a worse condition than I received you, she'd have my head.'

His niece didn't seem to hear his warning. 'Thank you, Uncle Duncan! I'll go to tell Grandmama. She was asleep when I went into her room earlier, but I'm sure she'll want to know.'

She raced away, narrowly avoiding a maid carrying a tray of freshly baked cakes as she went. Belatedly, it occurred to Duncan that his mother might not be pleased at the prospect of her granddaughter throwing herself down a snowy slope, but he was soon distracted by Jane's unconscious frown.

'Is something wrong?'

'No, no. Not at all.' She began to gather up the scraps of leftover pastry. She seemed to be thinking about something, however, as a moment later she spoke again. 'Where do you think would be the best place to go?'

It was a casual enough question but Duncan understood her intent. Although trying to hide it, he could tell she hesitated at the idea of leaving the house and having to be on public display, even with her veil. With unfortunate irony, the ever-present screen of dark lace must invite comment almost as much as the scars would have done, although he would never embarrass her by pointing it out.

'There's a slope in the woods behind the house,' he said

with deliberate indifference. 'It's smaller than the one in the park everyone else will be using, so we should have the place to ourselves. I think that would be better, considering Charlotte has never been sledging before.'

Jane nodded. Her expression didn't change but he thought he saw a whisper of tension leave the set of her mouth, the lips he would have given anything to kiss again softening the smallest degree.

'I haven't been sledging in a decade,' he went on. 'I hope I can still remember how, or else Charlotte will be in for a disappointment when I can't show her anything.'

He was trying very hard not to look at Jane's mouth, but she didn't help matters when she suddenly broke into a smile. 'Don't I recall you fell off quite spectacularly once?' She raised her eyebrows, sending them under the frilled edge of her cap. 'When you were quite young, chipping a tooth? I'm sure you told me something like that.'

Ruefully, Duncan rubbed the back of his neck. 'That's right. Perhaps I'm really not the best choice of teacher.'

Something stirred within him. He must have told her that story not long after they'd first met, and yet she had remembered. It was a throwaway comment on her part, probably, but it reminded him how intimate they had once been, in the days when he'd been closer to her than anyone else alive.

That was another memory he shouldn't waste time pursuing, he told himself gruffly. He was intent on holding himself back from fresh heartache, not hurtling towards it, and the momentary slip reminded him yet again of the need never to relax his guard. She'd crushed his hopes once with her kind, gentle rejection and he didn't intend to suffer the same thing again, self-preservation demanding he ignore the persistent ache inside that wanted to offer himself to her anew.

She pushed back her chair and stood up, brushing down her apron. It was covered in flour and he saw her black sleeves were speckled too as she reached up to adjust her cap.

'I'll just go to change my gown. I'm not sure what one is supposed to wear to go sledging, but I suspect it isn't this.'

With a pleasant nod to the kitchen maids, Duncan followed her to the door. 'Whatever you have that's warmest would be my advice. I may ask my mother if I can borrow her fox fur stole.'

Jane glanced back at him over her shoulder. The corridor was empty: all the maids were occupied elsewhere, readying the Christmas provisions that so richly scented the air, so there was no one else around to hear her snort.

'Don't do that. You'd look much better in mink.'

Warmth kindled in his stomach. When she looked at him so teasingly, she was irresistible. The urge to touch her was maddening, like an itch he couldn't allow himself to scratch, and so it felt like the most devious of temptations when a perfect opportunity fell into his lap.

'Wait a moment. You have flour on your face.'

'Have I? Where?'

Immediately, she stopped walking and tried to scrub it away. She only succeeded in smearing it further, however, and with his heart pounding like a bass drum, Duncan realised he had already lost.

'It's still there. Shall I…?'

She was half turned away from him but he saw a trace of colour creep into her flour-streaked cheek. 'If you wouldn't mind. I'd rather not give anyone any more reason to stare.'

He nodded, his mouth suddenly dry. There was a momentary pause and then he stepped towards her, willing his hand to remain steady as he lifted it to her face.

Jane flinched as his fingertip grazed her skin although she didn't pull away. She kept her eyes averted, refusing to meet his, but she couldn't hide her deepening blush, flushing crimson as he gently brushed away the flour from her cheek and jaw.

Duncan gritted his teeth. Her lips were slightly parted and he could have sworn he heard her draw in a sharp breath when he touched her, the first time in three years he had felt her warmth beneath his fingers. With her face so close and slightly upturned, he could see her scars more clearly than ever before and his chest tightened to imagine how much each one must have hurt. More than anything, he wanted to kiss them—both to soothe any lingering pain and to show Jane that *everything* about her was precious, including the parts about which the world had made her feel ashamed, but of course, he could not.

Every sinew in his body wanted to drop his hand to her waist and pull her nearer, but instead he stepped back, reluctantly obeying the alarm bells ringing in his ears. 'There. Perfectly respectable once more.'

'Thank you.' Jane smiled weakly, her gaze still fixed over his shoulder. As far as he was aware, there was no masterpiece hanging behind him, so there must have been some other reason for her fascination with the corridor wall, one that might also have explained the odd pitch of her voice. 'Shall we meet in the hall in half an hour? That'll give me plenty of time to dig out my thickest cloak.'

'Very good.'

Inclining his head, he invited her to walk ahead of him. It was best she couldn't see him at that moment, he decided as she began to glide away. She might have noticed the ticking of his pulse above the collar of his shirt, spurred into a gallop by so small a contact as running a fingertip over her cheek but still enough to make his knees feel like water. She was a torment and a delight wrapped up in one unwitting package and he braced himself for another afternoon in her company as he followed her towards the stairs, trying—and failing—not to notice the subtle sway of her waist as she walked.

Jane had always been fond of children, so it was a quiet pleasure when Charlotte's hand slipped into hers as they trudged through the snowy woods. In large part it was the little girl's obvious liking for her that she was so glad of, but she couldn't deny another less noble reason for being grateful that Duncan's niece was there.

While Charlotte chattered like a cheerful bird both adults could focus on her rather than each other, and that was a far safer prospect while Jane felt in danger of getting carried away.

He only touched my cheek. It's not as though he kissed it.

Her veil would prevent him from seeing how she bit her lip at the thought and for that she was thankful indeed. He'd once known her so well and there was a possibility he might still have been able to read her face with one glance, immediately seeing that she was thinking things she shouldn't.

'Are we almost there? We've been walking for *ages*.'

Charlotte sounded as one might after a two-hour hike through a mountain pass and Jane smiled at Duncan's answering laugh.

'It's been about ten minutes. Surely your legs aren't tired already?'

He strolled along beside them, his boots crunching through the snow as he shortened his strides to match his niece's slow pace. Under one arm he carried a sledge: a bulky old-fashioned thing that must have been heavy but he held it with no trouble at all, the effortless strength of his bicep something Jane admired out of the corner of her eye.

'They aren't yet but they might be soon,' Charlotte told him piteously. 'I could be too tired to sledge when we get there.'

'Oh, dear. That would never do.'

Duncan looked grave. Fleetingly, Jane wondered if he was going to suggest they return to the house, but then her heart turned over when he flashed her the briefest of conspiratorial smiles.

'Here. Let's see if we can't take the weight off a little bit.'

Transferring the sledge to his other arm, he took Charlotte's free hand. 'If Miss Stockwell will help me? On the count of three!'

Jane understood at once. On his *three!* she and Duncan swung Charlotte into the air between them, the little girl kicking up a shower of snow as she squealed. She landed again, giggling, and Jane knew she would never forget how handsome Duncan looked when he grinned.

'Is that better? Did that give your legs a rest?'

'Only a little one. I think they might need another!'

He laughed. 'I'm not so sure. Look—we're almost there.'

He pointed through the frost-laden trees. A small clearing lay a short distance away, spread out beneath a steep bank. The snow there looked deep and undisturbed and Charlotte gave a squeak of delight as Duncan let go of her hand and allowed her to run towards it.

'Be careful. Remember what I said about your mama and my head.'

The girl scurried away, leaving Jane and Duncan behind. The snow was indeed much thicker now the trees had thinned and it was a struggle to pick through, the hem of Jane's red cloak darkening to a sodden crimson as she walked. Duncan didn't seem to be having quite so much trouble; the long legs she had always thought so highly of let him move far more easily, although once or twice their shoulders brushed together as some unseen dip made them stumble, each accidental touch sending shockwaves beneath the bodice of her gown.

Charlotte was almost dancing with excitement when they emerged into the clearing. 'Are we going to the top of the hill, Uncle Duncan?'

'Yes. Lead the way.'

Together they clambered up the bank. Calling it a hill was exaggerating slightly but Jane supposed it must have looked much bigger to Charlotte, the little girl glowing as they reached the top and Duncan carefully positioned the sledge.

'Hop on.'

His niece didn't need to be told twice. She leapt onto it the moment he stepped back, snatching up the piece of rope he held out to her.

'Hold onto this and keep your arms tucked in. If you lean forwards, you'll go faster.'

Duncan set a foot on the back of the wooden seat. 'Are you ready? Then—off you go!'

He pushed firmly, sending the sledge shooting over the crest of the bank. Charlotte gave a shrill squeak and then she was gone, carried away down the slope at a speed Jane suspected would have made Mrs Fitzjames wince.

Duncan stood with his hands on his hips, observing with interest as his niece raced away. 'What do you think? Will she fall out?'

'I doubt it. She was clutching onto that rope for dear life.'

Charlotte was picking up speed. She flew over a series of hidden bumps, each one making her scream, and then ploughed directly into a snowdrift at the base of a bare tree.

There was a moment of stillness. Then—

'Can I go again?' a distant voice floated up the bank, cutting through the cold air, and Jane echoed Duncan's laugh.

'Of course,' he called back. 'Wait there.'

He turned to her. 'I'll just go to get the sledge. It's too heavy for her to manage by herself.'

Jane nodded. Duncan waded away and she watched him go, feeling a different kind of admiration as he reached where Charlotte lay in a crumpled heap and gently set her back on her feet.

He always was good with children, she reflected, touched to see him wrap his niece in a hug that was enthusiastically returned. *He'll make a wonderful father one day, to children of his own.*

Abruptly, she pressed her mouth into a tight line. That didn't stop the rush of sadness that swept over her, however, and she bunched her fingers into a fist, digging her nails into her gloved palms.

Seeing him with his family was precious but at the same time it made her ache for what she couldn't have. To make her own family with Duncan was what she wanted and the power of that want caused her eyes to prickle behind her veil, constant grief for Deborah already lying heavy beneath her ribs. She'd known that being under the same roof as him would be difficult but she hadn't realised quite how much, the future she'd been forced to sacrifice now seeming so very far away. She would never feel she'd made a mistake in choosing Deborah's safety over her own happiness but it would probably never lose its sting either, the fact she'd been backed into such a wretched corner impossible to forget.

'Were you watching? Did you see?' Charlotte called out as she skipped closer and Jane gave herself a stern internal shake.

'I was and I did. I'm very impressed.'

Having dragged the sledge up behind him, Duncan now repositioned it at the top of the slope. 'On you get. Let's see if you can hit that other mound of snow this time.'

Charlotte scrambled aboard. Lifting his leg, Duncan once again set his foot on the seat and with a sharp shove sent the little girl shrieking away down the bank.

As they followed her progress through the snow, Duncan casually addressed Jane over his shoulder. 'Are you tempted to have a go yourself?'

'I think not. I may, however, gather some of that holly.' She pointed to a tree a short distance away, wreathed with berries and gleaming green spikes. 'I promised the girls I'd show them how to make Yuletide decorations this afternoon and I have a feeling I'll need more supplies.'

He smiled, the upward quirk of his lips doing something strange to her insides. 'Good idea. I find, when it comes to those three, it's always best to have plenty of spares.'

He retreated to retrieve his niece from her second pile of snow and Jane moved away likewise. In the chilly December wind, the holly leaves seemed to beckon to her and she wasn't sorry to go, glad of a few minutes to collect herself after her previous slide into regret.

It wasn't easy to gather the leaves. The spikes were vicious and the stems thick and even after a while of twisting and pulling she'd still only managed to amass a small pile. Behind her, she could hear Charlotte's repeated ventures down the slope, much screeching and laughter splitting the quiet, and it was only when another unexpected voice piped up that Jane turned back round.

'Sir?'

A maid emerged from the trees at the bottom of the slope. Duncan was engaged in excavating Charlotte from her latest drift but he looked up at the servant's approach. 'Dinah? What are you doing here?'

From atop the bank, Jane heard the maid reply. 'The mistress asked me to bring Miss Charlotte home, sir. She's worried about her catching cold and requests you send her back now.'

'Does she?' They were too far apart for Jane to hear Duncan sigh, but she knew he must have done by the movement of his shoulders. 'Since having influenza, my mother sees illness round every corner. Charlotte seems well enough to me, but I suppose we can't disobey a direct order.'

The little girl made a sound of protest but Duncan shook his head. 'Your grandmama has spoken, I'm afraid. You'll have to go along with Dinah. Miss Stockwell and I will follow once she's finished gathering all the holly she needs. We won't be far behind.'

With obvious reluctance, Charlotte took the maid's outstretched hand, but not before looking up the slope to wave to Jane, who flourished a holly bough in return. The servant dipped a curtsey and she and Charlotte withdrew, two cloak-swathed figures cutting through the trampled snow to disappear into the woods.

Jane returned to her task. Her fingers were starting to hurt from snapping the tough branches and she was about to reach for her final leaf when Duncan's voice came from behind.

'Have you got enough?'

She started. She hadn't heard him approach, despite the crunchy ground, and she hoped he hadn't noticed how she'd jumped.

'I think so. That's all I'll be able to carry in my cloak, anyway. I should have thought to bring a basket.'

Twisting off the last prickly sprig, she dropped it onto the pile. If she held up one corner of her cloak she'd be able to make a sort of pocket in which to carry them, although she didn't have the chance to try before he spoke again.

'The snow up here is still so pristine. Between Charlotte and the sledge, the stuff at the bottom of the bank is as churned up as a farmer's field.'

Jane looked up. Duncan was gazing around, one hand shielding his eyes from the wintry sun. 'It's beautiful, really.'

'I think so too. I love when snow is as deep as this.' She pushed the toe of her boot down into it, her foot almost disappearing beneath the carpet of white. 'It reminds me of making snow angels with my sister, when we were about the same age as Charlotte. Those were happy times.'

She hadn't meant to sound wistful. It was supposed to

be a mere passing comment, but she realised that more than a touch of sadness had stolen into her voice when Duncan slid her a quick, searching glance.

'You could always make one now.'

'What? An angel?' Hurriedly, she forced a laugh. She didn't want him to know how close to the surface sorrow lurked for her, the loss of both Deborah and any future with him pressing on her heart. 'I couldn't. Auntie would say it was beneath my dignity.'

'I disagree. I think she would want you to take happiness wherever you could find it.'

For a split second he looked so serious that Jane felt her breath catch. He seemed so earnest in his concern for her that she wasn't sure what to say, but then he smiled.

'What if I made one too? Would that make a difference?'

'You?' To her surprise, she laughed again, albeit this time far more genuinely. 'A lieutenant of His Majesty's navy, rolling about in the snow?'

'Why not? It's Christmas, after all. If not now, when?'

As if to prove his intentions, he swept off his hat and hung it on one of the tree's berry-laden branches. 'Come on. We'll do it together.'

He held out his hand, and in a dizzying moment of foolishness she was sure was a mistake Jane allowed herself to take it.

The next thing she knew, she was flat on her back in the snow.

A damp chill seized her but she was too shocked to pay it much mind. The sky above was a perfect clear blue peeping through the skeletal treetops, a sight almost as beautiful as the unblemished snow, but it was Duncan's chuckle in her ear that was the best thing of all.

'I'm sorry. Weren't you expecting that?'

She turned her head. Her bonnet had come off, she realised belatedly. Her veil lay on the ground beside her like a shadow but she couldn't seem to make herself reach for it. Duncan was too close for that, lying next to her and his hand still very near hers, and when he looked over at her all such tedious thoughts of veils and bonnets instantly fled.

'So?' he asked her. 'What now?'

Jane groped for the right answer, difficult to find when a pair of warm brown eyes were fixed on her face. 'Now we move our arms and legs to make the shape of the angel's skirt and wings.'

'If you say so.'

They were too close together to fully outstretch their arms and she felt a thrill skitter through her when his hand accidentally brushed her waist. The snow scrunched up around them and her sadness of moments before faded into the background as she wriggled, the whole thing too ridiculous to allow any unhappiness to keep its grip.

'Am I doing it right?'

One glance at Duncan was enough to force out any lingering gloom. He looked more like a fish squirming on a hook than an angel and she couldn't hold back a laugh, louder and more real than any before.

'No! What on earth are you *doing*?'

His grin could have lit up the darkest room. 'My best, which is obviously not good enough.'

He fell still, his arms and legs still outstretched. Somehow, in their inelegant writhing, they had shuffled even closer together and another laugh died in her throat as she felt his fingertips come to rest, *just* touching hers.

She lay quietly, trying to catch her breath. She didn't want to move. In that moment, everything was perfect: the azure sky overhead and the gleaming beauty of the snow, Duncan lying beside her as if none of the past three years had happened. Anyone stumbling across them now would have thought they were a couple in love and the desire to be so again came so hard and piercing she almost gasped aloud.

Duncan's voice broke the spell. 'Oh.'

'What?'

She turned her head to look at him, feeling how the snow had dampened her uncovered hair. He was staring straight upwards, into the overhanging branches of the tree, and she followed his suddenly sharpened gaze.

'Up there. I've just noticed.'

Her heart turned over. 'Is that…mistletoe?'

'Yes. I think it is.'

His voice was carefully controlled, but even so something in it made her shiver. It was as though he was pretending to be calm rather than truly feeling so, and she imagined her face must have given a similar impression as she met his eye.

He didn't speak further. He looked at her and she looked back at him, neither one able to move.

A rising sea of tension welled up around them. Jane felt it in every nerve, every vein filling with anticipation instead of blood as she watched Duncan's gaze flit from her eyes down to her mouth and stay there, a strange kind of hunger growing inside her that she didn't know how to name. She'd felt it before, however; it was the same ungovernable desire that had struck every time they'd been alone together in the months before she'd had to turn him away, and just because three years had passed since she'd last felt it didn't mean she'd forgotten what came next.

When their lips met it felt *right*.

The air was freezing and a chill had seeped into her wet clothes but Jane felt as though she was on fire as Duncan pulled her into his arms right there in the snow. She went willingly, her mouth seeking his with impatience she wasn't too proud to fight, although, even if she'd tried, she knew she would have failed. Every regret, every pent-up fear and burden of grief was lifted as he kissed her, one hand around her waist and the other sliding up to cup her ruined cheek.

She stiffened when he touched her scars, suddenly afraid, but he was not to be deterred. He didn't falter. With gentleness that reassured her more than any words, he traced his thumb over the raised welts, never stopping the soft but certain questing of his lips as he stole her every breath.

Her cloak was tangled around her. Snow had found its way into one of her boots but she didn't care, her entire consciousness wrapped up in the sensation of being in Duncan's arms. It was where she belonged, the last dregs of her rationality told her, and by the way his fingers tunnelled into her half-tumbled hair she thought he must have thought the same. It was impossible for her to feel the shame her scars usually inspired in her when he stroked them so reverently and she abandoned herself to his caress, her hands sliding beneath his coat and everything in her willing him not to stop…

It came as a crashing disappointment when he drew back.

He was breathing hard and when she forced her eyes open she saw his were glazed. He looked very much like a man who would have preferred to continue rather than restrain himself and she shuddered at the frank craving in his face. For a snatched moment it seemed he was balanced on a precipice, unsure which way he would fall, but then he gave a shaky sigh and released her from his hold.

He sat up and Jane tried to follow suit, although her limbs didn't want to cooperate. Her mind lagged three steps behind, not recovered from its kiss-induced stupor, and if Duncan hadn't offered her his hand as he got to his feet she might never have been able to stand.

She found she couldn't speak. Her legs shook alarmingly and her head felt full of gauze, any hope of forming a sensible thought not yet returned.

How did that happen? What did it mean?

Duncan didn't seem to know the answer to either question. He was uncharacteristically quiet himself as he picked up her bonnet, brushing the snow from her veil before handing it to her with a self-conscious nod.

'We ought to go back. The girls will be wondering where we are.'

Still half stunned, Jane peered up at him. Was that all he was going to say? He had just kissed her, shown her that the scars she was so embarrassed about apparently meant nothing to him, and now he wanted to return to the house without any further discussion?

'I… Yes.' She managed a dip of her head that could have been taken as agreement. 'You're right. I wouldn't want your mother to worry either.'

Duncan retrieved his hat from the tree. It seemed a good idea to cover her face, certain he would be able to see her confusion, and so she replaced her bonnet like-wise, pulling the veil firmly down to her chin. Her holly leaves still lay in a pile and she bent down to collect them, noticing as she straightened up again that the snow around them was in a state of scandalous disarray.

She felt Duncan close behind her. His presence affected her like a physical touch and she wanted nothing more than to lean back against him, rest her head on his chest and let him fold her into his arms. Confusion reigned, however. Whether that was something he would *want* to do she didn't know, and to break the silence that now threatened to fall between them she gestured weakly at the ground.

'I'm not sure we were successful. They don't look much like angels to me.'

'Don't they?' His voice close behind her stirred the hairs at the back of her neck. 'I suppose looks can be deceiving…or so I've always thought.'

Chapter Four

Christmas Day began early for Duncan. It was still dark when he heard muffled giggling and shuffling on the other side of his bedroom door, which would certainly have roused him if he hadn't already been awake. As it was, the sounds of his nieces preparing to ambush him were welcome indeed, providing a distraction from the other thoughts that swirled relentlessly inside his head.

What did it mean that Jane had let him kiss her? Surely he'd made a colossal mistake, forcing open a window that for the wellbeing of his own heart he should have left firmly barred?

He had no idea of any answers. Ever since their adventure in the snow Jane had been shyer than before, blushing every time he sat opposite her at the dining table or held open a door for her to walk through, and he couldn't tell whether it signified anything. All he knew for sure was that he loved watching her cheeks glow that fresh rosy pink, and it was growing harder and harder to curb the urge to kiss her again just to see her colour rise.

The whispering on the landing grew louder. It seemed

he was to be burst in on at any moment and he quietly pushed back the blankets and got out of bed, noiselessly pulling on his dressing gown as he crept towards the door.

Without warning, he yanked it open, prompting a chorus of startled squeaks from the other side.

'Why are you lurking about outside my bedroom? Is something happening?'

All three girls were still in their nightgowns, their hair in disarray, but there was nothing sleepy in their barely lit faces as they bounced up and down.

'It's Christmas! It's Christmas Day!'

'Oh, yes. Of course it is. Thank you for reminding me.'

He smiled at his nieces' excitement. Maria and Eliza were hopping from one foot to the other, swept up in their older sister's enthusiasm, and Charlotte herself seized his hand. Some lunatic had trusted her with a lantern and the flame bobbed alarmingly as she moved, throwing wild shadows on the wall behind her head.

'Grandmama said we had to wait for you and Miss Stockwell to come down before we could open our gifts from Mama and Papa,' she told him urgently. 'Will you come now?'

'If I must. There seems little chance of me being allowed to go back to sleep.'

The eager prancing intensified. 'Thank you, Uncle Duncan! I'll tell Miss Stockwell too.'

Quickly, Duncan shook his head. 'No. Don't disturb her. Let Miss Stockwell come down when—'

He was too late.

Charlotte had dropped his hand and slipped across the

landing faster than an eel. Jane's bedroom door was just a few steps away and he could only watch as the little girl knocked on it smartly, the lantern swinging precariously from her free hand.

'*Charlotte*,' he hissed, trying to convey authority in a whisper. 'Wait…'

He was cut off by a creaking of hinges. The door opened a crack, and then his heart skipped as Jane's tousled head appeared round the jamb.

'Goodness. Is it time to get up already?'

She opened the door a little wider. Maria and Eliza rushed to her, jostling Charlotte out of the way, and if he'd been less distracted he would have worried the lantern might be overturned.

Instead, however, he barely noticed the peril. The girls were babbling to Jane but suddenly he couldn't make out what they were saying, his attention snatched up by something else entirely.

The light from the lantern wasn't strong but it illuminated her in the doorway as though she were a painting in a frame. The intimacy of it made Duncan's mouth run dry: her face was soft with sleepiness, unguarded and still warm from her bed, some of her hair come free from its plait to surround her in a mass of untidy waves. Her feet were bare and he saw her shiver as the cool air touched her skin, her nightgown surely too thin to provide much protection from the cold…

She might as well be wearing nothing at all.

He tried to dismiss the thought but it was too accurate to deny. Jane's sheath of ivory linen didn't leave much to the imagination and he had to battle not to let his eye linger on the ribbons at her throat, just one careful pull away from falling open to reveal the dip between her collarbones. He'd kissed her there before—heatedly, never wanting to stop—and the desire to do so again almost brought him to his knees.

She glanced up. He was afraid she'd see the longing in his eyes despite the gloom and, sure enough, she seemed to hesitate as she caught sight of him at his door, the nod she gave him not quite fully at ease.

'Good morning. Or should I say, Merry Christmas.'

'The same to you.'

He sketched a bow, glad of an excuse to avert his gaze. Her nightgown was not only thin but clinging too, giving an excellent idea of what might lie beneath, and every second he spent looking at her was a second of extreme discomfort.

Fortunately, his nieces had no understanding of either tact or timing.

'So you'll come down now? Both of you?'

Three pairs of keen eyes flicked from Duncan to Jane and back again. It would have been a challenge for any suggestion of romantic tension to survive such scrutiny and he wasn't sure whether to be disappointed or relieved when Jane took a half-step back into the darkness of her room.

'Yes. Just give us a few minutes to dress. I'm sure I speak for your uncle too when I say we wouldn't want to keep you waiting.'

'That's right.' Duncan took a matching step towards

safety, although not before temptation got the better of him. One last glimpse of her made his throat tighten, the barely concealed line of her waist and hips firmly imprinted in his mind as he shooed the children away. 'We'll be down very soon.'

The church was full, as Jane had expected, and her usual unease at being out in public wasn't helped by how often members of the congregation kept turning to stare.

She was used to that, of course, but on that snowy Christmas morning she knew her veiled face wasn't the only reason she was attracting attention. The man sitting beside her in the pew was to blame for that, if blame was the right word to use, but all the same she couldn't suppress a thrill every time Duncan's leg brushed against her skirts.

Is it wrong to feel like this in church? And on Christmas Day, no less?

With her hands clasped demurely in her lap, she hoped nobody would guess how much she wanted to slip one into his palm. There had been much muttering when Miss Stockwell had arrived arm in arm with the still pale and tired-looking Mrs Fitzjames, and when she'd seated herself beside the older lady's son the ripple of interest among the congregation had grown stronger, those with long memories recalling how at one time an engagement had seemed inevitable. It would be nothing short of a miracle if Lieutenant Fitzjames renewed his addresses now though, Jane imagined her audience was thinking, not since her face had been damaged beyond repair, while he was still the most handsome single gentleman in not only Wilton but possibly Wiltshire and beyond. They would make an odd pair and there was no point in trying to deny it…although after what had happened when they'd taken Charlotte sledging, perhaps it was possible that Duncan wouldn't be swayed by something so skin-deep…?

She'd barely been listening to Reverend Dawkins' festive sermon and she started when Duncan suddenly rose to his feet, a starburst erupting in her stomach as his hand grazed her arm. Apparently, it was time for the final carol and she scrambled to stand, almost dropping her hymn-book as the organist struck up the first notes of 'Hark the Herald Angels Sing'.

The singing began and she was forced to bite back a laugh as Charlotte led Eliza and Maria into an enthusiastically loud but entirely tuneless rendition that hardly resembled any carol ever heard. Mrs Fitzjames peered at them in mild alarm and their nurse tried to impose order with a stern look from the end of the pew, but Duncan's eyes creased at the corners, his mouth curling upwards in the way Jane loved most. *His* voice was a pleasure to listen to: deep and resonant, it was everything his nieces' squeaking was not, and she could have stood and let it wash over her all day if he hadn't subtly bent his head in her direction.

Under cover of the organist's tinkling, he muttered into her ear, 'Voices like angels, don't you think?'

The nearness of his lips to her lace-covered cheek almost made her shiver, but all the same it was impossible not to smile. 'Absolutely. I assume, from the similarity in pitch, they must have inherited such talent from you?'

Duncan laughed, converting it hurriedly into a cough when his mother slid him a sideways glance. There was something in Mrs Fitzjames' expression that Jane couldn't quite place, and she quickly turned her attention back to the hymn before she could receive an impenetrable look of her own.

The sermon came to a close and Yuletide greetings and Merry Christmases echoed around the church as the congregation filed out into the cold sunshine. Several people turned in Jane's direction and she made sure to keep her head down as she guided Maria and Eliza through the open door, their nurse and grandmother following closely behind. Charlotte walked ahead with her uncle, her hand entirely swallowed by his, the sight of him carefully escorting the little girl making Jane's heart melt anew.

He really would be the most wonderful father, she thought longingly. If only there could be a way—

'Jane?'

A voice from behind made her turn. Someone was strolling towards her, a tall figure in an expensive black hat, and her spirits plummeted as she realised who it was.

'Cousin Franklin. A Merry Christmas to you.'

Her second-cousin spared her a brief bow. He was looking at the twins with only the barest of interest and she found herself bristling at his dismissive nod.

'Whose children are those?'

Jane inclined her head towards where Duncan's mother stood near the churchyard gate. She was watching with polite patience, although Jane thought she caught a glint of dislike in the other woman's eye. Mrs Fitzjames evidently recalled how Deborah had been treated by the callous son who thought only of his inheritance, her mouth pressed into the thinnest of lines. The twins didn't seem to care much for Cousin Franklin either; they pulled on Jane's hands, trying to drag her away, and she was obliged to let them be scooped up by Miss Vine and borne off to join their uncle, who had likewise turned back to watch.

'I'm staying with their grandmother, Mrs Fitzjames, for Christmas,' Jane explained unwillingly, conscious of Duncan's attentive gaze. 'You might recall your mother speaking of her. They were good friends.'

'I can't say that I do.'

Franklin shrugged. His indifference couldn't have been more obvious and it stoked the resentment already circling in her chest. He cared nothing for what had been important to his mother, she saw all over again. To him, Deborah had been nothing more than an obstacle between him and his father's fortune, and she felt a fresh spike of anger that such a strong, compassionate woman had been valued so little by her only son, the very man who had forced her to sacrifice her own happiness in order to stave off his malice.

'I'm glad to have seen you,' he went on, oblivious to her rising emotion. 'I wanted to remind you of our agreement. You remember you need to have removed yourself from Maybury Place permanently by the twenty-seventh of this month?'

Jane's insides shrank. 'Yes. I remember.'

'That's only two days from now. I wouldn't want you to feel you hadn't had enough notice.'

Franklin's scant pretence at consideration wouldn't have fooled a child. There was a hint of a threat behind his false smile and she felt it keenly, the sorrow she'd managed to push to the back of her mind while spending time with the Fitzjameses returning sharply to the fore.

Her face was covered but a glance at Duncan showed she must still have somehow betrayed her discomfort. A light frown creased his brow and he began to move towards her, casually enough not to draw attention but so unmistakably resolute she felt her pulse begin to flutter.

Her second-cousin hadn't noticed. 'The snow is beginning to melt. I'm certain you'll be able to travel to your parents in Bournemouth by then.'

'My parents live in Bristol, sir.'

'As I said.' Franklin waved a careless hand, although his eyes were cool as ever. 'Don't forget: the twenty-seventh. Two days, and then I'm afraid you must be gone.'

'I won't forget. You can be assured of that.'

There was no way Duncan wouldn't have caught the end of their unpleasant conversation as he approached, but when he came to stand at her elbow his face was determinedly impassive.

'Jane. If you're ready, we ought to return to the house,' he said civilly. 'It's cold and I don't think you're dressed warmly enough to stand around for long.'

'No. I believe you're right.'

He held out an arm and she took it without hesitation, glad of the support. She didn't want to spend another moment in her relation's odious presence and she suspected Duncan felt the same, although the good manners that so often set him above other gentlemen wouldn't allow him to leave without a word.

'Mr Franklin.' He bowed solemnly to the other man. 'Please accept my sincere condolences on the loss of your mother. She was a fine woman and I'm sure the neighbourhood will miss her greatly.'

'Oh.' Cousin Franklin looked faintly surprised that anyone should bother to admire his mother, making Jane's blood begin to heat again. 'Thank you, Fitzjames. It was good of *your* mother to take Jane in for Christmas. I would have done so myself, but...'

He tailed off. Clearly, even he wasn't tactless enough to finish that sentence with the truth—that he didn't care a fig what became of her, at Christmas or any other time— but Duncan's response came quickly enough to cover any awkward pause.

'It was no hardship. The circumstances of her coming to us were regrettable, but Miss Stockwell's company has been—and always will be—a pleasure.'

His arm tightened imperceptibly around her fingers and Jane felt herself glow. It was a sweet thing to say and he seemed to mean it, his words lightening some of the oppressive weight Franklin's ruthlessness had set onto her shoulders.

'Well. Quite.' Franklin didn't look as though he necessarily agreed with Duncan's sentiment. Having a near penniless woman under his roof was something he actively wanted to avoid rather than embrace, and he stepped back quickly as if afraid Duncan would offer to share his good fortune. 'I bid you both a Merry Christmas. Good morning.' He tipped his expensive hat and strode away, sliding a little on the slippery ground.

He was right that the snow was beginning to melt. In places, the white carpet had been reduced to a grey slush and as she watched him leave Jane knew she would soon have no excuse but to do the same. Her time with the Fitzjameses was running out, and there was nothing she could do to hold back the hours before she'd have to wave them goodbye.

The weight on her shoulders slid down into her gut. The idea of parting from Duncan again was too painful to entertain, and although she knew she was just saving up unhappiness for another day she couldn't help but try not to think about it as he began to lead her back towards his mother and the girls.

'Come on,' he said gently, as if he understood how seeing Franklin had tied her innards up in knots. 'Let's go back. Dinner will be cooking, and if there's anything that smells more delicious than a Christmas goose I'm sure I've never found it.'

Seated comfortably beside the fire, so full of goose and Christmas pudding that he could hardly move, Duncan suspected he might have fallen asleep if he hadn't been busy watching Jane out of the corner of his eye.

She knelt on the hearthrug, playing some complicated game with Eliza and a new doll, but although she was smiling he could tell her mind was elsewhere. It was no mystery where her thoughts had strayed and he realised the knowledge had made him unconsciously grit his teeth.

Couldn't Franklin let her have Christmas Day in peace, at the very least? Was that too much to ask?

He'd guessed immediately why her second-cousin had cornered her in the churchyard and on approaching he had been proven right. The miserly wretch had wanted to drive home the message that she was unwanted and in so doing had dented any enjoyment she might have otherwise found in a day meant to spread gladness, not crush it into the ground. For Jane to be happy was all he wanted and seeing a fresh crease between her eyebrows hurt, the little furrow a sign of suppressed grief he ached to smooth away.

Beneath his waistcoat, the question that had been nagging at him since the day she'd let him kiss her in the snow pressed harder against his ribs.

I wonder what she'd say if I were to propose again?

Unseen by anyone else in the parlour, he pressed his fingertips against his tired eyes.

Not that I have any intention of doing so. It's just an idle thought.

Yes, she had let him kiss her. Yes, her liking for his company seemed to have survived their three years apart… But liking wasn't enough. If she hadn't wanted to marry him *then,* there was nothing to say she would want to *now*, the reason for her previous rejection still not something he fully understood. A sensible man would want to avoid the potential for more pain and he was nothing if not rational, the need to spare himself fresh agony telling him to keep his distance before everything went catastrophically awry.

And yet…

If he'd been alone in the room, he might have groaned out loud. The gnawing beneath his ribs intensified with every orbit of his mind around the same central point and he feared that if he didn't act soon there was a very real chance that he might run mad. He had to know for certain how she felt, even if only to bolster his own defences, and the only way to find out was to leap headfirst into the abyss.

He stood up.

'I think the girls are getting restless,' he announced a little too loudly. 'If I took them for a walk, Miss Stockwell, could you be persuaded to come with us?'

Jane glanced up at him in surprise. In reality, his nieces didn't appear agitated in the least: Eliza was entirely consumed by her fireside game and Maria dozed in a chair while Charlotte flicked quietly through a new picture book. It was difficult to imagine three children who looked any *less* restless, although to his immense relief his eldest niece came to his rescue.

'Oh, yes! You must, Miss Stockwell.' Charlotte slid down from her chair to kneel persuasively beside Jane. 'Say you'll come. I want to show you my new skipping rope, but Grandmama says I mayn't use it indoors.'

'I should think not,' said Mrs Fitzjames sleepily from her own armchair. 'Some of these ornaments are older than I am and I'd like to keep them intact.'

Jane was quick to surrender. 'In that case, yes. Of course I'll come.'

To Duncan's unfortunately strong delight she rose from her crouch by the hearth. The girls' nurse roused herself likewise, ready to get up from the sofa where she sat knitting, but he stayed her with a hasty hand.

'There's no need for you to venture out into the cold, Miss Vine. I'm sure Miss Stockwell and I will be able to manage between us.'

The nurse looked covertly pleased to be excused, although his mother's expression as he ushered Jane and the children from the parlour was less easily deciphered. She watched him go with the faintest hint of a smile and he was damned if he could tell whether it was amusement or pleasure at the prospect of having half an hour to herself that prompted it—or perhaps something else altogether, her eyes following him closely until he left the room.

The park was far busier than he'd hoped it would be. It seemed that half of Wilton had decided to take a post-dinner stroll and he sensed Jane's unease as they walked the central promenade, aware that many of the people they passed gave her veil a second glance.

The cold wind plucked at it and swiftly she pulled the lace back down over her face. 'This breeze is a menace. Perhaps I shouldn't have come.'

Duncan turned to her. 'Do you want to return to the house? We can always go back.'

'No, no. I wouldn't interrupt while the girls are enjoying themselves.'

Right on cue, three small cannonballs flew past, one with a skipping rope dangling forgotten from a pocket. Several glovefuls of grey, mushy snow were traded and then his nieces ran off again, leaving only a trail of boot-prints and echoing giggles in their wake.

He watched their retreating backs as they charged away. 'Hmm. I think there might still be some work to be done before they can be called young ladies.'

Jane huffed a laugh. It didn't ring entirely true, however, and Duncan gathered his nerve.

'I know something's bothering you,' he began cautiously. 'I can tell. You've been quiet since we left church and not even finding a coin in your Christmas pudding made you smile for long. Do you want to talk about it?'

For a moment she didn't reply. She carried on walking beneath the snow-covered trees, her shoulder almost brushing the sleeve of his coat, but then he heard her sigh.

'I can't stop thinking about having to leave Wilton,' she murmured. 'I like it here, and returning to Bristol will put my parents under more financial strain than they are already. Given the choice, I wouldn't go back.'

Duncan nodded, intending to look thoughtful rather than show the breathless anticipation that had begun to simmer. 'I suppose you really *have* to leave? It seems cruel you should lose your home too, so soon after your great-aunt's passing, especially since it seems so against your wishes.'

A snort came from behind the screen of black lace. 'I think you heard dear Cousin Franklin. My wishes are irrelevant. There's no alternative but to go; I have no employment here so I couldn't afford to take rooms, and besides, my mother would never agree to me living alone.'

She seemed to huddle into herself, her shoulders rising to touch the bottom edge of her veil. Usually, knowing she was unhappy made him want to take her in his arms and this occasion was no exception, although for the first time another feeling rose to challenge its supremacy.

His hands were clasped behind his back and he felt their palms prickle with sudden, anxious sweat.

He wasn't going to propose, he assured himself resolutely. The risk was far too great: she'd turned him down before and the after-effects of her refusal had followed him across the sea, a constant source of sorrow that still sat inside him like a lump of ice. To ask again would be the act of a fool, but he was as human as anyone else and the need to be sure that his suspicions were correct refused to be ignored. Confusion and uncertainty were almost as bad as heartbreak and equally hard to withstand, and if he let the chance to shed such a burden slip through his fingers he would only have himself to blame.

'What if there was a way for you to stay here in comfort and respectability?' he muttered, hardly able to speak through dry lips. 'If there was somewhere else you might call home?'

The turn of Jane's head towards him was so sharp he wondered whether it had hurt her neck.

The inscrutable curtain of lace fluttered slightly. No words came from behind it but he knew she was staring at him, almost able to *feel* her eyes boring into his.

'I think I would be glad of it, although I can't imagine how such a thing could be managed. Can you?'

His breath stalled. 'I… I couldn't say.'

Inwardly, he cursed his lack of transparency. She'd met his cautious hint with one of her own and he was no closer to understanding her, left with no choice but to take a more forthright—and dangerous—approach.

'Come through here. Off the path.'

His heart was beating too hard to hear if she made any reply, although when he hesitantly reached for her hand, she took his so readily there was no need for words. The feeling of her fingers twining around his was more potent than the strongest wine and it made his head spin, only the knowledge that they were in public stopping him from lifting her veil and kissing her right then and there.

'Girls. Through here.'

Nodding for his nieces to follow, he turned off the path, leading Jane by her unresisting hand. She seemed to be floating along beside him with little comprehension of where they were going and it made it easy to steer her through a broken section of hedge and into the trees beyond.

Once a safe distance from the path, he beckoned the girls closer.

'Look.' He pointed with a not entirely steady finger to a sapling a few yards away. 'There's a young oak over there that looks perfect for climbing. Why don't you try? I won't tell Grandmama if you won't—just be careful not to fall.'

Three little faces lit up. Climbing trees was strictly forbidden and a sanctioned chance to break the rules was enough to send Charlotte and the twins scurrying off, their skirts flying as they hurried to leave him and Jane alone.

'If I didn't know better, I'd think you were trying to get rid of them.'

It sounded as though Jane was attempting to appear calm, although her body gave her away. With her hand still held captive in his, he could feel how it shook, a tell-tale tremor that hinted her tense expectation was every bit as strong as his.

'Only for a moment. I'd like to speak to you without an audience.'

With a glance to make sure the children were in no danger, he drew her behind a tall shrub, his blood roaring in his ears. The gentle pressure of her fingers gave him courage, however, which was just as well, as for what he was about to do he needed all the courage he could find.

Very carefully, giving her plenty of time to twist free if she chose, he stepped closer. Her bonnet moved, tilting upward as she looked at him, and he gently shook his head.

'No hiding now, Jane. If you'll permit me, I'd rather look you in the eye.'

A beat of tension crackled in the air. The only sounds were the swishing of bare branches and the distant giggles of his nieces somewhere in the background, but then Jane lifted her free hand, the stiff fabric of her bonnet rasping softly against her glove as she pulled it from her head.

She looked up at him. Her eyes were wide and in them he thought he saw the same complex jumble of emotions that burned in his own chest. There was a very real possibility that he was wrong, that wishful thinking had clouded his judgement, but he'd come too far to back down now.

'Jane,' he choked out, his pulse racing so fast it made it speaking difficult. 'Since my return—'

He wasn't able to finish his sentence before she wrapped both arms around his neck and brought his face down to hers.

She kissed him as though nothing mattered more. Her hands cupped the back of his neck and his initial shock subsided in a burst of fireworks as her fingers slid beneath his collar to stroke the sensitive skin of his nape, his own hands flying up to take possession of her as she leaned against his chest.

No thoughts were necessary. He didn't need to think while he held her, revelling in the warmth of her body and hidden curves rediscovered by his questing palms. She felt just as she had the last day she'd been in his arms and he tightened his grip so this time she wouldn't slip away.

He could have stood there for ever, kissing her until she saw stars; a constellation had certainly spread out behind *his* closed eyelids as her mouth moved over his, and if he hadn't heard a faint sound from somewhere behind them he wasn't sure he would have been able to stop. They had waited so long and it was a wrench to have to make himself draw back, listening intently to what had suddenly become an extremely unwelcome noise.

'Wait. I think someone's coming.'

Jane blinked up at him, her eyes unfocused and her

cheeks flushed a delicate pink. Her lips were rosier than usual and so soft-looking he had to bite the inside of his cheek to stop himself from claiming them again, although a second later they parted in dismay.

'I don't want to be seen like this. Where's my bonnet?'

She stumbled back, her obvious panic rising as she cast about. Her bonnet must have dropped from her hand when she'd kissed him and Duncan urgently scanned the melting snow around them, his concern growing as the sound of chatter and crunching boots came closer.

'Over there. It must have rolled…'

Jane scrambled for the black shape caught in a nearby tree's roots, but she didn't get there in time.

Two women appeared from around the other side of the shrub, both starting when they realised they weren't alone.

'Oh, Lieutenant Fitzjames. You gave us a fright!'

They smiled at him, although he saw the shape of their lips stiffen when they caught sight of Jane. She'd managed to pull her bonnet on but the veil was snagged awkwardly on the brim, leaving her face exposed, and he felt a stab of horror as he watched their eyes fix immovably on her damaged left cheek.

Both women stared as though they had never seen anything more fascinating than Jane's rapidly reddening face. She stared back, although stricken rather than intrigued, and Duncan felt something inside him twist.

He stepped forward, deliberately blocking her from their line of sight. What he wanted to do was demand they remember their manners, but he knew Jane wouldn't appreciate an even more unpleasant scene.

'My apologies for startling you.' His voice was clipped but he couldn't seem to summon much more than the barest civility. He could *feel* her dismay as she stood behind him, all delight and wonder drained away, and he could have cursed the two interlopers for destroying what should have been a moment to cherish.

'Merry Christmas, ladies. Don't let me delay your walk.' He forced what he imagined was probably a wintry smile. It was the best he could do, however, and he was glad it had the desired effect when the women began to flutter away.

'Merry Christmas, Lieutenant... And to you too, ma'am.'

He thought he sensed Jane give a weak nod, although he didn't turn to check. He wanted to be sure they were alone before he encouraged her to take comfort in his arms, soothing the sting of the women's hurtful ignorance with all the sweet words she deserved, and he watched with narrowed eyes as they walked away.

The wind had died down. The branches no longer scraped and creaked above their heads, which had the unfortunate effect of making it possible for both Jane and Duncan to hear every word the two ladies said as they retreated.

'That was Jane Stockwell! I don't recall the last time I saw her face. Did you see those scars?'

'That's why she always wears the veil. She was pretty before the accident, but now, poor thing...'

'Perhaps we shouldn't feel too sorry for her. That was

Lieutenant Fitzjames she was with. He can't like her, though, surely?'

There was a faint laugh, a note Duncan only just caught before its maker disappeared around a frostbitten tree. *'Oh, I doubt it. A man that handsome wouldn't settle for her when he could have a wife who was more of a credit to him. I know her great-aunt and his mother were friends, so most likely they're just acquaintances—what chance is there that so mismatched a pair could ever be anything else?'*

Chapter Five

Jane's fingers shook so hard she could barely hold her quill. The neat handwriting her tutors always used to praise when she was a girl would have won no awards now, the scrawl she'd made across the parchment in front of her rendered almost illegible by despair.

Her packed bag stood beside her bedroom door, dimly visible in the light of the single candle guttering on her desk. All that remained was to leave the note she was writing on the post tray for the servants to find in the morning, and then she'd slip out of Mrs Fitzjames' house before anyone awoke. The night-time darkness would cover her flight and by the time her absence was noticed it would be too late for anyone to try to stop her from collecting the rest of her possessions from Maybury Place and boarding the first coach that could cut through the melting snow, bearing her away to Bristol and leaving Duncan behind to appreciate his lucky escape.

Her eyes clouded with tears but stubbornly she blinked them back.

It's for the best. I know it is.

Creeping away in the middle of the night was a discourtesy she had apologised for in her note, but it was infinitely better than the alternative. If she tried to leave during daylight Duncan would doubtless feel honour-bound to try to make her stay and she couldn't allow him to make such a mistake. She had been carried away by a fantasy, almost letting herself believe that her future could be happier than she'd ever thought, but the mortifying encounter in the park the previous afternoon had forced her to confront the truth.

She signed her name at the bottom of the page, hardly recognising her own signature. It was little more than a squiggle but that was all she could manage, and she hoped Duncan would be able to read it as she folded the letter and sealed it with a smear of wax.

She stood up. Her knees ached from sitting still for so long in the cold room as she'd agonised over what to write, but the pain would be worth it. After her explanation Duncan would finally understand everything: why she'd had to turn down his first proposal as well as why she thought it necessary to run from the possibility of a second, and although she knew he'd feel some misplaced disappointment she would not be changing her mind.

With quiet steps, she crossed to the door. The house was reassuringly silent. Not even a servant stirred at this hour and with her throat as raw as her red-rimmed eyes she made herself pick up her bag and tiptoe from the room, taking great care not to glance towards Duncan's closed bedroom door as she crept out onto the landing.

She stole down the stairs, listening hard for any movement. Her heart was beating far too loudly but nobody appeared as she reached the hall. The post tray stood in its place on the sideboard and she dropped her letter into it, determined not to allow herself a moment to reconsider.

Her insides clawed at her, the pain making her wince, but she didn't falter. Every time she was tempted to hesitate, she thought again of the two women in the park, who in their unwitting cruelty had given her a glimpse into the future she'd tried to deny.

Duncan deserves more than a wife who'll be whispered about wherever she goes. He might not mind so much now, but as time goes on...

Her lower lip tried to tremble and she clamped it firmly between her teeth. Crying would solve nothing. Action was what was needed—when she reached Maybury Place she could weep as much as she liked; but she had to get there first, and so with one last burning glance around the holly-laden hall, she reached down her bonnet and veil from their hook beside the front door and, bag in hand, slipped out into the night.

'Damn it—damn it all!'

Duncan hadn't meant to shout but boiling frustration made it near impossible to hold himself in check. He'd read Jane's letter twice now and the second scan didn't make it any less infuriating, although the growl it tore from him did succeed in bringing his mother into the hall.

'*Duncan.* I don't think the girls need to overhear that.'

She came towards him, her eyebrows knitted into a

frown. 'What's the matter? Why are you bellowing and pacing about like a lion in a cage?'

Unwillingly, he halted his stride. He had absolutely no desire to tell her why he was uttering profanities in her entrance hall for the whole house to hear. The contents of the letter cut too close to the bone and he didn't wish to share it while confusion and dismay ran riot, although he had to say *something* to stop his mother from peering at him with such growing concern.

'Miss Stockwell has gone back to Maybury Place,' he answered shortly. 'She left in the middle of the night, apparently without a word to anyone.'

'Did she?' Mrs Fitzjames' eyebrows raised upwards from their frown. 'I assume that note in your hand explains why?'

It was too late for him to hide it, but all the same he found himself flattening the folded piece of parchment against his leg. Whatever mess was unfolding with Jane was no one's business but his and hers, although the sudden roll of his mother's eyes suggested she disagreed.

'For goodness' sake, Duncan. Do you take me for a fool?'

At his look of bemusement, she pursed her lips. 'I've known you were head over heels for her since the first day you met. If there's trouble between you now, you might as well tell me. I may be able to help.'

Duncan stared at her. 'How did…?'

'One only has to look at you. And at her, for that matter, to see she feels the same.'

Mrs Fitzjames smiled. It was the same shrewd one she'd

worn when he had left the parlour for his walk with Jane the day before and he could have kicked himself for not realising what it had meant.

Torn, he distractedly folded and unfolded the paper. Part of him wanted to keep his counsel as he always had, not in the habit of confiding the inner workings of his mind to anyone, but another acknowledged he was in desperate need of advice.

With a sigh that held both trepidation and regret, he handed his mother the letter. 'I'm not so sure of that.'

Mrs Fitzjames took the sheet without a word. A large, comfortable chair stood in one corner of the hall and she retreated to it, sinking down into the cushions as Duncan resumed his restless pacing at the foot of the stairs.

There was a period of torturous silence as she read.

With nothing else to do, he tried to concentrate on slowing his breathing. It had sped up when he'd first seen the letter and was still fast now, anger quickening his pulse.

If those busybodies at the park had just held their tongues…

His jaw hardened. Why had they felt it their place to comment on Jane's appearance, or the entirely fictitious effect it might have had on his opinion of her? She had clearly been upset as he had guided her and the children back to his mother's house, but any attempt to talk to her had been politely rebuffed and he'd resolved to try to speak with her again once she'd had time to gather herself. He'd been so sure he could comfort her by and by, not for a moment suspecting she might think the gossips spoke truth, and it had certainly never crossed his mind that such outright nonsense would cause her to flee—

'Oh.' His mother's voice cut through the silence. 'Of course,' she murmured, more to herself than to him. 'How stupid of me—and Deborah too, come to that.'

'What do you mean?' Mid-stride, Duncan wheeled round to face her. 'What do you mean, you were stupid?'

Mrs Fitzjames' eyes were still on the letter. She looked as if she was realising something important for the first time, understanding beginning to dawn.

'Both Deborah and I knew there was something between you,' she said slowly, still studying the page. 'Neither of you openly admitted it, but there was no need. We were certain there would be an engagement before you went back to Southampton, but when you left without Jane we thought we must have been wrong about your intentions towards her. I had no idea you'd proposed and she had turned you down, and apparently neither did Deborah.'

Duncan held back a grimace. It wasn't pleasant to have his past pain revealed; the day Jane had rejected his proposal was one he'd rather forget and he didn't relish his mother learning of it now. It was an unavoidable discovery if he wanted her advice, however, and he tried not to notice the intense sympathy in her gaze as she peered up at him.

'My poor boy. And that poor, poor girl!' Mrs Fitzjames tutted pityingly. 'She was utterly miserable after you left, you know. We thought she was disappointed you hadn't asked for her hand, but now I can see her heart was breaking at having to let you go. If Deborah had suspected she'd rejected you for her sake she would have insisted Jane go after you…which, I realise, is the very thing Miss Stockwell wanted to avoid.'

She got up from the chair, the letter still in her hand. Her face was pallid, the after-effects of the influenza lingering, but he could tell it wasn't only her past illness that made her look so grave.

'I had no idea about any of this. I'm so sorry you've been hurting all this time, bottling up your suffering, and I didn't see it.' She held the letter out to him and when he took it, she laid her hand on his arm. There was guilt in her eyes and it pricked at his conscience, aware that any failings were his alone.

He patted her hand with rough tenderness. 'It isn't your fault, Mother. I didn't want you to see. I didn't want anyone to. But however I felt then doesn't matter. What concerns me is what I should do *now.*'

He glanced down at the paper, uncertainty and unhappiness clouding his mind. Jane's signature peeped out from under his thumb, so uncharacteristically untidy he knew she must have scrawled it while in great distress.

'I never knew her reason for turning me down until I read this,' he admitted. 'Now she says she can't marry me because I deserve a better wife than she would make. Would a second attempt at winning her even be something she'd want? I won't keep trying to chase her if she doesn't want to be caught, however much I might desire to.'

It was tempting to sit down on the stairs and put his face in his hands, but Duncan was not that kind of man.

Giving up easily wasn't in his nature—if he'd known for certain Jane would welcome another advance he would already have gone to find her, but he had no such assurance. The very last thing he wanted was to make her feel like prey, hunted against her will, the thought of causing her further upset something he would not entertain.

'My goodness. And I thought I'd raised you to use your brain.'

His mother's tut—of impatience this time, rather than sympathy—caught him off-guard. 'Pardon?'

'You heard me perfectly well.' There was more than a touch of exasperation in her tone. 'Can you really not see? If I were in your shoes, nothing in that letter would give me a moment's pause. It isn't that she doesn't want you—quite the reverse. She loves you so much she thinks you deserve the very best, and if you think that's her, then surely there's no cause to delay?'

Duncan's heart slammed to a stop.

'Is that truly your interpretation? You really think it would be safe to propose again?'

It would be the one thing he'd been hoping for above all else, and his thoughts must have been obvious by how quickly the shrewd smile he'd glimpsed earlier returned to his mother's wan face. 'I believe so. But of course, we both know there's only one way to be sure.'

Dragging the two trunks packed with all her worldly possessions down Maybury Place's staircase and into the entrance hall made her arms and back hurt, but Jane didn't mind the discomfort. The pain in her muscles helped to distract her from that in her heart, although nothing could completely blot out the ache beneath her ribs.

Ellen lingered near the open front door, uneasily wringing her apron through her hands. 'Please, ma'am, let me help you. You shouldn't be doing that on your own.'

'You have too much work to do already, thanks to Cousin Franklin. I won't burden you further with mine.'

The maid looked as though she might have been thinking of arguing and Jane turned away quickly before anything more could be said. She didn't have the energy to defend herself, not while grief closed in from all sides, being back in Great-Aunt Deborah's house reminding her with vivid cruelty of everything she'd lost. There were ghosts in every corner, of love, laughter and hopes that were now no more than spectres of happier times, and if she stayed too long she feared she might not able to hold back her despair.

A glance out of the front door showed her carriage was yet to arrive. Almost nobody worked on Boxing Day and she'd had to lay out almost every penny she had left to persuade one of the local cabs to take her to the coaching inn on the other side of town. From there she would travel post to Bristol, only stopping to change horses along the way, and once back under her parents' roof she could try to pick up the pieces of her smashed and scattered dreams.

I hope he won't be late. The sooner I can leave here the better.

The walls felt as though they were drawing closer. Waiting was suffocating; it gave her time to dwell when what she really wanted was to think as little as possible.

One thought in particular bothered her more than the rest—*Has Duncan read my letter yet?* passing through her mind so repeatedly it set her teeth on edge.

With bleak decisiveness, she reached for her bonnet and veil. If she had to wait for the carriage, it would be much better to do so outside. The fashionable road on which Maybury Place stood was unusually busy that morning, many of Great-Aunt Deborah's former neighbours out walking off the excesses of their Christmas dinner from the previous day, but even enduring the sidelong stares of passersby was preferable to staying inside. The image of Duncan's final smile might not be able to find her if she went out into the greying slush that had once been snow, her longing to see him one last time perhaps carried off by the chilly breeze.

'I'm going to wait on the drive, Ellen. I'll come back in for my things when my carriage arrives.'

Pulling on her bonnet, she swept her veil into place. Her red cloak was draped over one of her trunks and she swung it round her shoulders, trying to ignore a pang as she tied the ribbons at her throat. The last time she'd worn it had been the day Duncan kissed her as they lay in the snow and she flinched away from the memory, too raw and too recent to yet view with anything but regret.

The cold hit her the moment she stepped outside. It was at least just above freezing, however. The deep snow-drifts had been reduced to dirty piles pushed to the sides of the road, turned into slurry by cartwheels and horses' hooves, and the people walking past the front gate weren't dressed quite so much for arctic conditions as they might have been a few days before. More than one head turned in her direction as she emerged—a husband muttered to a wife while one nursemaid shepherding a gaggle of children traded significant looks with another, their scrutiny following her as she drifted down the front steps and onto the gravelled path.

She walked with little purpose, allowing herself to be carried along by unthinking steps. The front gate grew closer and she ran an ungloved hand over the iron scrolls she'd touched a thousand times or more, pretending not to notice the curious glances of a group of older gentlemen on the pavement beyond. Standing so close to the road gave anyone passing the house ample opportunity to gaze at her and she reflexively checked her veil was in place as she turned back, unwilling to let anyone see the unhappiness written across her face just as clearly as her scars.

She had almost reached the halfway point between the house and the end of the drive when she heard the front gate squeak open behind her.

'The air is icy this morning. Why are you wandering around outside?'

The gravel beneath her boots crunched as she whirled round.

Duncan stood just inside the gate. He was slightly flushed, as though he'd been running, but she hardly noticed, the instant squeezing of a fist around her lungs coming as a sharp distraction.

'What are you doing here?'

The words jolted out on instinct, the first thing that came to mind, but Duncan declined to answer.

'I asked my question first. Why are you here, shivering in Deborah's garden when you could be warm inside with me?'

Bewildered, Jane stared up at him. He'd taken a pace towards her and she saw a faint gleam of sweat below the brim of his hat, more proof that he'd run from his mother's house to appear before her now. The real mystery was *why* he'd come when her note had explained everything, his presence a bittersweet joy that would now force the painful goodbye she had hoped to avoid.

'I... Didn't you read my letter?'

Duncan dipped his chin. 'I read it. My question still stands, however, or perhaps I should rephrase it.'

He paused. A carriage rolled past on the street beyond the gate, its wheels creaking and horses' tack jingling as it went, although he didn't seem to register the noise. His eyes were on the clouds gathering above them and it seemed for all the world as though he was hoping they might tell him what to say.

In the end he chose simplicity. 'Is this really where you want to be?' he asked frankly. 'If you're truly set on returning to Bristol I won't try to stand in your way, only no letters this time. If you don't want me, tell me so yourself—face to face, with nothing standing in between.'

The hand around her chest clenched tighter. He was looking at her now rather than the sky, so directly she felt she might as well not have been wearing the veil at all. Somehow, his eyes found hers even through the layer of lace and they held her steady, immobilised by weary longing and unable to speak anything but the truth.

'It was never that I didn't want you,' she heard herself say in a voice she scarcely recognised as her own. 'As I wrote in my letter, I wanted to accept your proposal more than I'd ever wanted anything in my entire life, but I *couldn't* leave my great-aunt. She was so ill and I knew Franklin would do nothing to care for her, and after all she'd done for me, I couldn't let her suffer alone.'

She saw Duncan's mouth move but her own hadn't yet finished. 'I couldn't tell you why I'd refused,' she continued, three years of secrets now flooding from her lips. 'Auntie might have found out and I never wanted her to know. She'd have been devastated if she'd discovered I'd traded my happiness for hers and would have either insisted I leave or spent the last few years of her life living with the most horrific guilt. Franklin's conduct had already made her so unhappy... I had to do what I could to make things better for her before she died.'

Heat had begun to build behind her eyes. She didn't want to cry but having Duncan so close when she'd never thought to see him again was a blessed curse. He was so handsome in the morning sunshine, the light turning his dark gaze almost golden, and the desire to throw herself into his arms was like a knife thrust directly into her soul.

She gritted her teeth as he came closer. There was something in his face she couldn't immediately unravel: compassion, definitely, but another emotion lying just beneath it that was much harder to name.

'I understand all of that,' he said with clearly determined patience. 'I wish you'd told me at the time, but I understand. What baffles me is why, now there's nothing to come between us, you still won't let me make you happy.'

She swallowed agonisingly. 'I explained why. In my letter—'

'Oh, hang *your letter*! Forgive me, but your notions as to how I think and feel aren't worth the paper you wrote them on.'

To her amazement, he pulled off his hat, frustratedly running a hand through his hair. His patience had clearly evaporated; he looked like a man on the edge of his endurance, a state that, judging by their concerned expressions, had also been noticed by a pair of elderly matrons passing by the front gate.

'Damn it all, Jane,' he growled in a tone she was alarmed to find extremely attractive. 'I never loved you because of your face. I loved your face because it was part of *you*. You may have some scars now, but what is that to me? If this is the face Jane Stockwell possesses then this is the one I love, and if anybody has anything to say about it, I am not inclined to listen—not now nor at any point in the many joyful years together I hope we'll have, if you would just stop thinking you know what's best for me.'

He pinned her to the spot with a powerful glance. 'Do you *want* to marry me? Yes or no?'

Her heart catapulted up into her throat. She'd never seen him so heated, his startling declaration taking a hammer to the wall she'd thought necessary to build between them. With every word he tore down another brick, her hesitations shrinking from the punishing blows he rained down upon them, but still she didn't dare believe it was safe to give way.

'Yes. But—'

'No buts. I want to marry you, and you want to marry me, and now that's out in the open there's really nothing more to be said.'

He sounded slightly breathless. His eyes were alive, however, alight with triumphant hope, and Jane knew she didn't have the strength left to resist.

On the other side of the ironwork fence, the inquisitive matrons' walk had slowed to a crawl. They were all but craning their necks to watch whatever drama was unfolding in Maybury Place's front garden, and on any other occasion Jane would have hurried away from their stares.

This time was different.

Duncan hardly blinked as she reached hesitantly upwards. He didn't seem to want to miss even a fraction of a second, every thread of his focus fixed on her trembling hand.

Even as her fingertips inched towards her bonnet she was assailed by a barrage of doubts. The hurtful conversation she'd overheard in the park the day before played again, trying to persuade her to reconsider, but now she wasn't alone in beating it back. Duncan stood in front of her as immovable as a rock, willing her on with the ghost of a smile, and her entire world shifted as she saw the unfeigned pride in his eyes.

She heard the two women mutter to each other as she slid the bonnet from her head, her face laid bare to both their curiosity and the winter's chill. Probably they were speculating as to why the left side of her countenance was so marred by faded red welts, but Jane realised she didn't have to care. The handsome man coming towards her was the only thing she had any interest in, his arms outstretched, ready and eager to gather her in, and it was an unspeakable effort to hold him off with one upraised hand.

'Wait. There is *one* thing more that must be said.'

Duncan stopped, obediently obeying her flat palm, aside from one hand that crept around her waist. He seemed to be having trouble keeping his composure; his grip was firmer than any calm man's would be and she felt a cascade of sparks glitter down her spine at the urgency of his touch.

'What would that be, Jane?' he murmured, his voice so low and intimate it made her wilt. 'You're worried what someone else entirely irrelevant thinks? Perhaps the Prince Regent, or the man who delivers my coal?'

'No. That's not what I was going to say.'

'Then what?'

He had subtly drawn her closer, her hand now resting on his chest, and she felt the wild leaping of his heart beneath his coat. If she lifted her chin she'd be close enough to rise on her tiptoes and kiss him, and when she looked up at him she saw the same thought cross his mind.

'Just that I love you. That's all.'

'That's all?'

He peered down at her incredulously, and then a swarm of butterflies took flight in her stomach at his disbelieving laugh. 'There's nothing *that's all* about it. Did you know I've been waiting years to hear that?'

'Shall I say it again then? Just to make sure?'

'In a minute. There's something else I'd like to do first, and I don't think it'll leave you with much chance to speak.'

He bent his head, his lips almost touching hers. They were out in public in broad daylight, a small but scandalised audience snatching glances from the pavement, but somehow neither factor seemed much of an obstacle. His hand was securely on her waist and the other one snaking round to curl deliciously in her now uncovered hair, and her eyes drifted closed as she prepared to be carried into bliss.

'To be clear, though. You'll marry me? You accept?'

His mumble grazed her mouth, its warmth sending another ripple through her. A deep yearning was building, his kiss so tantalisingly close yet still out of reach, and she had to steady herself before she replied.

Fortunately, she had a firm, solid chest to lean against.

'I never expected to enjoy Yuletide again after all the sad things that have happened at this time of year,' she whispered, her eyes still closed as she surrendered herself to his dependable hold, 'but now… You've given me the best gift I ever could have wished for. Yes, Duncan. I accept.'

* * * * *

If you enjoyed these stories, why not check out these other Historical collections

Under the Mistletoe
by Bronwyn Scott and Marguerite Kaye

Regency Christmas Parties
by Annie Burrows, Lara Temple and Joanna Johnson

A Gilded Age Christmas
by Amanda McCabe and Lauri Robinson

Regency Reunions at Christmas
by Diane Gaston, Laura Martin and Helen Dickson

Regency Christmas Weddings
by Christine Merrill, Liz Tyner and Elizabeth Beacon

THE CHRISTMAS HUSBAND CHARADE

Samantha Hastings

For Jennie Ferguson

Chapter One

23 December

The draught of cold air that entered the mail coach caused a shiver to run down the honourable Miss Julia Sullivan's spine and the hairs to stand up on the back of her neck. At the same time, she was both frozen and entirely aware of the handsome gentleman who was the last passenger to enter the carriage in London. His beaver hat gleamed and his burgundy coat had three capes on it. His golden hair peeked out from underneath his hat and his white smile would have stood out in even the most crowded ballroom.

Not that Julia had been in a ballroom for the last three years. Not since she had jilted a very eligible baron at the altar.

No. Her father had forced her to become a governess to teach her a lesson in humility and filial obedience. Overnight Julia had gone from a beautiful sought after débutante to the governess drudge of the most unpleasant woman in all of England. Mrs Heap loved to *heap* Julia with tasks that should have been done by the housekeeper or a housemaid. But since Julia depended upon that woman for her bread, she had not been able to tell her no. The little Heaps had also given her plenty to do. Nor did Julia ever manage to teach *them* obedience, but she was excessively fond of the children. And she did teach them writing, reading and arithmetic; and while the little Heaps rarely did what she asked them to do the first time (it was usually the fifth or sixth time), they were carelessly fond of her. Which made her miss her much younger half-sister Amelia even more.

Julia let out a long and loud sigh—one that exhaled all of her frustration and grief over three years of drudgery. She'd been called back home for a second chance—that was what her father had written. In his brusque, businesslike writing, he had failed to mention what the 'second chance' was for. But if he thought he could bully her again into a marriage not of her choosing, he would soon learn that her resolve had only grown through her struggles. And that she'd carefully kept every coin that she'd earned, and although it was not enough to live on indefinitely, Julia could support herself long enough to find a new position.

On the opposite seat, she noticed two rough-looking men staring at her. Their clothes were rumpled and unwashed, as were their faces. The one on the right was missing several teeth as he smiled at her in a way that made her feel quite unwell. The man on the left had a long beard which appeared to still have bits of his last meal in it. He glared at her: it was even more frightening than his companion's smile. Julia folded her arms across her chest as if to make herself smaller. If only her father had sent a manservant to accompany her on the public coach, Julia might have felt safer. Her eyes darted to the newest traveller. She couldn't help but be glad that the clean and handsome young gentleman had joined them in the mail coach. She felt less chary with him there.

'Surely you are too young for such sighs, miss?' the woman who sat next to her on the bench said. She was not much older than Julia, but she was holding a young daughter or son and was apparently about to give birth a second time at any moment. Black curls framed her heart-shaped face and one of her front teeth was rather forwarder than the other. Still, she was undeniably pretty. The woman's husband, however, looked to be nearly twice his wife's age and was not at all handsome. His face was gaunt and his frame appeared painfully thin. He would not provide his own family or Julia much protection on this journey. But at least the woman had someone to look after her safety.

Julia couldn't help but wish that a man was travelling with her. Her former betrothed, Joshua, Baron Ballantine, had been handsome and thirty-six years old, compared to her scarce eighteen years of experience. The gulf between them had seemed impassable and that was before she'd seen him in the arms of another.

The woman cleared her throat and spoke again. 'And where are you travelling to, miss?'

'I am going home to Pickwich.'

'So am I,' said a deep voice.

Julia looked across the aisle to see the handsome gentleman on the other side who had filled her belly with butterflies and made her feel safe in the mail coach. His eyes were unique: one green, the other blue, and both startlingly attractive in his otherwise pale face. His lips twitched into another smile as if he realised that she was gaping at him. But it wasn't just because of his looks. It was the eyes. She'd only seen that particular shade combination once before in her former betrothed. This man had to be his much younger brother, Devin Ballantine, who was a busy barrister in London. Julia had only met him once, three years ago—the night before the wedding when she had called it off. He was the one who had threatened to sue her family for breach of promise. Then her father had promptly disowned her.

Devin was thirteen years younger than his brother and, if the rumours that circulated around Pickwich were true, not from the same father. The younger son had golden hair, whereas Joshua's was dark brown and looked black in certain lights. The shape of their faces and the strong lines of the jaws were the same. Julia had once fantasised about kissing Joshua's jaw—or kissing him at all. He had never made the smallest attempt to touch her, or kiss her, while they were engaged. She had told herself that it was because he respected her too much.

She knew now that while Joshua might have respected her, he hadn't loved her. And the small hope that their acquaintance would blossom into something more when they were married had died the moment she saw him kissing his true love.

Like a pantomime, she saw Devin's eyes widen and

his mouth open slightly as he realised why she was going to Pickwich and *who* she was. Julia must not have made much of an impression on the young barrister the first time that they met. Not that they had ever spoken to each other. Julia had entered the dining room where both families were eating and declared that the wedding was cancelled. Joshua had followed behind her and formally released her from the contract. Pandemonium had followed. It was difficult to remember which parent had yelled more—Joshua's mother or her father. Even her soft-spoken stepmother had been disappointed in her. And Devin had pushed for a lawsuit.

Julia watched as the surprise left his face and his mouth twisted into a look of disgust. She was the young woman who had jilted his elder brother and caused a great deal of scandal, not only in the village of Pickwich but in London Society. Devin turned his gaze out the window and Julia followed suit. She had no desire to make a scene in front of strangers. Particularly not the two frightening men who were seated next to Devin. The man with the missing teeth gave her another horrifying smile and his partner eyed her reticule like it was a Christmas pudding. Julia swallowed uncomfortably. Her former charge Felix Heap would have called them *bridle culls*, a fancy name for thieves.

The woman spoke again. 'I'm Mrs Mack and my husband and daughter and I are going home to his curacy in Tiddleford.'

'I am Miss Sullivan.'

Devin bowed his head. 'Mr Ballantine.'

Mrs Mack turned to the two rumpled men across from her. 'And you, sirs? What are your names and your destination?'

'None of your business, ma'am,' the bearded one said in a deep voice.

Mrs Mack opened her mouth as if shocked by their lack of civility. But she did not speak because her daughter woke up with a loud scream.

At first, Julia was relieved to have the attention of the other passengers on the toddler and not on herself. But when the child continued to wail and holler for the next half an hour, she couldn't help but wish for the uncomfortable silence to return.

The girl's parents were useless in comforting the child.

Mr Mack just kept repeating, 'Do something, Mary.'

And Mrs Mack would respond, jiggling her child in her arms, 'I am trying to. Hush, Lizzy, go back to sleep.'

Lizzy then would reply at the top of her lungs something indecipherable, except for the word *dolly*. Obviously the child wanted her doll and none of them would receive any peace until then.

Clearing her throat, Julia said in a loud but polite tone of voice, as to be heard over the wailing child, 'Where is her dolly? Perhaps it will help her stop crying.'

Mrs Mack's face turned red as if she'd committed the grossest of crimes. 'I must have forgotten it at the posting inn last night. I can't find it anywhere.'

Lizzy's wails redoubled at this news and Julia wished that she hadn't attempted to intervene. Mr Mack loudly scolded his wife again and the child continued to cry.

The three men on the opposite side of the mail coach all gave her matching glares. The last thing she wanted while travelling alone was their attention. Julia resolutely stared out through the small rectangular window at the thick snow that continued to fall at a steady pace. She could no longer see any grass or weeds, nothing but a blanket of white that softened the countryside and frosted the tops of the cottages.

Another shiver ran down her spine. She hoped that they would arrive in Pickwich soon. The snow seemed to grow heavier by the hour. The speed of their vehicle slowed and Julia worried that she would have to spend even more time in the company of the tantrum toddler, the unpleasant parents, a pair of bridle culls, and a man who hated her. She wished again that her father had been kind enough to send a male servant to travel with her or even a maid to lend her countenance.

Her heart leapt in her chest, straight to her throat, when the carriage finally came to a stop. By now it was snowing too hard for her to tell if they were in the village of Pickwich, but they must have been. She grasped her reticule tighter and waited for the door of the carriage to open. She could hardly wait to go inside the posting inn and wait for her father's driver to pick her up and take her home. She knew the proprietors of the inn, and she would be safe with them until a servant was sent to fetch her. There would probably even be warm soup and a fire in a private parlour. The hot stone at her feet had long lost any warmth and her coat was not keeping out the cold. She only wished that her body wasn't so aware of Devin's disapproving eyes upon her and the sinister men's smiles. Julia couldn't wait to remove herself from their company.

Strangely, it was several minutes before the groom opened the door of the mail coach and by then Julia could see her white breath in the air.

'My name is Joe and I'm here to tell you that the carriage is stuck,' he said in a low, guttural voice.

'How long will it take to clear it?' Devin asked.

Joe sneezed and then shook his head. 'The snow is too deep and it's still falling heavily. Our only choice is to go and wait out the storm at the closest inn.'

Julia touched her throat. She was eager to get home for Christmas and the safety of Broadwick Abbey. 'For how long?'

The groom shrugged his shoulders. 'A day or two at least. Possibly longer. But there isn't time to dawdle. The snow is coming down thick and you'll all have to walk to the nearest village, Hooting. It ain't more than a mile away.'

'You want us to walk a mile in deep snow?' Mrs Mack declared in dismay.

Goose bumps formed on Julia's arms and her chest tightened. She was already cold and she was about to follow a stranger into a snowstorm to an inn where she didn't know anyone. Her circumstances had changed from bad to worse.

Mr Mack cleared his throat. 'What about the horses?'

Joe coughed into his hand before he answered, 'It will be hard enough for the beasts to make it through the snow holding the mail without a rider on their back.'

'But we's paid for a coach ride,' the bearded man said. The expression on his face was murderous.

'And youse welcome to stay in the coach,' Joe said, raising his scarf to cover his mouth and red nose. 'You'll freeze to death, but it's your choice. I'm leaving with the driver, Mr Denard, and the horses this very moment to stay the night at the posting inn. If you want to live, you'll keep close to us, so as not to get lost in the snowstorm.'

Despite being scared and half frozen, Julia had worked too hard for that horrible woman to die now. Without waiting for another word of complaint from her fellow passengers, she stepped out of the carriage and realised that the snow was well above her knees. The reason that Joe had taken several minutes to open the door was that he had removed the snow first. Trembling, she wrapped her arms around herself. But nothing she did kept out the cold or her fears.

One by one, her fellow passengers exited from the stuck mail coach. Joe deftly climbed up the carriage and offered to throw down their bags. Julia would have happily left her small portmanteau behind, but if she did, she would have no dry clothes to change into when they reached the nearest posting inn. Devin easily picked up his own small trunk and slung it over his shoulder. His eyes briefly met hers as if to challenge her to ask for his help.

She would rather die. If he hadn't tried to sue her for breach of promise, perhaps Papa would not have disowned her and sent her to live with Mrs Heap.

Besides, Devin was treating her like a heartless jilt, when Julia had been forced to end her engagement or live as the unwanted third in a ménage à trois. She deserved better in a marriage and she would not settle for anything less than love if she were to be engaged a second time. Scooping up her portmanteau, she carried it in her arms like a recalcitrant child and struggled through the snow after Mr Denard and the horses.

After a few minutes of trudging through deep snow, she glanced over her shoulder and saw that all of the coach passengers were walking and that Joe was at the back of the group making sure that no one left the road—including the pair of bridle culls. Not that Julia could see a road underneath all the snow. Devin gave her another glare and she returned her gaze to the horses and Mr Denard. She didn't look back again. It took all of her strength and determination to keep going.

Chapter Two

Sitting in the crowded mail coach, Devin Ballantine hadn't remembered how beautiful his brother's betrothed was and it irked him to no end. In his mind, he'd reduced his memory of Julia Sullivan to only her flaws: she'd had two red spots on her chin, she'd been little more than skin and bones, and she'd cried as she called off the wedding. Sir Eustace had started yelling and so had his own mother. Then Julia's face had turned completely red with embarrassment and tears—not pretty at all. Despite the havoc she was causing his family, Devin couldn't help but feel a bit sorry for her.

His beloved elder brother, whom he looked up to, had not shown any emotion at all. He'd merely accepted his jilting like the gentleman that he was, ignoring their mother's insistence that he refuse to release her from the already signed marriage contracts—which were legally binding. The contracts stipulated how much Joshua would receive as Julia's dowry portion and her yearly pin money, as well as her future widow's portion. Mama had then pressed Devin to sue Julia Sullivan for breach of promise—and the end of the engagement brought more than just embarrassment for Joshua.

Unpleasant and unflattering rumours about his brother had reached Devin all the way in London. People said that something must truly be wrong with the baron if a young heiress would rather be a governess than a baroness. Baron Ballantine had to be mad with an uncontrollable temper or plagued with the pox. Because of the scandal, his brother had not returned to London for the yearly Seasons but stayed in the small town of Pickwich on his estate. His brother's close friend and steward, Roger Ashby, had even moved into Riverdale House to keep Joshua company and his spirits up. And his brother, now nine and thirty, was still unmarried and without an heir.

Despite the usual tittle-tattle about younger sons, Devin had no aspirations towards his elder brother's title or estate. He wasn't even sure if he was the late baron's son— questions and gossip about his paternity had followed him since school. Although, the man he had called Papa had treated him with nothing but love and kindness before he died. And his mother swore that there was no truth in the rumours.

Besides, Devin was a hard-working barrister and in the last five years had begun to make a name for himself at the London bar. He intended one day to become a judge. And Devin found country life to be quite dull. He loved the hustle and bustle and the sound and the grind of a large city. He thrived on never knowing who or what would come through his door and request legal representation.

Unfortunately, he recognised the two men sitting beside him in the coach. Angus Rhys had been sentenced to three years of hard labour for house-breaking. He'd had an additional year added to his sentence for breaking the arm of a fellow inmate. But it was Timothy Pip that put Devin's nerves on edge. Rhys's partner had been on trial for murder at the same time. Ultimately, his barrister had been able to reduce the charges from manslaughter to breaking and entering because of the lack of an eyewitness. The only person in the house at the time of the theft had been an older woman who had died from a stab wound.

Despite his animosity towards Miss Julia Sullivan, he couldn't help but wish that she'd been on a different mail coach. At least one of these men was a murderer. And he wished that he wasn't so damned attracted to her—the one woman that he could never have.

There was a little pink in Julia's cheeks from the cold, but her complexion was peaches and cream without a blemish to be found. Her hair was light and could have been called brown or blond, but the closest colour he could think of was honey. Sweet, rich honey with the sunlight shining through it. Her figure was still slight, but with feminine curves that he very much appreciated. And like a fool, he'd smiled at her. He was only a man after all and she was a beautiful woman with large blue eyes that a fellow could get lost in.

His heart hardened. Poor Joshua had gotten lost in

her blue eyes and much good it had done him. Although Joshua had never complained, Devin was still angry on his behalf. He glared at the vixen and she had the audacity to smile back at him. He would like nothing better than to bring her down a peg or two.

Devin was fuming by the time he got out of the cold mail coach and picked up his trunk. Miss Sullivan's portmanteau was nearly as large as herself and he wanted her to ask for his help, just so that he would have the pleasure of refusing her. It was petty of him, but it might have made him feel a little better. But the minx didn't. She hoisted her portmanteau and trudged through the snow without a glance back at him.

A small stirring of admiration for her spunk grew in his chest, but he pushed it down and trailed after her. He needed to keep a close eye on her with a murderer on the loose. Mr and Mrs Mack were in front of him and squabbled the entire way as their child continued to cry for her doll. The two house-breakers behind him talked in low tones. He felt their gazes on his back as if they eyed him like a pigeon waiting to be plucked. Devin would definitely be bolting his bedchamber door tonight and he would tell Julia to do the same. No matter how much he resented her past actions, he had no wish for her to be robbed or stabbed. This pair of crooks were capable of anything. Joe followed behind the thieves and Devin wondered if it was for the other passengers' safety or his own. He didn't like having his back to those men.

Instead, he watched Julia Sullivan scramble through the snow to keep up with Mr Denard and the horses. Her skirts were soaked through and Devin could have sworn he heard her teeth chattering from ten paces away. Still, she didn't complain or slow down. Not that either would have done her any good. The horses were laden with the mail and Devin was determined not to assist her. Aside from keeping her safe from the two thieves.

Holding his own trunk aloft, Devin's shoulder ached where he'd fallen off a tree and dislocated it as a lad. He was beginning to lose the feeling in his fingers and his nose felt frozen enough to snap off, when he finally saw a small light in the distance. Trudging through the snow, he wished that he had stayed in London for Christmas. But his brother had begged him to return to Riverdale House and Devin didn't wish to disappoint him. Poor Joshua had gone through enough disappointments in life. Their father had been bedridden and died young, leaving Joshua with a great responsibility at a tender age. Then his brother had become engaged to Julia, only to have her call it off in the cruellest of manners.

No.

The snow did not matter. Devin would be there for his brother—always. Joshua had been more of a father than an elder brother. His brother had asked very little of Devin, yet given him everything. These thoughts gave Devin the energy to make the final steps toward the posting inn.

Four feet of snow rested against the walls of the building and covered part of the windows. A small path was carved through the snow that led from the stoop to the door. Already new snow had begun to collect there.

'In you go, missy,' Mr Denard said to Julia. 'I have to take care of the horses and keep an eye on His Majesty's mail.'

She gave the man a nod as if speaking was too difficult. Devin watched Julia walk to the door, but she could not open it because she carried her portmanteau with both hands.

'What is taking so long?' Mr Mack demanded, his arms full of his family's trunks.

'I don't have a free hand,' Julia explained.

Mr Mack huffed impatiently. 'Mary, open the door.'

'But I am holding Lizzy.'

Devin realised that another marital fight was brewing. He decided to avert disaster by pushing forward and opening the door for them all.

'Thank you,' Julia said in a low, sultry voice that caused him to jump and something inside his chest to snap. She passed right by him and went straight to the fire. She placed her portmanteau on the floor and then sat upon it with her hands outstretched to the blue and orange flames.

Neither Mrs Mack nor her husband said a word of gratitude to him. Nor did the two thieves. Their eyes were on his trunk as if trying to see what was inside of it. Instinctively, Devin stepped closer to his property. Despite the inn being very small, he had no intention of sharing a bedchamber with these men. If he did, he'd be lucky if he still had his nightshirt in the morning.

Devin glanced around for the proprietor or a tapster, but it wasn't until the little girl started crying that she was hungry that a small man with a most impressively long red beard came out of the back room. There was snow in his whiskers and Devin assumed that the man had helped Joe and Mr Denard put the horses in the barn first. The back door opened again and Mr Denard came through it. He did not engage with the angry and disgruntled passengers but merely went up the stairs and presumably to his room. Devin wished to do the same. He didn't want to spend another moment in the company of his fellow passengers.

Everyone began speaking at the same time. The two rough men wanted blue ruin to heat up their insides. Mrs Mack wanted food for Lizzy. Mr Mack wanted a private room for his family. And the proprietor rubbed his eyes and then his beard as if he hadn't expected to have any customers on such a snowy day.

The proprietor held up his hands as if he was being robbed by a highwayman. 'Quiet, quiet. I can't possibly hear you all at the same time. This is a small but respectable inn. My name is Peebles. My wife is making stew at this very moment for your supper and I will happily serve you spirits at the tap after you pay for your stay.'

Mr Mack harrumphed. 'But we don't know how long we will be stuck here.'

Mr Peebles smiled. 'Denard says at least two nights. So please show me your coins and then I can lead you to your rooms.'

Julia stood up and moved from the fire, but the warmth of it was still in her rosy cheeks. She held up her reticule as if to take money from it. 'I should like my own room. I am happy to pay for it.'

'A private room for my family,' Mr Mack said.

'We can share,' the two men said.

'I require my own bedchamber as well,' Devin added.

Mr Peebles held up his hands again as if to silence them all. 'My inn is small with only four rooms. The driver and groom have already claimed one. I have three rooms left.'

Devin looked at the quarrelling couple with the wailing child, the two thieves, and then to Julia, who stood all alone. He couldn't leave her unprotected. But what should he do? She couldn't stay with the thieves. Her only option was to share a room with the family, but Devin had heard Mr Mack yell at his wife for the majority of the trip. He didn't seem a particularly pleasant or safe man to be around either. Devin could perhaps share with the two thieves, which would be awful for him but allow Julia her own room—but then she would be all alone and that wasn't safe either. She should have had a maid with her and a footman accompanying them both. Sir Eustace had been negligent in sending his daughter to travel by herself. And Devin wouldn't be able to sleep without knowing that Julia was safe and protected.

Which left only one option.

Devin would have to share a room with her—but she was a single young woman and her reputation would be ruined. Devin briefly glanced at Mr Pip whose hands curled into fists. Better her reputation sullied than for her to be met with violence or be violated. Or was there perhaps a way to protect her without ruining her reputation…?

There was only one thing to be done. Devin would have

to pretend to be her husband. It would only be for two nights and as long as no one in Pickwich ever learned the truth, there would be no harm to her reputation. And Julia would be safe both nights under his protection.

He released a loud sigh, quite like the one that she'd given in the carriage. 'No more games, dearest Julia,' Devin said, holding out his hand to her. She took it reluctantly, her eyebrows raised in a question. 'My wife and I will share a room—as you all know, we are both from Pickwich and going to meet my family. We had a small disagreement and therefore did not sit together in the coach. You heard her loud sighs.'

Julia jerked her hand back. 'Yes, we did have a fight, *dearest* husband. That is why I must have my own private room. I do not wish to see your face.'

Mr Peebles shook his head. 'There is not another room to be had, ma'am.'

'You're welcome to share with us, luv,' Mr Rhys said with a jeer.

Julia stepped away from the two thieves and closer to Devin. He watched as she looked at the other passengers and then to him. She must have realised that he was her safest option. 'Very well, *husband*. But you'd better keep your hands to yourself! I have not forgotten our fight.'

Mr Rhys guffawed. 'Now, I couldn't promise that, lass.'

Devin found his own hands curling into fists. Neither Rhys or Pip were going to lay a finger on Julia under his watch.

'That settles it, then,' Mr Peebles said. 'Mr and Mrs—'

'Ballantine.'

Julia flinched a little at his side but remained quiet. Devin cursed his own stupidity. He ought to have used a false name.

'You may have the room at the back. And Mr and Mrs—'

'Mack.'

'You and your little girl can have the middle room,' Mr Peebles said. 'And the two gentlemen can have the room closest to the stairs and the tap. It's directly across from where Joe and Mr Denard will be staying. Joe's a real light sleeper, iffen you know what I mean.'

Devin knew exactly what the proprietor was saying. He was warning the two thieves that they were being watched.

Devin stooped down and picked up both his and Julia's trunks. 'Lead the way, Julia.'

Chapter Three

Julia shot Devin a cold glare before walking up the stairs and opening the door to the back room. There was no fire in the hearth and one dirty window. The bed did not appear much more promising. It was a good thing that she had packed her own sheets, a piece of advice she had Mrs Heap to thank for. And separate sheets would give them a little space on the sagging bed. Not much, but looking down the hall at the grumbling other passengers entering their bedchambers, Julia couldn't help but think that Devin was the best of a bad lot. But why in heaven's name had he begun this charade? If they were caught sharing a room by anyone in Pickwich, both of their reputations would be ruined.

'Why did you tell the other passengers that we were married?'

Rubbing his face with one hand, Devin sighed. 'I recognised the two men who sat by me on the mail coach from the criminal court. Angus Rhys is a violent criminal and Timothy Pip is a known murderer. I thought that you would be safer in my company than by yourself.'

Drat. He'd just confirmed her fears and suspicions. A shiver ran through her entire body. But the most annoying thing was that Devin *did* make her feel safe. Not that she had any intention of telling him that. 'And when did I become Julia, *Devin*?'

He scoffed. 'I would have thought a goose-cap like yourself would be more upset at becoming my wife than by me calling you by your given name—since the idea of marrying a Ballantine is so repugnant to you.'

Julia's fingers clenched into fists. She pressed so hard into her skin that she could feel little crescent-shape indentations from her fingernails. She did not blame Joshua for not telling his brother the truth: Julia wouldn't have wanted to confess such a personal thing to this judgemental man either. Between clenched teeth she managed to say, 'You have as much sense as a hedge-bird. Why did you use your real name? What if someone from home learns about our ruse?'

'I am not used to deceit like your lovely self.'

'You do not know what you speak of, basket-scrambler. And all I can say is that I hope that you never become a judge, for you are not very good at seeing the truth that is right before your eyes. One that a stranger discovered before you.'

Devin's nostrils flared. She'd hit a sore spot. Joshua had confided to Julia, when she was his betrothed, that his little brother was eager to be a judge in the highest courts in London one day. He'd also bragged about how hard-working and intelligent Devin was at his barrister career, but she was not about to tell him that.

'What is the truth? If I can believe anything from your treacherous lips.'

Julia's treacherous lips pinched into a thin line as she shook her head. 'I do not give other people's confidences, chaw-bacon. But I will say that your brother loved another and I released him from an engagement that he did not desire. Therefore, you had no right threatening to sue my family for breach of promise. And because of you, I was cast off by my father and forced to become a governess for the meanest woman in the world.'

'And my brother and my family's name has been dragged through the dirt. I lost clients because of it.'

'Perhaps you belong in the dirt, hedge-bird,' Julia retorted. 'But I am no simpleton, so I shall start the fire and then we may change out of our wet clothes so that we do not catch our deaths!'

Pivoting on her foot, Julia turned to the cold hearth and took off her damp gloves. She wasn't precisely certain what *chaw-bacon* meant or *hedge-bird* for that matter. But she'd heard Mrs Heap's grooms insult each other with those phrases. And *basket-scrambler* had something to do with charity. It was one of Mrs Heap's favourite things to say about her acquaintances.

Julia took a deep breath. Most governesses did not start fires. That was the job of a footman. But thanks to Mrs Heap, there was no position in the entire household that Julia had not had the ostensible pleasure of learning. She put the tinder into the fireplace and then struck the flint until the sparks caught fire. She blew a little to help the flame grow and once the tinder was all alight,

Julia added the wood that was next to the hearth in a log-cabin pattern. She opened the flue before standing up, something she should have done from the very start, but Devin irritated her so much that she'd forgotten. At least she'd caught her mistake before their room had been filled with smoke.

While she was making the fire, Devin must have put her trunk on the opposite side of the room from his. Julia was half tempted to insist that he leave while she changed her dress, but it would only cause suspicion from the other passengers. For why would a husband not get into dry clothing before getting a drink? And why would he need to leave his wife alone to dress? But perhaps the biggest reason that she did not ask him to leave was that she felt more secure in his company than by herself. At least she knew him, or of him, and while he was awful, he did not appear immoral. The other passengers were all complete strangers and criminals.

Julia cleared her throat to get Devin's attention. 'I am going to take off my wet things. I will look at the door and you may look toward the window, and therefore we won't see anything untoward.'

He smirked at her. 'Perhaps my brother made a narrow escape if your body is untoward-looking.'

Clenching her teeth, Julia was cold, wet and irritable. She was not about to rise to Devin's bait, even if every bit of her wished to put him in his place. 'Yes, he did. Now I am going to turn around and for the sake of your ramshackle eyes, you should as well.'

Spinning on her foot once again, Julia felt for a brief

moment like she was dancing. Her lips twitched into a small smile. How she had loved dancing and parties in London. But in her last three years living in Town she had not attended any parties. It was hard not to feel resentment towards the entire Ballantine family. If only Joshua hadn't allowed his mother to push him into an engagement that he did not wish for. If only Devin knew that Joshua had been relieved when Julia ended their betrothal rather than threatening legal action. If only her father had not decided to punish her by making her serve as a governess to the most unpleasant woman in the world. If only she could have explained to her stepmother the real reason she had called off the engagement.

In the last three years, Julia had discovered that lingering on *if-only*s was a waste of time. They did not change her current situation and she was currently shivering from the cold. Without glancing over her shoulder, Julia took off her bonnet, scarf and coat. Instinctively, she sidled closer to the heat of the fire. Then she sat down on her trunk and took off her wet boots and sodden stockings. Her toes were shrivelled like an old woman's. She would have been embarrassed in anyone else's company, but she did not care what Dreadful Devin thought of her. And besides, he wasn't looking.

Getting back to her feet, she carefully slid her damp dress over her head. It was her warmest garment and she did not want to wrinkle or dirty it. She carefully laid it out on the bed and caught an eyeful of Devin—his body certainly was not dreadful. His shoulders were broad and she'd never seen a man without his shirt on. Julia's entire body seemed to tighten at the sight and her breasts felt strangely tender. She forced herself to turn back to the door and she carefully pulled off her stays until all she had on was a chemise that barely reached her knees. It was damp too, but she felt far too vulnerable to be naked for even a moment with a man in the room. Even a man who hated her. But then a shiver ran through her entire body, and Julia decided that being dry was more important than her modesty. She opened her trunk and took out another chemise. With a deep breath, she lifted the damp chemise over her head and then traded it as quickly as she could for the dry one. She could not put on her stays, for they were wet, so she grabbed the drab governess gown on top of the pile in her trunk and pulled it on.

Devin stooped to pick up his dry shirt and noticed Julia's reflection in the window. She was in only a thin chemise with her figure underneath illuminated by the light of the fire. Her legs were long and luscious, her bottom was heart-shaped, and the flare of her hips seemed to be in perfect balance with the side angle of the swell of her breasts. She looked younger and softer, probably because he wasn't seeing her shrewish face. It was hidden by her hair that had half fallen out of her chignon.

He nearly swallowed his own tongue when she took off the chemise and he saw the back of her glorious body naked.

It was only for a second, for she put on a dry shift and then her gown. But it was enough for the image to be seared in his mind. Devin needed to get out of this room and fast. Silently turning from her, he put on a new shirt and buttoned it up, before taking off his damp breeches and putting on a new pair of smalls then pantaloons— which were uncomfortably tight. He tucked his shirt into his breeches and put on a waistcoat and coat; for even with the fire, the room had a chill in it. He then rifled through his trunk and pulled out a pair of stockings and dry shoes.

Devin closed the lid with a loud snap and then went to the door. He meant to leave without a backwards glance at her. But his eyes involuntarily found her sitting by the fire with her honey hair completely down and her delicate hands outstretched. Such an image felt too intimate for a stranger to see. Particularly one who hated her and desired her in equal measure. He needed to leave before he forgot the damage that she'd done to his family's name and his own career. She was too damned tempting.

'I'm going down to the tap for a drink and to check on those two men,' he said and slammed the door behind him.

Leaning his back against the door, he took a few deep breaths before walking down the dark, narrow hall. He heard voices in the last room—the one with the shifty men. Devin paused and listened at their door.

'Everything is going wrong, Pip!'

'Hold your counsel, Angus. No one suspects any havey-cavey business and let's keep it that way while we're here.'

'We shouldn't be here. We're like sitting ducks for a pair of Bow Street Runners.'

Devin held his breath, waiting for the partner's answer.

'If the mail coach is stuck, no runner is going to make it

through that storm. Just hold your counsel and make civil whiskers. The other passengers will be none the wiser.'

'But what if—'

'No more *what-if*s, Angus. Keep your mutton mouth closed and we will brush through just fine. No one is going to look through our things.'

'And if they do?'

'We'll say that flash-cove Ballantine planted the goods here.'

Devin startled at the sound of his name and decided that he had lingered too long at their door. As quietly as he could, he descended the creaky stairs and was surprised not to see Mr Peebles at the tap. Curiously, he went back to the door where the man had come out earlier and found it ajar. Pushing it open, Devin saw that the man was alone in the kitchen and appeared to be attempting to cook, but the smell emanating from the pots on the stove would not have tempted a starving pig.

Mr Peebles glanced up at Devin. 'What do you need, Mr Ballantine?'

'Where is your wife, Mr Peebles?'

The proprietor stroked his beard that was already liberally covered in flour. 'You have caught me in a small prevarication, sir. We didn't think that no one would be coming to the inn today and she has gone off to help our daughter deliver her baby at a nearby farm. There's no one here to cook but myself.'

Some of the dismay that Devin felt must have shown on his face.

Peebles held up both hands. 'Now, don't you fret, sir. Your dinner will taste better than it smells.'

Devin sincerely doubted that. 'Would you mind if I poured my own glass of wine at the bar? I don't drink from the tap.'

'Certainly,' he said with a false smile. 'You'll find the red to be the finest in the house.'

Bowing his head, Devin left the dirty and smelly kitchen and returned to the bar, where he located the bottle of red wine. He poured himself a glass and took a sip. It was a very fine French wine and as a servant of the law, he was also certain that it had never paid a duty in any port. Sighing, Devin brought the glass back to his lips. He was snowed-in with a woman he both desired and loathed and whom he was pretending to be married to for her safety, a pair of violent criminals, a quarrelsome couple with a whiny child and a proprietor with bootlegged booze.

What could go wrong?

Chapter Four

Julia sat close to the fire until she felt as if she was being dried out like the clothing she'd hung in front of it—both hers and Devin's. Still, it was nice to finally feel warm and it was even nicer to experience some peace and quiet. Although she would feel more comfortable when Devin returned to their room.

She hoped that little Lizzy was fed and happy, but she doubted it. Even at the advanced age of eighteen during her Society début, Julia had felt uncomfortable living in an unfamiliar environment and being surrounded by strangers at parties. She was too old for dolls, but she always sewed when was sad. Every time she held a needle, Julia remembered her late mother and her kind patience as she taught her daughter needlework. Julia did not have a doll to give to the small girl, but she could sew her one with the scraps in her kit.

Opening her trunk, she took out her sewing box and selected a patch of peach silk for the face. Julia threaded her needle and carefully sewed on a smiling mouth. She tied off her stitch before finding two black buttons that did not quite match each other, but made rather nice eyes. She attached them just above the mouth and then set that piece of scrap aside. For the dress, Julia picked a crimson velvet and laid it out on the wooden floor. She would have preferred to use a pattern, but she was a clever seamstress and she could work without one.

Besides, having something to occupy her hands and her head kept Julia from thinking about Devin's scowl and his shirtless back. Both were terribly distracting. Blinking, she forced herself to focus on her current project. She took out her late mother's silver chatelaine. In almost all of Julia's memories of her mother, Mama wore the chatelaine attached to the waistband of her dress. The fashion of high-waisted gowns made it impossible for Julia to wear the chatelaine the same way, but she could still use the sharp scissors and the other beautiful sewing instruments on the silver chains.

She was cutting out the doll's dress when Devin opened the door without knocking—a thoughtless gesture but which made sense from such a brusque and unpleasant man.

'Stop playing with scraps. 'Tis supper time and the only food that we'll be eating for the rest of the day,' Devin said as he stood in the door-frame. 'And fix your hair respectably before you come down. You look like a hoyden.'

Julia's hands tightened on the scissors and she would have very much liked to stab Devin with them at this moment. 'Your word is my command, *husband*.'

He flinched and then shut the door with a loud thud.

She wrapped the chatelaine up and put it away in her

sewing kit before touching her hair. It was long and thick and difficult to get to cooperate. When she'd had a lady's maid, the servant had been able to pin her curls into submission. But Julia had not enjoyed the services of a maid in three years and she'd learned how to arrange her thick and unmanageable hair into a serviceable chignon at the bottom of her neck. It was neither attractive nor comfortable, so whenever Julia was alone, she always took her hair down. She ruthlessly twisted the hair into a knot and pinned it.

There was no mirror in the room, so Julia glanced into the window for a shadow of her reflection. Her gown was dark and shapeless—which was to be preferred, since her stays were still not dry. It did, however, seem monstrously unfair that Devin looked nice enough to attend a London party and Julia didn't appear presentable for a dinner in a small inn.

Sighing, she put on her shoes and left the room. Once she was in the hall, she heard Lizzy crying for her doll again and Mr Mack hollering at his wife to make the child stop. As if yelling at his spouse would help the situation. She passed the last door in the hall that belonged to the two bridle culls. It was across the hall from the driver and groom's door. Instinctively, she felt for her mother's pearls around her neck. They were still there. But she'd left her silver chatelaine, which was Julia's most precious possession, in her trunk. She couldn't bear to lose it.

Turning around, she returned to her assigned bedchamber and unwrapped the chatelaine, and then pinned it on her dress at her high waistline. A proper lady would not be wearing her sewing instruments to dinner. But there would be nothing proper about tonight's dinner and she felt safer with the sharp scissors within reach.

The Macks opened their door and Julia saw that the very pregnant wife was still holding the small girl, who whimpered unhappily. Even in the poor light, she could see how weary Mrs Mack was.

'Would you like me to hold your daughter?' Julia offered. 'I can assure you that I am quite good with children. I am—was—a governess.'

'Oh, you must mean before you were married,' Mrs Mack said with a tired smile. 'I was a governess as well. That is how I met Mr Mack. He was the uncle of my charges.'

Julia held out her arms and Mrs Mack exhaled as she handed over the cranky and no doubt tired child.

Lizzy outstretched her arms back to her mother. 'Mama! Mama!'

It seemed that the young girl was going to throw yet another screaming tantrum if Julia didn't do something and quickly. She bounced the girl up and down. 'What is your name, poppet?'

The little girl stopped whining. 'Lizzy.'

Julia was not about to say that her name was Mrs Ballantine. She would rather be boiled in figgy pudding first. 'And I am Julia. Are you hungry? Should we go have some dinner?'

Lizzy nodded.

With her free hand, Julia pointed for the Macks to go downstairs. She and Lizzy followed behind them. As Julia supposed, the inn wasn't large enough to have a private parlour or dining room. Two tables had been pushed together with mismatching chairs. At least the tablecloth and dishes appeared to be clean. She felt Devin's presence behind her before she saw him.

'How charming it is to see you with a child in your arms, *wife*.'

He said *wife* like *knife*—sharp and cutting.

Julia continued to bounce the little girl who had laid her head against Julia's shoulder. The child would be asleep soon. No doubt she'd cried herself into exhaustion. Another experience that Julia could relate to.

'If only you would give me a child to love, *husband*.'

Devin's face flushed red and a tense silence followed. Then one of the bridle culls laughed. The sound grated on her ears.

'Your wife is a corker, Ballantine.'

Devin pulled out a chair for Julia. 'That she is.' And as she sat down, he whispered in her ear so only Julia could hear. 'I would be more than happy to fill you with a child, wife.'

Julia felt her own colour rising at his innuendo, her chest tightened, and an odd feeling of butterflies entered her stomach. At least Lizzy had finally fallen asleep. Devin took the seat next to her and his knee brushed hers. He did not move his leg as it rested against Julia's limb and caused her internal temperature to heighten once more. Dreadful Devin cast her a mocking look as if daring her to scoot away from him.

She would burn to a crisp before she moved one inch for that man.

Never before had Devin been attracted to a woman holding a child. He'd never believed that motherhood could be sensual, but there was something extremely attractive about a beautiful woman cradling a sleeping child. Julia hummed low and rocked back and forth in her chair. Devin couldn't decide if it was the sounds she was making or the studied kindness of calming another woman's child. He'd believed Julia to be wholly selfish and clearly he was wrong about that. He also tried not to think of the fact that she wasn't wearing any stays. That her lovely figure was entirely her own. Although the plain dress of a governess did little to ornament her body, Julia was so lovely that it did not matter.

The need to touch her was overwhelming and Devin couldn't resist brushing his knee against her leg. He expected her to flinch or move, but she didn't. It annoyed him that his touch did not bother her in the slightest. But then he saw that her neck was a lovely pink. She was not indifferent to his touch. For a moment or two, Devin allowed himself to fantasise about burying his head into that pink neck and kissing her until she made some humming sounds for him.

Devin grabbed his wine glass and gulped rather than sipped. What had he been doing? Fantasising about the very woman who had ruined his brother's life and mired his family in scandal. Devin had even lost clients over it.

No. He would not give into this siren. Nor to his base desires. Besides, he had no wish to kiss a woman that his brother had. It felt incestuous. At least that was what he tried to convince himself. However, it made a rather unconvincing argument even for a barrister.

Mr Peebles took the lid off the pot of what Devin assumed was supposed to be the soup, though it smelled like burnt peat moss. Even the two thieves wrinkled their noses at it.

Mrs Mack attempted a civil smile. 'Did you make it yourself, Mr Peebles?'

'My wife——' Peebles began to lie but then caught Devin's glare '——has been called away, but I followed her instructions to the letter.'

'I wonder which letter of the alphabet that was,' Julia said in an undertone that only Devin could hear.

He nearly chuckled but kept his mouth firmly closed. He would not laugh at her wit or be charmed by her mouth. Although her mouth was a very pretty shade of pink and her lips were full. Devin wondered how they would taste.

Better than his dinner—that was for certain.

Blissfully unaware, Peebles dished out his stew into everyone's bowls and then filled their glasses with the fine red wine. It was an excellent vintage, but it did not hide the fact that the dinner was inedible and Devin was famished. He'd had a large meal for breakfast but not had a bite to eat since.

'Where is Joe, Mr Denard?' Mrs Mack asked.

The coach driver glanced up from his soup bowl. 'A bit of a head cold so he stayed in our room.'

'I shall bring up a bowl to him,' Mr Peebles said.

Devin didn't think that even a man with a head cold would be able to eat this slop. He watched as Julia toyed with her spoon in her free hand, but somehow she managed to never bring the thick green gloop that Peebles considered stew to her mouth. She did sip her wine and gave little contented sighs that were driving an already hungry man mad with both annoyance and lust.

Unable to control his temper or his desires any longer, Devin turned and whispered in her ear, 'Stop making those noises at the dinner table. It is most unseemly.'

Her eyes widened as if in surprise and then they narrowed at him in what he hoped was fury with a dash of disgust. Devin needed her to hate him—because Julia tempted him too much.

She hissed back at him, 'The only unseemly sound at this supper, husband, is the slurping of your soup. Did your mother forget to teach you manners?'

'Gammon.'

'Hell-born babe,' she whispered back, her tone venomous.

'Is everything all right?' Mrs Mack asked from across the table.

'Yes,' Devin and Julia said at the same time.

'I am sure that it is nothing more than a lovers' quarrel, Mary,' her husband said.

Devin felt even more irritated.

'My sister ended up in Bailey's Jug after a lovers' quarrel,' Mr Rhys said with a jeer.

'Quiet, Angus,' Mr Pip said, stroking his sinister beard. 'You're a trifle disguised.'

Devin did not think that Angus was a little inebriated, he thought that the man was well and truly foxed. Why else would he tell a group of strangers that his sister was in a prison?

'Oh dear,' Mrs Mack said, bringing her napkin to her lips.

'Oh dear indeed,' Mr Rhys agreed with a wink, his cheeks unnaturally red. 'But it were worth it for her, since she won the argument with the help of her kitchen knife.'

An awkward hush fell over the horrible dinner. What did one say after a stranger admitted that his sister had murdered her husband?

'Are you suggesting I borrow one of Mr Peebles's kitchen knives, Mr Rhys?' Julia asked.

'Only if you want to win your argument with your husband.'

And then he heard Julia make another of her infernal sounds. It was half snort, half laugh, and entirely charming. Devin found himself holding in a laugh. Then Julia giggled and the rest of the table laughed. It was too ridiculous not to. Including the very bosky Mr Rhys. Perhaps Devin could use the man's inebriation to learn more about the stolen goods they were hoarding. 'Angus, is it?'

The man pointed a thumb at his chest. 'Angus T. Rhys III.'

'The third what?' Julia quipped and Devin had to purse his lips to keep from smiling.

'No idear, my fine lady, no idear!'

Everyone laughed again, including Peebles, who laughed longer than the rest. Devin picked up his wine glass. 'To Mr Rhys's sister and the winning of all marital arguments.'

Mrs Mack glanced at her husband as if seeking permission before she picked up her glass. Julia had hers raised defiantly and the last person to lift their cup was Mr Pip. He had to be the brains of their two-man crew. The group echoed his toast with laughter and then sipped from their glasses.

Julia was still holding the sleeping girl but managed to keep her wine glass raised. 'To the Christmas season and to warm fires and new acquaintances.'

Everyone drank a second time with more enthusiasm than they had to his toast.

The rest of the meagre meal passed without interest or incident. Peebles cleared the table and Mrs Mack took back her sleeping child after thanking Julia warmly. Then she turned and harangued Devin. 'You are so lucky to have such a kind and thoughtful wife. See to it that you don't forget it.'

For a woman who had been a wet dish-rag to all of her older husband's complaints throughout the day, it surprised him that Mrs Mack would attempt to take him to task for his treatment of his supposed wife. 'I won't.'

Judging from the ill-assorted company, it was going to be a long evening. Angus T. Rhys III was back to the tap with another pint of blue ruin and Timothy Pip was standing near him as if to shield his partner's thoughtless words and behaviours from the group. Peebles, presumably, was in the kitchen cleaning up after the glue-stew he'd cooked. Which left himself, Julia, Mr and Mrs Mack and their sleeping daughter.

'Would you be interested in a game of whist?' Julia asked.

The Macks agreed and for the next couple of hours Devin learned to not bet any money against Julia. Not that they were playing for money. Mr Mack was a curate who did not believe in gambling, which proved fortuitous for the man because Julia would have taken both his shirt and his shoes. She was a card shark and Devin was glad that he was her partner. He stood up and bid farewell to the Macks, and Julia followed suit. As a gentleman, he should have followed behind her up the stairs, in case she were to fall.

He didn't.

Devin walked up without a glance behind him and tried not to regret his moment of pettishness when he realised that he'd missed the perfect opportunity to glance at her behind on the way up if he'd allowed her to go first. He did, however, open the door for her. She did not thank him.

'Please keep your eyes focused on the window' was all that she said.

Opening his own trunk, Devin made a rather poor effort to focus on his own gear and nightshirt. But truthfully, his gaze was on her reflection in the glass, her naked slender calves and her beautiful bare arms, before she covered them with a nightgown that was primmer than a granny's. The garment was so long that it brushed the ground. The cuffs nearly covered her fingers and if the neckline had been any higher, it would have been over her saucy mouth.

He pulled his own nightshirt on and watched as she bent over to add more logs to the fire—he most definitely should have let her walk up the stairs first. Then Julia pulled the pins out of her hair and shook her honey curls seductively. Despite being covered from her neck to her toes, Devin was on fire for her. She acted innocent, but he wondered if Julia knew what she was doing to him. If she had, she would probably have laughed in his face.

'I packed my own sheets, so there is no need for us to touch.'

'As if I would ever touch you.'

She sniffed and then climbed into bed on the side of her sheets. He entered the opposite side and saw that she had cocooned herself in linen. Devin knew that sleeping in the same bed as a beautiful woman that you couldn't touch would be dashed uncomfortable. But this was bordering on torture. Julia fell right asleep and made more sweet little noises that inflamed him. She even mumbled a few words that Devin couldn't quite understand. He saw her curls flared over the pillow and he longed to touch them. She was only an arm's reach away from him, but she was untouchable.

Julia had belonged to his brother and then she had betrayed him. Only a complete and utter fool would long desperately for her caress.

Chapter Five

Christmas Eve

Julia woke up in the early morning feeling overheated. Huffing, she threw off her coverlet, only to realise that the cause of her discomfort was the large, handsome man who still slept soundly beside her. Although her thin sheet separated them, his body gave off heat like a stove.

Devin had lied.

He was touching her. Or at least the entire side of his body was pressed up against hers most agreeably—*annoyingly*. Whichever word applied, Julia felt very hot and bothered. She'd never slept in the same bed as a man before and her curiosity threatened to overcome her good judgement. His facial features were softer as he slept—highlighted by the sunrise and the dim light of their dying fire. Julia's hands began to shake with the overwhelming need to touch him. To feel his hot skin against hers. She wondered what it would be like to be kissed by Devin. To have his strong arms around her and to bury her face in his broad chest. She lifted her hand to touch him but paused over his rising and falling chest.

What if he were to wake up?

Or, worse, move back over to his side of the bed?

Julia liked having his body close to hers—for *safety*. Shoulder to shoulder. Arm to arm. Torso to torso. Leg to leg. She dared not shift or move a muscle which might cause him to turn away from her.

She tried to go back to sleep, but now that she was awake, Julia felt quite hungry and altogether aware of the man sleeping beside her. Not that she regretted not eating the slop that had been served at supper. It had been inedible, but clearly Mr Peebles was not to be trusted in the kitchen and since his wife was away, Julia would have to take charge of breakfast. Thanks to Mrs Heap, she was able to boil eggs, make bread, and assist in simple meals. When Julia had balked at being treated like a kitchen maid, Mrs Heap had threatened to throw her out on her ear.

Rubbing her ear with her free hand, Julia swore that never again would she allow someone to have so much power over her—including her tyrant of a father. And certainly not Devin.

If she stayed beside him much longer, she might lose control of her body. Julia got out of bed. She resolutely did not look at Devin's face while he was sleeping. Therefore she did not see his hair charmingly mussed and a stupid, open-mouth expression that was somehow warming her belly. No, she took off her nightgown and put on her stays, yesterday's now dry gown, an apron and her mother's chatelaine. This dress was her warmest and this inn felt chilly. Julia was tempted to leave her hair down just to taunt Devin, but she plaited it instead so that it would not get in the way of her cooking.

Slipping into her shoes, Julia decided that since it was Christmas Eve, she would be generous. So before leaving, she added two more logs to the dying fire. No doubt her act of kindness would irk Devin more than her insults had.

Julia went down the stairs and found Peebles in the kitchen. The stove was lit and he was boiling a pot of water—that could be helpful. Still, the wooden countertops were covered in dried bits of food from the night before and Julia would not trust herself to eat from any dish that Peebles had washed.

As if by instinct, Mr Peebles held up his hands when he saw her, then swept her an exaggerated bow. 'Mrs Ballantine, how may I help you?'

She shook her head. 'I thought perhaps that I might help you.'

His eyebrows raised and he stroked his dirty red beard. 'You know how to cook, ma'am?'

'A little. Would you please pour that boiling water in the basin and I shall wash the dishes. Then you can fetch me eggs, flour, yeast and salt. Now, please tell me that you have butter.'

Devin woke up with a start. Instinctively he reached across the bed for Julia, but she wasn't there. Had Pip or Rhys kidnapped her in the night? His pulse quickened and he threw off his coverlet, getting to his feet ready to do battle for her life. Blinking, he noticed that her stays and gown were no longer hanging near the healthy fire—Julia must have added logs to it. If she had been in trouble, the irascible young lady would not have stopped to make sure that he was warm. Devin sat back down on the bed and released a long sigh. Julia must have already gone downstairs for breakfast. She had not eaten a bite the night before.

His eyes went back to the hearth where his clothing was hung up in an orderly fashion. Why had she stoked the fire? He had certainly given her no reason to be kind to him.

What sort of game was she playing?

Was the vixen trying to entrap a second Ballantine brother with her wiles, only to discard him again?

Well, Devin was not about to fall into her traps. Nor be swayed by the gentle swell of her hips and the sweet curves of her bosom.

No.

He would treat her with common courtesy and no more. Julia Sullivan wasn't worth his jibes, he reminded himself. The way she had treated his brother showed him that she was beneath him.

Oh dear, that was not a good phrase for him to imagine first thing in the morning. Luckily, the air was mighty cold when he stripped bare and put on his fresh clothing. He took out his toothbrush and paste and cleaned his teeth, before brushing his hair. Not that he was trying to impress anyone—especially not Julia. It was merely good hygiene.

Devin made sure that his purse was in his coat pocket when he left his room. He would be a fool to leave it unattended with two thieves in the inn—even in its secret compartment. He walked to the end of the hall and stopped when he reached the door of Rhys and Pip. Holding still and quiet, he heard two very distinct snores. One was short and staccato. The other long like a bullhorn. At least if they were asleep he didn't have to worry about their shenanigans yet.

When he reached the bottom of the stairs, he saw Mr Mack sitting next to his daughter near the hearth, while Mrs Mack was setting the table. Devin was about to ask where his wife was—where Julia was—when she opened the door to the kitchen carrying a tray of boiled eggs in decorative bowls. He watched silently as she set two eggs in front of each mismatched chair.

The vixen had surprised him again. Not only did she know how to cook, she had made the effort to prepare all of the passengers a meal. Not just herself. Those were not the actions of a selfish person. Could he have been wrong about her personality? Perhaps she had been too young to understand the ramifications of her actions when she jilted Joshua?

'Ah, Devin, you're finally awake,' she said with a sly smile that made his neck stiffen. 'I thought that you were going to be snoring logs until the afternoon at least.'

Any kind thoughts he had entertained about this saucy woman fled his mind. 'You can't blame a man for sleeping in, when his wife mumbles and makes noises all night long.'

Devin saw red blotches form on her cheeks. Probably because Julia knew that he was not lying. The woman did talk in her sleep. She'd awoken Devin more than once. She hadn't shut up, until he'd snuggled up beside her.

Mrs Mack gave a high nervous laugh. 'Is there anything else that I can help you with, Mrs Ballantine?'

His body had a visceral reaction to Julia being called by his surname. His teeth clenched and his chest tightened, as did other unfortunate areas.

Julia turned away from him, which was a relief. 'Yes, Mrs Mack. I am going to slice the bread. Can you check the jam and butter that Peebles found to make sure that they aren't spoiled? The proprietor is as helpless as my husband when it comes to domestic matters.'

Devin grabbed the sides of his face but managed to keep his tongue between his teeth. He took a deep breath before asking, 'And how may I assist you, *dearest wife*?'

'By falling off the nearest cliff,' Julia said without missing a beat. 'But at the moment, glasses of milk would be much appreciated. Make sure that you use the cups that are still wet. I washed them thoroughly this morning with boiling water and soap—I would not trust the other tumblers.'

He tipped his head slightly to one side. '*You* washed the dishes with your hands?'

Laughing at his question, Julia wiggled her delicate hand that was not holding the tray. 'It would have been much more difficult to wash them with my feet, and less clean too.'

Mrs Mack giggled again, a high and grating sound.

Raising her eyebrows, Julia walked past him and back into the kitchen. Mrs Mack followed her, still chortling.

Mr Mack snorted and patted his little daughter's brown curls. 'Never underestimate what a woman can do or the reasons for her actions.'

Devin's temper boiled like a kettle of water. Who was this man to give him advice on treating a woman, when he was hardly a stellar husband himself? Not that Devin was a husband or that Julia was his wife. But the point remained the same. Mr Mack was hardly a deft hand with women either.

The man continued as if not noticing the freezing glare that Devin had directed at him. 'I have found that a humble apology goes a long way. I gave one this morning after my irritable behaviour yesterday.'

Devin raised his eyebrows. 'And she frankly forgave you?'

'Instead of telling my wife what to do, I asked what she needed me to do and she told me.' Mr Mack lifted his daughter onto his knee and bounced her. 'My wife needs me to take care of Lizzy today because holding her is hurting her back… No marriage is perfect, Mr Ballantine, or family for that matter, but I wake up every day determined to do better and I think it does make a difference.'

'Faster, horsey!' Lizzy said in a loud voice.

Chuckling, Mr Mack jiggled his leg even quicker.

Stewing like the smelly soup from the night before, Devin entered the kitchen to see that Julia had transformed the dirty room into a clean space with wonderfully smelling fresh-baked bread on the counter. He located the wet glasses in the drying rack and carefully carried four of them to the table in the taproom, before returning for an additional five tumblers. He found fresh milk in a bucket by the door of the kitchen but assumed that Julia would not wish for him to pour a bucket at the table. He located a pitcher and dumped the milk into it, then returned to the taproom and carefully filled each cup.

The smell of good food must have awakened not only the pair of thieves but the driver as well. Everyone in the inn, save for Joe who was sick, sat down for breakfast together. Unbidden, Devin felt a bout of pride that Julia had prepared a meal with such meagre resources. His eggs were perfectly boiled and the bread was soft and delicious. Not a slice was left at the end of the meal.

'What an excellent repast, Mrs Ballantine,' Mr Mack said but pointedly looked at Devin as he spoke. Like the man expected Devin to compliment the woman he thought was his wife.

Julia smiled and Devin felt a flash of annoyance. 'I couldn't have done so without the help of your wife. Thank you, Mrs Mack.'

Devin was in no mood for niceties. 'Mr Denard, do you need help freeing the carriage this morning? I should be happy to assist you, so that we might continue onto Pickwich as soon as possible.' He glanced at the other passengers. 'And the other destinations, in time for Christmas tomorrow.'

Mr Mack looked out the window. 'The snowstorm has finally stopped. Do you have a sleigh, Mr Peebles?'

The mail coach driver spoke before the innkeeper

could. 'Can't depart today. Joe is too sick to get out of his bed this morning. We can't leave until tomorrow at the earliest and only then if every man here does his duty and helps clear the roads.'

Mr Peebles cleared his throat and tugged at his buttered beard. 'I should like to help, Mr Denard, but I must spend the afternoon preparing supper.'

'Nonsense, Mr Peebles,' Julia chirped from Devin's side. 'Every woman in this room knows her duty too and will ensure that the meal is prepared and edible.'

Devin snorted but managed to keep in his guffaw. Mr Denard and Mr Mack made no such attempt. But it was truly Julia who got the last laugh, for she made all the men clear the breakfast table and scrub the dishes with hot water and soap as she watched them closely. And then she gave Mr Peebles a broom and instructed him to sweep out the taproom.

After tidying up, Devin returned to their shared room and put on his overcoat, hat, scarf and heavy boots. It was going to be a miserable day. As he passed Julia in the narrow hall, their shoulders brushed and she jumped away from him as if scorched by a flame.

'Try not to miss me, wife.'

'Believe me, I won't, husband,' she said and shot him a cheeky smile that kept him warm for the rest of the afternoon.

Chapter Six

Julia made the bed that she had shared with Devin and tried not to think about how tense he made her feel. Her insides were wound up like a ball of yarn, impatient to be released.

Such nonsense!

Devin would be gone all afternoon and she did not wish for him to think that she had shirked her responsibilities. She tidied the rest of her room and would have helped Mrs Mack with her own chamber if the good woman hadn't already told her that she was putting her daughter down for a nap. Julia went next to the bridle culls' room and was unsurprised to see it disordered. At least Devin took good care of his togs.

She huffed before stepping over the dirty garments to the bed. It was too messy to remake: she had to start again. She tore off the coverlet and sheets, straightened the saggy mattress and heard a clatter. Something had fallen out of the bed. Her first thought was a varmint and she grabbed her throat to stop herself from screaming and waking little Lizzy—who was a most unpleasantly behaved child without a nap.

Shaking her head, Julia realised that a mouse would not have made such a loud sound. She gathered her courage and got to her knees. Underneath the bed was a beautiful diamond necklace that she doubted belonged to either man. Her breath quickened. She wanted no trouble. Not while they were isolated at this unknown inn. She put the necklace back underneath the mattress and determined to tell Devin.

Julia took a deep breath before making the bed and tidying the room. Her pulse was heightened, but she didn't wish for anyone to guess that something was wrong. She quietly closed the door and was about to go back to her own room when she realised that she hadn't tidied the driver and groom's room. Perhaps she could bring the sick man some tea.

She knocked quietly on the door across from the thieves' room, but there was no answer. Julia slowly opened the door and saw Joe sound asleep in bed and the mailbag by the door. She could tidy the room and get him some tea when he woke up.

Returning to her room, Julia remembered that it was Christmas Eve, the night of gift-giving, and she wanted to finish the doll for Lizzy. Julia sewed the dress together, along with arms and legs, and finally the head. She braided ribbons for the hair. Now all she needed was some stuffing and she knew just where to find it. Using the scissors from her chatelaine, Julia cut a small hole in Devin's pillow and pulled out the feathers and carded wool. She stuffed the doll until it was full and then carefully sewed the final piece shut.

Lizzy would have a Christmas Eve gift after all.

The door to her bedchamber swung open abruptly and Julia gasped in surprise—it was only Devin—and he gave her an exasperated look. His face was red from the cold and his expression could have frozen milk. 'Have you already forgotten that you have a husband for Christmas?'

Julia covered her mouth with her hand and got to her feet. She was so relieved that it wasn't Rhys or Pip that she could have kissed Devin. Instead, she added another log to the fire and helped him take off his cold and wet things and his boots. 'You poor, totty-headed man.'

He gazed at her warily. 'Why were you scared of me just now?'

She shrugged her shoulders. 'I wasn't. I am not. Scared, that is. Of you.'

Devin walked to the fire and held his hands near the flame. 'You have cut me to shreds with your words and your wit dozens of times in the last twenty-four hours. Perhaps you could tell me the truth.'

For a moment, Julia thought that Devin meant the truth about why she called off her engagement to Joshua. But then she realised he was asking about why she was afraid now. She opened her mouth to tell him but then shut it.

'You can trust me.'

Those four words seemed pretty ironic coming from a man who didn't know her and didn't trust her in return. But Julia was truly scared of the thieves.

'I was tidying the rooms and I found a diamond necklace in Mr Rhys and Mr Pip's room when I made the bed. I put it back, but I think it has been stolen.'

Huffing, Devin rubbed his face with his hands. 'I am certain that it has.'

'I think that we should lay information in Pickwich about those bridle culls.'

Sighing, Devin shook his head. 'Those what?'

'*Bridle culls*, at least that is what little Felix Heap called thieves. He was one of my charges when I was a governess, and he learned the term from one of the young cockney grooms.'

A small smile played on his lips. 'An apt term.'

'What do we do about the criminal pair until we reach Pickwich?'

One word melted his frozen heart: *we*.

Julia didn't ask what *she* should do, but what *they* should do. They weren't truly married, but at this moment they were no longer strangers who hated each other. They were partners in crime—or, rather, to report a crime.

'Will Rhys and Pip know that you entered their room?'

'Of course they will. I cleaned it and made the bed. It was a disaster before.'

'But they didn't see you in it. For all they know any person in the inn could have entered their room and tidied it.'

She scrunched up her nose in the most adorable way. 'Won't they realise that all of the men were helping with snow removal? Which would only leave myself or Mrs Mack as suspects.'

'And the sick groom,' Devin pointed out. 'Unlike your snoopy self, I don't think they have searched his room.'

Julia touched her heaving bosom, her face a beautiful picture of indignation. 'I wasn't snooping, I was tidying.'

'You were brilliant and clever to put the necklace back where it was.'

His compliment seemed to catch her off guard and instead of smiling, she regarded him with suspicion.

'What are you waiting for?' he asked.

'The insult at the end.'

'There is no insult.'

'How unlike you.'

'I know,' Devin said and remembered Mr Mack's words from before breakfast about trying to be a better person each day. His behaviour the last two days had been petty and embarrassing. He was a twenty-six-year-old man and yet he had acted like a spoiled boy, who was petulant because he couldn't have something that he wanted very badly—Julia. She was off-limits to him, as a woman formerly betrothed to his brother. Still, Devin's behaviour towards her had been unworthy of a gentleman. 'I am trying to do better.'

She inhaled sharply and Devin realised that his compliments were far more staggering to her than his rudeness had been. Only now, he no longer wished to injure her feelings. Julia was right. Devin did not know the reason for the end of the engagement with his brother—although, he still wished that it had not been the night before the wedding and that somehow she could have prevented the scandal that followed.

Julia said when they arrived at the inn that she had caught Joshua with his true love and broken off the wedding. When Julia told him this, Devin had been too angry to listen or to try and understand her side of the story. But if that was the case, Julia had sacrificed a title and her own happiness for his brother Joshua. And for her trouble, she'd been disowned and forced to become a governess. Julia wasn't the villainous vixen he had created in his mind but the heroic heroine.

It felt as if his entire world had been turned upside down. Devin would have to ask Joshua for *his* truth, but something deep inside of Devin's heart believed that his brother's words would match Julia's. But why had Joshua not confided all of this to him three years previous? Did his elder brother not trust him with the truth? Did he think that Devin would not love and accept him no matter whom he loved? Joshua was welcome to marry a barmaid or a servant for all he cared. His brother's happiness meant more to Devin than their family's position in Society or even his own reputation and business prospects. It hurt him deeply that Joshua had not confided in him. Perhaps if he had, Devin would not have behaved so poorly towards Julia.

The beautiful woman across from him gave him a sceptical look and Devin remembered Mr Mack's other piece of advice about listening and asking what his wife needed. 'What do you need me to do?'

'I—I thought you would tell me.'

'I have learned that telling you things is rarely helpful—for either of us.'

Julia laughed in his face and Devin found his own lips twitching with amusement. Warmth filled his chest. 'You're right. But I do not wish to put you into any danger.'

Another misconception on his part. Julia didn't purposely try to hurt people, even taciturn strangers. Devin *was* trying to be better, but he was still a man with pride. He flexed his arm muscles. 'I am not afraid of those men.'

This time she giggled and his entire body hummed in awareness of her.

'I thought we could stay together for the rest of the time at the inn and then perhaps you could contact the local constable when we arrive in Pickwich.'

Devin wanted nothing more than to stay by her side. Before, he hadn't been a true gentleman, but he was determined to be one now. He returned her steady gaze and felt his pulse race. He needed to calm down, even if that meant jumping back into the snow. His eyes moved to the floor and he saw that Julia had dropped whatever sewing she had been working on. Devin stooped to pick it up and saw that it was a doll. 'For the Macks' little girl?'

'To replace her lost one.'

As he held the delicate doll, Devin realised that he did not know Julia at all. But oh, how he wanted to. If only she wasn't the woman who had jilted his brother.

Chapter Seven

Julia didn't know what to think of Devin's abrupt change in behaviour. Perhaps the cold had addled his brain. She left the room so that he could change into dry clothes. Her entire body seemed to tremble as she went down the stairs to the kitchen to start making supper.

Mrs Mack was feeding Lizzy a slice of bread and jam from the second loaf Julia had baked this morning.

Julia was relieved that no other person was in the kitchen. She was not ready to see Mr Rhys, Mr Pip or even Mr Peebles. 'You must be very hungry.'

'Yup,' Lizzy said with jam on her cheeks.

'And very lonely without your dolly.'

Lizzy stuck out her lower lip and nodded.

Julia pulled the doll she had made from her pocket and gave it to the little girl. 'I thought that you could keep Molly company. She's been lonely too.'

The little girl held the doll with awe-like reverence. 'Molly's bootiful.'

'I made her myself, just for you.'

Mrs Mack placed a gentle hand on Julia's shoulder. 'You are too kind, Mrs Ballantine. I am deeply touched.'

Blushing, Julia always felt a little awkward accepting compliments. 'Well, it is Christmas Eve after all,' she said brusquely. 'And we have a supper feast to prepare.'

Julia had displayed all of her cooking skills at breakfast. Happily, Mrs Mack was the youngest daughter of a vicar and had often helped prepare dinner at home. She took charge and Julia was relieved to follow her lead. Julia chopped vegetables and stirred sauces. While slicing and dicing, she couldn't help but think that perhaps she had been rather spoiled for the first eighteen years of her life. Julia hadn't been able to make a pot of tea or do the smallest of menial tasks. Such things had never been required of her. Despite the loneliness and heartache of the last three years, Julia was grateful that she'd learned how to take care of a house, cook a meal and dress herself. No matter what the future held for her, she was capable of adapting. If only she didn't miss Amelia and her stepmother so much! If only Papa would have allowed them to write to her.

She put down her knife and set the table in the taproom. Julia wondered what her sister was doing right now to celebrate Christmas Eve.

She sighed loudly.

A familiar deep voice from behind her said, 'Surely you are too young for such sighs.'

Julia spun around to see Devin. He had changed and freshened up and looked handsomer than ever. She was still wearing an apron and her hair was falling out of its plait. Conscious of her harried appearance, Julia touched the side of her head.

Devin walked closer to her until the tips of his shoes brushed the hem of her gown. 'What was the sigh for, fair Julia?'

Her hand moved to her neck, which felt very hot. 'It's silly, really.'

'Tell me.'

She didn't wish to mention her family, so Julia jerkily gestured to the plain table. 'It doesn't look very Christmassy.'

Devin nodded. 'I agree. How would you like me to remedy that?'

Again, he was asking how she wanted him to help her. It was flattering and a bit staggering. Awkwardly, she wrapped her arms around herself. 'I can't ask you to go back out into the cold for evergreen boughs and pine cones.'

He winked at her. 'You didn't ask me. *I* asked you.'

Then she watched him fetch his overcoat and return out into the cold air of December. She didn't know what to make of it. Or of him. Nor did she know what to say when he returned a quarter of an hour later with evergreen clippings and asked Julia to arrange them on the table however she liked. And she did. The greenery and pine cones brought cheer to the barren table—all it needed now was crimson ribbons.

'What can I fetch you?' Devin asked, as if he'd realised that Julia was not yet content with their Christmas spread.

'I was only going to get some red ribbon from my sewing kit upstairs.'

'I'll get it for you,' he insisted. 'I need to put my overcoat away.'

While she waited, Julia helped Mrs Mack bring the tureens and covered dishes to the table. Her heart was behaving most strangely and fluttering in a most unnatural way. Devin returned with her spool of crimson ribbon and Julia was grateful that she was still wearing her mother's chatelaine so that she could easily trim the ribbons. Devin did not offer to help this time, but watched her tie bows onto the boughs as if it were the most fascinating thing that he had ever seen. She felt her colour rise but felt absurdly pleased by it. And when they sat down for dinner with the other assorted passengers, the driver, and Mr Peebles, she pressed her leg against Devin's.

Not only to tease but because she felt warm and protected when they touched. After they had finished their hearty meal and the men had washed up, Julia found herself by Devin's side as the ill-assorted group sang Christmas carols. His voice was deep and low and entirely masculine. It caused her skin to tingle and the hairs on the back of her neck to stand up.

Mr Peebles left for a few minutes and then brought back a fiddle and began to play it. Mr Mack picked up his daughter and danced with her. Perhaps Julia had been over-harsh when she'd judged him. Mr Denard asked Mrs Mack to dance and they joined the jig. Julia grabbed Devin's hand before Mr Rhys or Mr Pip got any ideas. She tugged him to the dance floor and with one twirl, he pulled her into his arms. Her breath caught and every bit of her body was aware of him from her hair to her toes. Devin's handsomeness. His strength. His acts of kindness that afternoon.

Dancing with Devin was entirely different than dancing with Joshua. His elder brother was a refined dancer and a good partner. Joshua made you feel relaxed in his company, like he was a friend from the very beginning of your acquaintance. He was the sort of person who you felt as if you could confide anything to. She'd first noticed Joshua at church when she was scarcely more than a child. He'd been twenty-nine to her scarce twelve years, but he had bowed to her as if she were a lady and an adult. Julia's younger self had fallen in love with the *idea* of him and six years later when her father had arranged the marriage with their neighbour, Baron Ballantine, she had not said no.

Devin must have been at school, for she had no memories of him at church. Or of having met him before that disastrous night three years ago. He was only five years older than herself and handsome enough for any girl to fall in love with. As he brought her closer to him, Julia half wondered what would have happened if only she had met Devin first. Or if her father had attempted to make a match with him rather than Joshua. How different everything might have been.

Chapter Eight

Julia danced with Devin a half a dozen times before they went up to their bedchamber. That must be the reason why she felt out of breath. It was not that she was nervous about spending another night in the same bed with him. With shaking hands, she removed her dress and stays and put on her warm nightgown. Julia dressed fast enough to see the back of Devin without his shirt on or his snug breeches, although he wore smalls. His legs were strong and muscular and Julia could have watched them longer, but unfortunately, he pulled his nightshirt over his shoulders and it covered past his knees.

'Shall we go to bed?'

Unable to form words, Julia nodded. She slid into bed without even adding logs to the fire. Devin did not forget that it was December and stacked several pieces of wood onto the flames before joining her in bed. There was no candle in the room, but the light from the fire was enough to see the chiselled lines of his nose, chin and cheeks. It was almost as if he'd been carved into perfection.

Devin climbed into bed on the other side and caught

her staring at him. He took her hand and held it in his much larger and warmer one. 'Don't worry. I have bolted the door. The thieves won't enter our bedroom tonight.'

Julia brushed her thumb over the calluses on his fingers. Touching them made her skin tingle. His wrist bumped her chatelaine and then he pulled back his hand.

'You don't have to sleep with scissors on you. I would not touch you without your permission. I mean, I won't touch you. Not at all.'

Julia was glad that it was dark, for she felt herself blushing as she picked up the sharp scissors on the end of the silver chatelaine. 'I'm wearing my scissors for protection not from you but from the thieves. And because this was my mother's chatelaine and I remember her wearing it nearly every day. I would rather Mr Rhys and Mr Pip steal my pearl necklace than this.'

Devin didn't speak for a few moments and Julia wondered if he had either fallen asleep or if he'd misunderstood her. 'Can you tell me about your chatelaine?'

She wasn't sure exactly what she was supposed to say. 'Well, um, you pin it to the waistband of your gown and when you're sewing you have all the needed instruments right at your fingertips. Chatelaine in French roughly means *lady of the castle*. Not that my mother spoke French. She was the daughter of a factory owner and had no fancy airs.' Julia held up the scissors that were on the first chain. 'Obviously these are the scissors.' Next she showed him the tweezers, thimble, magnifying glass, miniature knife, mirror and the little nut-shaped case that her mother said was her good luck charm.

'Have you ever opened the good luck charm to see what is in it?' Devin asked.

Julia was still holding the nut-shaped silver case between her fingers. She felt around its decorated silver casing to find a small latch that she'd never realised was part of a mechanism. Her mouth fell open. How could she have not noticed it before? Her curiosity got the better of her and she slipped her thumbnail underneath it and popped the nut lid open. Inside the silver vial was a folded piece of paper. She gasped in surprise as she pulled it out and recognised her mother's careful handwriting on it.

'It's a letter from my mother addressed to me.'

The light from the flames was not enough for her to see the small penmanship, so she climbed out of bed and rushed to the fireplace. She had carried her mother's chatelaine for eleven years and never once found the hidden message that had been waiting there for her. Julia had never thought to look for one. Nor could she recall her mother telling her about it. Biting her lower lip, she held the letter to the light.

My dearest Julia,

A woman should always be prepared for any adventure. That is why I always wore my chatelaine, so that I could protect and take care of myself. It is my hope that I will always be able to take care of you, my dear girl, but my cough worsens and my body grows weaker. I would have left you in the care of my sister and her husband, but the law does not recognise the wishes of a wife. Only the power of a hus-

*band and father. And I don't think your father will
let you go because you are precious beyond measure in more ways than you know. Your grandfather
was a factory owner and he did not trust your father; he thought him a spendthrift baronet. So when
we married, he added a clause to the contracts that
your father could only use the yearly income from
my dowry of fifty thousand pounds during my lifetime. And in the event of my death, the money would
pass to my children—to you.*

*My dear daughter, I hope by the time that you are
reading this that you are old enough to understand
that your father only married me for my money. He
was very handsome and held a title and my head
was quite turned. It wasn't long after our marriage
that I realised how ugly he could be. But at least he
gave me you—the love and joy of my life. Perhaps
I should have told you, but I did not want to cause
problems for you with your father. When you are one
and twenty, take your inheritance and be happy. I
will watch over you, even from heaven.*
Love, Mama

Unbidden and unwanted, tears fell freely down Julia's
cheeks. How she missed her mother! Even the smell of
her lavender soap and the sound of her ragged breathing: Mama had said that her lungs were full of cotton.
Julia tried to sniff quietly, so Devin could fall asleep. She
didn't want him to see how vulnerable and upset she felt.
Her mind was a whirlwind. She was no longer without

her own funds. Nor was she dependent upon her father for money. She did not have to humble herself to him or be obedient to his dictates. She would not have to scrape and bow before the Mrs Heaps of the world either.

Julia was so intent upon her letter and her tears that she did not hear Devin leave the bed nor notice that he had, until he knelt by her side.

'Is everything all right?' he asked, his hand outstretched to her.

She realised that he would not touch her without her permission. So she held out a trembling hand to him and he encased it in a firm grip. His thumb gently rubbed the top of her hand. It had been so long since she'd been touched by someone who cared about her. Not since the day after her cancelled wedding when her stepmother had hugged her goodbye and Amelia had cried upon her shoulder.

Taking a deep breath, Julia nodded. 'I never expected to hear my mother's voice again and when I read her words, it was as if she were here beside me. Guiding me as she once did. It was a most unexpected and wonderful Christmas Eve gift.'

'I am glad. What I wouldn't give to hear from my late father once again.'

The mention of fathers made Julia remember her mother's letter. 'May I ask you a question as a barrister?'

'Of course.'

Julia wasn't sure if it was the heat of the fire or from her own embarrassment, but she felt hot all over. 'When a woman marries, doesn't all of her property and fortune become her husband's?'

'By English law, yes,' Devin said softly. 'All a woman has or expects to have becomes virtually the property of the man she has accepted as husband, and no gift or deed executed by her is held to be valid.'

Her eyes returned to her mother's letter, wrinkled with numerous little folds. 'Then, what my mother writes cannot be true. She and my grandfather could not have not have left his fortune to me.'

Devin released her hand and she missed his touch immediately. 'May I?'

Julia felt reluctant to let her mother's letter go so soon after finding it, but she trusted Devin completely.

Taking the letter, Devin nodded his head. 'Sounds like your grandfather had a very good family lawyer working for him. He must have set up what is called a separate estate or a separate property for your mother when she was a bride. The lawyer would have made a separate trust for your mother which is typically overseen by the Court of Chancery. A woman can have access to her funds or property once she applies for them through her trustee. There's usually more than one to make sure that everything is financially above board.'

'Then, her husband, my father, could not access the money?'

Devin's gaze returned to the letter. 'It appears that the yearly income from the separate estate was to be given to your father while your mother was alive. But he would have been unable to access the principal. Nor could his

creditors seize the property or money to pay his bills…
And after your mother's death the yearly income was to
go to her children—which is you. How old are you?'

'I turned one and twenty on December 6 this year.'

He gave a low whistle that made her overly warm body
even more aware of him. 'It would seem that your father
calling you home right now is probably not a coincidence.
Perhaps the trustees will not release next year's income
unless you are living under his care.'

'But the money should be mine, correct?'

Devin rubbed his eyes and shook his head. 'By law,
yes, but since women are rarely given access to a great
deal of money—in this case the yearly income should be
at the very least twenty-five hundred pounds—your father might have been able to persuade your trustees that
he is handling your fortune for you.'

Julia gritted her teeth. She would still be underneath
her father's thumb. 'There must be something that I can
do.'

His lips twitched and then he smiled. 'You should hire a
good barrister and make sure that all payments are given
directly to you… I happen to know a really good one who
would be happy to represent you.'

A laugh escaped her lips. Devin was talking about himself and despite the rocky start to their relationship, she
believed him. In their time together she'd discovered that
he was hard-working, intelligent and loyal to a fault. All
things that would make him a wonderful lawyer.

'How do I engage your services, sir?'

'I prefer that you call me Devin, or hedge-bird. That insult has really grown on me.'

Julia gave a watery chuckle. 'How do I engage your services, *Devin*?'

'Do you have a coin in your possession? Even a farthing.'

She scrambled to her feet and went to her trunk. She opened it and took out her purse—which only had a few coins in it. Sighing, she took out a ha'penny and placed it in the palm of his hand. 'You now work for me.'

His fingers closed around the coin, but his arrestingly mismatched eyes were staring into her very soul. 'With your permission, Julia, I will hold onto this letter from your mother until I have been able to contact the Court of Chancery and learn the names of your trustees. Then I will write directly to them as your representative and hopefully they will release the funds directly to you. If not, we can take the matter to court.'

'You will keep the letter safe?'

'Safer than your coin purse,' Devin retorted, pointing to her open portmanteau. 'You haven't even hidden it. Anyone could have stolen it, like the diamond necklace.'

Standing up, she climbed into her separate sheets and turned to look at Devin on the other side of the bed. She was so glad that he was beside her. Devin made her feel safe and he was quite nice to look at as well. 'Goodnight, Devin. And don't forget, I have given you a ha'penny to be my barrister, so now technically, you're my servant and I should be telling you what to do.'

His low chuckle set all of her nerves on end. 'You are my client, Julia. Not my master.'

She wanted to touch him again. Just to feel his fingers intertwined with hers. The warmth of his body near hers. With a deep breath, Julia scooted closer to Devin until their shoulders were touching. This might be the last night that they spent together and she didn't want to waste it. 'Or mistress?'

Devin squeezed his eyelids closed. 'Do you always play with fire?'

With the last of her courage, she took his warm hand and held it in hers. 'Are you going to burn me?'

Opening his eyes, he turned his head to look directly at her. 'I would never hurt you, Julia. You are too precious to me. I only wish… There's no point in wishing.'

His words caused her entire body to tingle with want; however, his expression was not one of desire but of regret. It didn't matter how much they cared for or were attracted to each other. There could never be a relationship between them. Julia had already embarrassed his brother and caused a great scandal.

She should have let go of his hand, but instead she held it tightly until she fell asleep.

Chapter Nine

Christmas Day

'Wake up, termagant,' Devin said fondly. 'It is Christmas Day and the mail coach is finally going to take us home.'

He'd awoken first this morning, performed his ablutions and changed his clothes. He'd even watched her sleep for a little while, but then realised that he didn't want to miss even a moment of her awake. Today they would part and whatever this wonderful feeling between them was would have to come to an end. He watched her yawn and stretch out her arms.

'I am not a termagant. I am your client, gull-catcher.'

His lips twitched in appreciation of her insult. 'Do you even know what half of the insults you hurl at me mean?'

Julia sat up in bed. Her complexion was rosy from sleeping and her braided hair delightfully mussed. Her body had been cuddled up next to him for most of his sleepless night. 'No. But a person does not need to know the definition of a word when you can clearly decipher its meaning from the context.'

'Since my clients come from all walks of life, I am familiar with London slang. A hedge-bird means a *vagrant* or a *vagabond*. And a gull-catcher means a *trickster* or a *cheat*.'

She got to her feet and not even her ridiculously prim nightgown could hide how lovely she was. 'I stand by every insult that I've called you. And *I* know what a termagant means. It refers to a *harsh-tempered or overbearing woman*.'

He smiled at her play on words. She *was* standing. 'Did you learn all sorts of vulgar terms and phrases in the servants' quarters as a governess?'

'Mrs Heap's servants were certainly a *rackety* group of people.'

Devin's grin grew even larger. Conversing with Julia was a bittersweet delight. She was sharp-witted and he never knew what she was going to say next. He was almost sorry that he'd helped clear the roads the day before because he was not ready to part from her yet. But perhaps it was for the best. His attraction to her was growing by the second and he did not know how much longer that they could have shared a bed without him losing control and kissing her saucy lips. In fact, there was nothing he wanted more now than to cover her mouth with his own. Not just because she was beautiful but against all odds he'd grown to like her. More than *like*. He loved her wit. Her generosity. The way she danced. How she laughed.

He even loved her tidiness. If she'd been any other woman he'd seriously contemplate courting her.

But she was the honourable Miss Julia Sullivan.

The woman who had jilted his elder brother.

'I shall pack my trunk while you change,' Devin said, forcing himself to turn away from her. 'And you'd better make it quick. I saw a new groom outside the window. Joe must still be too sick to leave the inn.'

Devin tried not to listen to Julia's breathing or the noises she made as she took off her nightgown and put on her dress. At least this time he did not sneak a glance. His attraction to her was too strong to tempt fate any further.

'I'm ready.'

He turned to see her holding her portmanteau with both arms. Her hair was freshly plaited and her lips newly licked. The urge to kiss her was almost overwhelming. Devin forced himself to take a deep breath and then took the portmanteau from her arms. 'Allow me to carry that for you. It's the least a totty-headed fellow can do.'

Julia giggled as he took her portmanteau and put it on top of his own. Devin set both trunks on the bed so that he could unlatch the lock and open the door for Julia. She winked at him as she went through the door-frame. Devin watched the lovely sway of her hips as she walked for a few moments before recalling himself and picking up the luggage and following her through the hall and down the stairs.

Breakfast was a miserable affair. Julia thoroughly disliked gruel and every minute brought her closer to saying goodbye to Devin. They were parting just when she was starting to—Julia couldn't name the feeling just yet. But it was unlike anything that she'd ever experienced before and it felt wonderful.

Devin was uncharacteristically silent at the table and then carried their luggage out to the mail coach. Julia and the other five passengers followed behind him.

The new groom tipped his hat to the group, but his eyes focused on Julia. 'Why, if it isn't the honourable Miss Sullivan! How are you?'

'Don't you mean Mrs Ballantine?' Mr Mack said.

The groom guffawed loudly. 'Miss Sullivan ain't Mrs Ballantine. She jilted Baron Ballantine at the altar three years ago and quite a stir it made from Pickwich to London. Particularly since her father is a baronet.'

'Then, you two are not married?' Mrs Mack said, pointing to Julia and Devin.

Julia felt her face go red and she wished that she could hide. What incredibly bad luck that someone from Pickwich had come to this small inn!

The woman covered her mouth with her hand as if this was more shocking than being held up by thieves. 'But you stayed in the same room for two nights.'

Devin finally found his voice. 'Only for her protection. I treated her like a sister.'

The groom gave a low whistle, but his eyes were positively dancing with glee.

Julia sighed. Such a juicy titbit of gossip would circulate through the town of Pickwich like wildfire and her reputation would be entirely ruined. Perhaps the groom would make sure that it reached London as well.

'Yes, I am Miss Sullivan and I am well but ready to go home. As is Mr Ballantine. How soon will we be leaving?'

'As soon as I tie up the trunks to the back of the coach,' the groom said, tipping his hat to her a second time. 'We'll be in Pickwich before luncheon. If you don't mind lending a hand, Mr Ballantine.'

Devin must not have minded, for he did not return to the carriage interior for several more minutes. When he did, Devin sat next to Julia but did not speak. All three Macks were on the opposite bench of the mail coach and had not conversed with Julia since the revelation of her single status, no doubt because they disapproved of her behaviour. It wouldn't surprise her if the Macks spread rumours about her. Instead, she was squished between Devin and the side of the carriage. They were on the same seat as Mr Pip and Mr Rhys and it appeared that he would protect her until she reached home.

Julia sighed loudly. She'd been so close to returning to her old life of privilege and parties, but now her reputation was ruined and not even a fortune could save her.

The ride to Pickwich only took a couple of hours, but it felt like an eternity.

Chapter Ten

Devin sat close to Julia in the coach, but he did not know what to say. Despite his best intentions, their predicament was entirely his fault. He should never have said that they were married or used his real surname. The moment those words came from his mouth, he had ruined Julia's reputation. And there was only one way to retrieve it: a real marriage. The thought of marrying her did not dismay him as it would have only a few days before. He longed to bed her and he enjoyed her wit. And as her husband, rather than her legal representative, Devin would have an easier time obtaining her yearly income from her trustees. He was only sorry to have taken away their choice in the matter and for the rift it would inevitably cause between himself and his only brother.

How he wished that he could go back three days and stop himself from his foolhardy declaration that Julia was his wife!

But then, he would not have gotten to spend so much time with her. Nor would he have discovered her penchant for interesting insults and her clever tongue. Groaning inwardly, he realised that this time the gossip and scandal would be entirely his fault. Not hers. He deserved to lose clients.

Devin prepared a speech in his head. The coach was uncommonly silent. The Macks' behaviour grated on his fraying patience. Neither Mr nor Mrs Mack would look Julia in the eye as their daughter sat happily between them holding the dolly that Julia had made for her instead of screaming like she had on their first journey. But it appeared that the Macks had already forgotten her goodness and kindness. All that mattered was her damaged reputation, which Devin was determined to restore.

When the coach stopped at a posting inn in Pickwich, Devin got out and helped Julia descend. Then he carried both of their trunks into the warm inn, where he saw Sir Eustace's driver standing near the bar. The man was no doubt waiting to take Julia to Broadwick Abbey. Devin couldn't allow her to go alone and face the disgrace. He set down the trunks, took Julia's elbow and whispered, 'I will take care of everything.'

'You will lay information about Mr Rhys and Mr Pip?'

He shook his head. The jewel thieves were the least of their worries. 'I meant about us. I will speak to your father and we will wed immediately. You needn't worry about anything.'

Julia jerked away from him, causing his hand to drop from her arm. 'Oh, Devin. I don't need another man in my life telling me what to do. I will go home by myself and contact you, as my barrister, when I return to London for help with my trustees. I've already paid you an entire ha'penny.'

He stepped towards her but didn't touch her. 'But your reputation—'

'Has survived worse. Happy Christmas, chaw-bacon.'

Devin watched her walk away and he could not stop her. Nor could he protect her. Shoulders sagging, he went to the constable's house and reported the stolen necklace. The constable went at once to the mail coach and, with the help of three grooms from the inn, hauled Rhys and Pip out of the carriage and into the local roundhouse.

Once he ascertained that thieves were in custody, Devin picked up his trunk and left the posting inn for the barn where he hired a horse to take him to River-dale House. The ostler tied his luggage to the saddle and Devin rode home feeling colder and more miserable than he ever had in his entire life.

He was met by a groom at the front of his brother's house, who took the horse's bridle and promised to bring his trunk up to his room. Devin walked into his brother's home empty-handed and alone.

Joshua strode forward to meet Devin and swept him up in a tight hug. 'I was so worried about you, brother.'

Behind them stood Roger Ashby, his brother's stew-ard. 'I nearly had to restrain the baron from riding out into the snowstorm to find you.'

Stepping back from his brother, Devin forced himself to politely smile at the man. 'I am glad you were so pru-dent, Mr Ashby, but would you mind if I spoke privately with my brother?'

Joshua jovially clapped him on the shoulder. 'Of course. Of course. Why don't you come into the library and I'll pour us both a glass of sherry? And Roger can go back to reading his book. He hates to be interrupted during the good parts.'

Devin could use a little fortified drink right then. He followed his brother down the grand hall and into the library. Books lined every wall and as a barrister, Devin couldn't help but appreciate how much wisdom had always been available at his fingertips. But what he needed to know now only his elder brother could tell him. Turning toward the credenza, he saw Joshua pouring them both a tumbler of sherry. His brother handed Devin one first and then lifted his own glass. 'To safe journeys.'

Devin tried to echo the kind sentiment but found himself tongue-tied. To ask his brother about his broken engagement felt like tearing the scab off an old wound to watch it bleed again. Yet Julia had insisted that she broke off the engagement because Joshua loved another. And Devin now trusted her: he believed that she had told him the truth.

His brother's eyebrows furrowed. 'What's wrong, D?'

One side of Devin's mouth quirked up at the old nickname. He took a long sip of sherry and then forced himself to ask 'Why did Julia break your engagement? Is it true that she found you in the arms of another woman? And if so, then why have you not married that woman?'

The smile faded from Joshua's face and he set down his glass on the nearest side table. 'Why do you ask?'

Devin drained the rest of his drink and then placed his empty tumbler next to Joshua's glass. Nervously, he raked his hands through his hair. 'Julia was on the mail coach with me. I—we were snowed-in together for two nights and I grew to know her...and to appreciate her wit and beauty. She insisted that she ended the engagement for your happiness and I need to know the truth because... because I'm falling in love with her.'

Joshua inhaled sharply. 'Julia is a very loyal person and I am grateful for her silence on the subject. It is not one that I ever meant to speak to you about. Perhaps I should have, only—' his elder brother swallowed and his face was tinged with red '—it is a private thing and I am not embarrassed by the person that I love, but the world would not understand. And I am afraid that you will not either.'

Rubbing the centre of his chest, Devin was a little hurt that his brother did not trust him with his confidences. 'I am your brother. You can tell me anything. And I don't care if you want to marry one of your former mistresses or turn a milkmaid into your baroness. I've never sought your title or your inheritance. I only care about you, Joshua.'

'And Miss Julia Sullivan, it would seem.'

Devin felt his own cheeks growing hot and he tried not to think of their terrible parting. 'Yes.'

His brother turned away from Devin, his gaze out the window, rather than meeting his brother's eyes. 'I think it is important for you to know that I have always been this way—for as long as I can remember... I have found men attractive rather than women.'

Blinking, Devin finally realised what Julia had been trying to hide. 'She caught you in a compromising position not with another woman but with a man.'

'I am not ashamed of my lover or of my feelings,'

Joshua said quietly. 'I am ashamed that Mama forged my name on the marriage contracts. And once the newspapers printed our engagement, I could see no honourable way out of it.'

'Did Mama know that you—that your heart was already taken by another?'

Joshua nodded. 'She thought that marrying a beautiful young woman would cure me. But I do not need to be cured. Nor do I want to be. This is who I am, Devin. Who I have always been.'

Devin's hands clenched into fists. 'Mama has much to answer for. I only wish… I wish that you had told me this three years ago. I am a barrister. I could have found a legal loophole since the signatures were forged. Or if nothing else, I would have taken your place as the groom.'

His brother glanced over his shoulder at Devin. 'You would have done that for me?'

'I would do anything for you, Joshua. You were more father than brother to me. There is no one else I care about more. And I hope that someday you will feel comfortable telling me who your lover is and knowing that I will always love and support you.'

Devin grabbed his brother in a bear hug.

They stepped back from each other and Devin could see that Joshua's eyes were filled with tears. 'I should have trusted you sooner. I am sorry that I didn't, brother. Roger is my lover and has been for the last twenty years—we have been as devoted to each other as any married couple.'

The wheels began to turn in Devin's sluggish mind. His brother's steward, Roger Ashby, had moved into Riverdale House not to console Joshua but because they were a couple.

'Actually, I am relieved. Nay, I am happy to know that you are with Roger,' Devin admitted sheepishly. 'Then, I do not have to feel guilty for harbouring feelings for Julia.'

Joshua raised his eyebrows. 'That must have been some snowed-in adventure for my stoic little brother to have fallen in love in only three days and two nights.'

'It was,' Devin said and they sat down. Then he told his brother the entire tale—leaving nothing out, even his sharing a bed with her and his insulting words. 'And since I had gotten us into a fix by claiming that we were married, I offered to speak to Julia's father and to take care of everything. I thought that she, too, had grown fond of me, but she glared at me, like she had from the very beginning of our relationship, and said, "I don't need another man in my life telling me what to do".'

Joshua exhaled slowly. 'I have some good news and some bad news. Which do you want first?'

'The bad news.'

'She didn't say *no*, because you never asked her to marry you.'

Scoffing, Devin shook his head. 'I promised to speak to her father and she did not wish me to.'

'Of course she did not wish you to speak to her father until you had asked her,' his elder brother pointed out in an annoyingly reasonable tone. 'The poor girl has never been proposed to. Her father told Julia that she was engaged to me and then you told her that she would be engaged to you.'

Devin felt as if he couldn't breathe for the second time that day. First at the realisation that his brother had been tricked into an unwanted engagement. And second that he'd behaved like a complete gudgeon with Julia. She'd lived for twenty-one years under her father's tyranny. Why would any woman in her right state of mind wish to spend the rest of her life under a dictatorial husband?

'I mucked it up terribly.'

Joshua nodded. 'You did. But I have not told you the good news yet.'

Sighing, Devin did not think that he could hear anything worse than the fact that he had ruined his chances with the woman of his dreams. 'Better get it over with, then.'

'We have been invited to the Sullivans' for Christmas dinner tonight. Lady Sullivan has extended an olive branch to our family to help hush the rumours that still circulate about the bad blood between our families. Perhaps you can try asking Julia this time. I would suggest that you at least become engaged before Sir Eustace learns of the days and nights she spent as your wife.'

'Good heavens, yes,' Devin agreed. 'And will Roger be accompanying us tonight?'

'Yes.'

'Excellent. That is how it should be. Our family is together for the holiday.' Devin got to his feet. 'I am going to bathe and then try to prepare a speech for Julia.'

Joshua stood up beside his little brother—well, *younger* brother—Devin was three inches taller. Joshua grasped

Devin's shoulder tightly. 'Maybe less speechifying and more listening to Julia next time.'

A laugh escaped his lips, but then Devin sobered quickly. 'Do you think that Sir Eustace will accept my suit? I am not a baron with an estate like yourself. I am only a London barrister.'

'You are my heir and I will make sure that Sir Eustace knows that after my failed attempt at matrimony, I am far too old and jaded to try again.'

Devin tried to swallow a lump in his throat. 'I don't want to be a bloody baron, so you'll have to promise me to live for a very long time.'

'I will,' Joshua said. 'Now, we both had best go and get ready for dinner tonight. My dear Roger hates being late by even a minute.'

The emotion that had threatened to choke Devin only moments before somehow turned into a breathy chuckle. 'How does he get Mama to arrive on schedule?'

'Roger simply leaves her if she is late.'

The image of their imperious mother being left behind was too much. Devin laughed loudly and Joshua joined in his mirth. They parted in the hall and Devin went up to his rooms. He was grateful to see that the servants had already begun filling a copper tub for him. He would need to bathe quickly. He didn't want to give Roger a bad opinion of him by being late.

Once the servants left, Devin deftly stripped out of his clothes and stepped into the steaming water. Leaning his head back against the rim, he felt lighter than he had in years. The truth really did set one free.

Chapter Eleven

'Have you not disgraced our name enough with a very public jilting of a baron?' her father demanded as soon as she stepped inside Broadwick Abbey. 'You spent two nights pretending to be Mr Ballantine's wife and you come home unengaged? The driver said that it is all over Pickwich and no doubt the scandal-mongers will see this sordid tale reaches London. You are ruined, daughter. *Ruined.* I ought to throw you out on your ear at this very moment so that you don't hurt Amelia's chances for a good match.'

Her half-sister, Amelia, would be ten years old now. Would they feel like strangers? Julia had adored Amelia from the day that she was born and doted on her. But she'd learned as a governess that children could be very changeable.

It had been three years since she'd last seen her father in person and he hadn't changed a bit. At least, in personality. He still yelled instead of speaking. Dictated instead of discussing. But his famously handsome physical features had altered. His face had more lines around the mouth and eyes. His light brown hair possessed more silver and he had a hint of a second chin. When he'd loomed over her in anger in the past, it had frightened her. But after living with Mrs Heap, nothing could scare Julia now. She'd faced the worst and managed to survive. She would not bend herself to another's will again. Not even Devin's.

'Fine. You can throw me out into the cold,' Julia said. 'But I will be taking my mother's inheritance with me.'

Cursing, Papa grabbed her wrist tightly. 'Who told you?'

She struggled against him. 'Mama.'

Her father tightened his hold. 'That money is rightfully mine. I was your mother's husband. That is the law of the land.'

Julia would not allow herself to cower. 'Then, you shouldn't have signed the marriage contracts before you wed my mother. No doubt my trustees will be shocked to learn that you forced me to become a governess for Mrs Heap.'

Her father did not make a sound, but from behind him her stepmother, Mildred, did. She was holding Amelia's hand. Her half-sister seemed to have grown at least a head taller and her dark brown hair was much longer, nearly to her waist. Her little sister did not return Julia's smile, nor did her eyes meet her gaze. Julia's heart plummeted in her chest. Her sister was looking at her like a stranger.

Her stepmother had always been a dainty woman with pale features and light coloured hair, but in this moment her countenance was ghostly pale. 'Are you spending your daughter's inheritance?'

Julia wrenched her wrist from her father's grasp. 'Papa could only do so while I was a minor. Is that why you finally sent for me to come home? So that you could convince the trustees to release the funds to you for my care and upkeep?'

Mildred released her daughter's hand and turned to face her husband. 'Is that true?'

Papa's face turned an angry red. 'You can't believe Julia. You know that she is a spoiled and foolish child. She embarrassed you and your dear friend Lady Ballantine when she jilted her son.'

'Instead of offering insults, Eustace, you should be begging your daughter for her forgiveness and clemency,' Mildred said in her quiet voice. She walked to Julia and hugged her. 'I am glad you are home, dear. I am only sorry that I allowed your father to send you away to become a governess in the first place. I was taught by my parents and the church that a wife had to be obedient to her husband—but surely, a wife should not be obedient if her husband is behaving wrong? Still, he is my husband and if he will not ask for your mercy, I must, for the sake of myself and my daughter.'

Julia did not wish to hurt Mildred or Amelia. She loved them. Even if Amelia wouldn't look her in the eye. Julia took a deep breath. 'I will not seek redress for the three years I spent as governess, but I will not let my father spend another farthing of the yearly income from my inheritance.'

'You expect your own family to live in poverty? Selfish, unnatural girl,' her father screamed. Spittle dangled from the side of his mouth and her father looked angrier than she had ever seen him before. But he didn't scare her. Julia was no longer dependent upon him because Devin had explained how marriage contracts worked.

Devin.

It had only been a pair of hours, but she already missed his comforting presence, his handsome face and the courage she had found while in his company. As much as she had grown to care for him, Julia could not exchange one keeper for another. She no longer wished to be subject and obedient to any man. She didn't need anyone to *tell* her what to do.

Julia lifted her chin. 'I expect my father to live on the income from his own property and, if that is not enough money, to seek employment, as I have done. Working for my bread has taught me to appreciate the smallest of services—from a cup of hot tea to a freshly washed glove. Perhaps it will do the same for you, Papa.'

Now what was she supposed to do? Go back to one of the inns in Pickwich and wait until the mail coach heading towards London arrived? Julia didn't know when Devin intended to return to the capital. She could stay in a hotel until he came back. He would know exactly how to contact the trustees and to see that her yearly income was given directly into her hands. She trusted him with her money. If only he had asked for her heart…

Picking up her portmanteau with both hands, Julia looked back to Mildred and Amelia. 'Might I trouble your servants for a ride back to Pickwich? I carried my bag for a mile before and it was quite exhausting.'

'You can't leave, Julia!' Amelia shouted and ran to hug her sister. Since Julia was holding the portmanteau in both hands, it was an awkward side hug, but it warmed Julia's heart. Amelia had not forgotten her after all.

Mildred came towards them and took the portmanteau and set it back on the floor, which allowed Julia to properly hug her little sister. 'How I have missed you!'

A tear slipped down one of Amelia's cheeks. 'I thought that you had forgotten me. You left and never came back. And you never wrote.'

Julia glanced over her sister's head to her father's angry red face. 'I did not have a choice, poppet. Papa arranged for me to become a governess.'

'If you had to be a governess, why couldn't you have been mine?'

The last three years of her life had been pure drudgery and Julia had no wish to repeat them. But if she did not let go of her anger, she would be reliving those three years every day for the rest of her life. She would not cede any more power to her father or the Mrs Heaps of the world.

'Your sister did not have a choice, Amelia,' Mildred said, her voice louder and stronger than before. 'But she does now. Please stay with us. You're family. At least through Christmas and Twelfth Night. Amelia and I have missed you so much and we want to hear about everything you've done since we parted.'

Her stepmother looked at her husband as if to see if he was going to countermand her offer, but for once Julia's father was silent.

Mildred linked arms with both Julia and Amelia.

'Come, we must get ready for dinner, for we have invited guests. Happily all of your beautiful gowns are still in your wardrobe, Julia.' She stopped walking and looked at her stepdaughter. 'The baron and his mother are coming to dinner. I was hoping to bury all of the bad feelings between us and our neighbours. It is what Christmastime is about.'

Three days ago, Julia might not have been able to bury her resentment towards the Ballantine family, but since meeting Devin she could. Julia realised that both families had suffered from the very public scandal and only through a show of friendship between them would the old whispers finally die. 'And Christmastime is about family.'

Amelia dropped Julia's hand and put an arm around her waist. They walked that way until they reached Julia's old room. Mildred opened the door and Julia entered the bedchamber. It was larger and finer than she had remembered. It almost felt as if this room belonged to a different person—or that in the last three years Julia had become a different person.

'I will have the maids run you a bath and my own personal maid will come and assist you to dress and arrange your hair… Perhaps you and Baron Ballantine will be able to patch things up.'

Julia thanked her stepmother and gave her sister one last hug, before they left the room. She was grateful for a long, hot soak in the bath, as well as for some silent time for reflection. There was no patching things up between herself and Joshua. He'd never been hers to start with. But perhaps she could with Devin. They had made a great team. Even when she had loathed him, she had been terribly attracted to him. His intelligence. His strength. His humour. And mostly his heart.

If he came tonight.

And if Devin *asked* her instead of told.

Chapter Twelve

Julia felt more nervous waiting for the Ballantines to arrive than she had when a criminal had winked and jeered at her. She touched her curls—they were beautifully arranged around her face. It was a great improvement on Julia's usual chignon. Nor was she wearing a plain gown in a sombre colour: her celestial-blue dress was three years out of fashion but still beautiful. The neckline was cut low across her bosom and the sleeves were short and puffed. The skirt was ornamented with three flounces. But what Julia loved best were the long gloves that had been tinted blue to match her gown. She felt transformed like Cinderella.

The sound of horses and a carriage caused her to jump. Mildred placed her hand on top of Julia's and lightly squeezed it. Her stepmother probably thought that she was embarrassed to see Joshua. But Julia could hardly tell her that she'd been compromised by her former betrothed's younger brother and, incidentally, had become besotted with him.

The butler opened the door to the parlour and announced Baron and Baroness Ballantine (Joshua and Devin's mother), Mr Ballantine, and Mr Ashby. Julia's family all stood and then bowed to their guests.

To Julia's surprise, Mildred walked up to Mr Ashby and shook his hand warmly. 'I am so glad that you suggested we make amends between the families, Mr Ashby.'

Mr Ashby, who was dark-haired like Joshua, bowed his head. 'I for one am pleased that you offered the olive branch and invited us to dinner this evening.'

The sour expression on Baroness Ballantine's face was less pleased. But Julia didn't care what she thought. Her eyes sought Devin's and she saw a smile grow slowly on his face until it reached his mismatched eyes that intrigued her so much.

'No one is as pleased as myself,' Devin said in a loud voice, 'for I have apologies to make to you all. You might have already heard the damaging rumours that have been spread throughout the village. Sir Eustace and Lady Sullivan, I am sorry that I claimed to be your daughter's husband on our journey here, but I can assure you that I did so for her safety from two known criminals and I did not compromise her in any way. I am a man of honour and Julia is a virtuous woman. I know that it is untoward, but I was wondering if I might have a private word with your daughter? I also owe her an apology for my behaviour this morning. I told her something rather than asked her, and I should like a second chance.'

Her father scowled and Mildred's gaze went from Devin's smiling face to Joshua's benign expression and back to Devin's in wonderment. Devin was not the suitor her stepmother had been expecting. Mildred rubbed her gloved hand over her opposite arm and answered for both of them, 'I suppose so, but not for long, Mr Ballantine. Unless you would like to speak to my husband first to ask for his permission to pay your addresses to his daughter?'

Devin shook his head. 'A woman can decide her own future.'

'Indeed? How the times have changed, Lady Ballantine,' Mildred said, glancing at the other matron for support. But the other lady did not speak. And her husband merely scowled. Mildred made a funny little sound, half cough, half giggle. 'Well, if there are no objections. I mean, unless Julia is not inclined to meet privately with Mr Ballantine.'

'I should like to speak with him, stepmother,' Julia said, moving across the room to Devin. Her pulse was racing like a rabbit jumping. When she reached him, he held out his arm for her and Julia curved her fingers around his elbow. 'I will take him to the Yellow Parlour.'

Mildred clapped her gloved hands together. 'Excellent choice, for that room is next door to this one. And allow me to remind you, Mr Ballantine, that the abbey walls are very thin. No more than ten minutes alone. For I must think of my stepdaughter's reputation.'

Which was hopelessly in tatters.

Broadwick Abbey's walls were made from thick stone, but Julia couldn't help but appreciate her stepmother's attempts at guarding what was left of her virtue and good name. The butler opened the door to the grand hall and they walked to the adjacent room and closed the door behind them. She released her hold on his arm. Julia's heart was thudding in her chest and her throat felt dry. She let out a long sigh of both nervousness and relief.

'Surely you are too young for such sighs, Miss Sullivan.'

Devin had repeated Mrs Mack's words from when they first met on the mail coach. Despite her trembling body, Julia giggled. Devin grinned at her in the sort of way that made her knees feel weak. 'I believe you know to the day how old I am, Mr Ballantine.'

'I know that today did not go how I would have hoped, and according to my brother, the blame is entirely my own,' Devin said, his gorgeous blue and green eyes burning into her own. 'I thought to make a proper speech, but Joshua warned me that was also a mistake. That I had talked too much and listened too little. So I mean to do better.' Devin lowered himself to one knee. 'Julia, what would you like me to do to make this right?'

She felt heat creep up her neck and into her face. Devin was humbling himself before her. He was asking Julia what she wanted. No man had ever done what she'd asked him to. None but Devin. She wrung her hands. She did not know what she wanted. Or, rather, she wanted more time. Julia had nearly been married to a stranger once before and she did not wish to do so for a second time. She had only known Devin for a few days. In that time they'd been strangers, enemies and then flirtatious friends. Warm feelings were already planted in her heart, but they needed time and nourishment to grow. And she wanted Devin to propose marriage to her not because he had compromised her good name but because he loved her and needed to be by her side. Yet how to put her thoughts into words?

Julia glanced down again at Devin on bended knee. She had once believed that she wanted power over the other people in her life rather than them having power over her. But it was not true. She did not want Devin to bow to her. She wanted to be his equal in all ways. So Julia carefully knelt and asked, 'Devin, what would you like me to do to make this right?'

'I should like to marry you, Julia, for you have stolen my heart and my wits.'

'You didn't have much of either.'

Devin chuckled and grinned lovingly at her, taking both of her hands into his larger ones. 'I would argue with you, termagant, but in my proposal this morning I lacked both… I suppose it was easier for me to pretend that I only wanted to marry you to save your reputation rather than to admit that I had fallen hopelessly in love with you.' He gulped and she could see his Adam's apple bob up and down. 'I spoke to Joshua and it appears that the blame of the engagement is entirely my mother's. He never asked you to marry him. Nor did he sign the marriage contracts—they were forged by my mother. And Joshua saw no way out of the wedding without disgracing you and our mother. But *you* were unbelievably brave. You saved my brother from a marriage he did not want and kept a secret that could have exonerated you and badly damaged his reputation. You paid for your bravery with three years of servitude and then I wrongfully accused you and threatened legal action. Then I treated you shabbily. I do not know how to atone.'

Squeezing his hands, Julia smiled back at him. 'And I treated you so nicely too, hedge-bird.'

His laugh echoed off the stone walls and perhaps even her diligent stepmother heard it. 'You're ruining my beautiful, heartfelt apology.'

'And you're ruining my courtship,' Julia countered. 'You haven't kissed me even once. That is, if you wish to court me and kiss me... I am not yet ready to accept your marriage offer, but I believe I will be, given time to get to know you better.'

Devin definitely wished to court her and to kiss her. He knew only one way to answer her query. He released her hands and gently cupped Julia's cheek, caressing her delicate skin with his fingers. Leaning his forehead against hers, Devin used his free arm to pull Julia closer to him, her body flush with his own. He brushed a gentle kiss against her forehead and he could feel her trembling in his arms. He rubbed a circle on her back. 'Whisht, darling. It's only a kiss.'

She stiffened in his arms. 'I've never been kissed before. What do I do?'

Devin made a row of kisses from her temple to her chin, before caressing her lower lip with his thumb. 'Take a breath or you'll faint and miss the entire thing.'

Julia moaned and made one of those sweet noises she had while sleeping that had inflamed him so. 'Rudesby.'

He kissed the tip of her nose. 'Peagoose.'

'Ramshackle,' Julia said but surprised Devin by putting her arms around his neck.

He nuzzled beneath her ear. 'Goose-cap.'

'Blunderhead.'

Unable to think up a suitable retort to deliver with his mouth, Devin gently brushed his lips against Julia's. It was even more marvellous than his fantasies. Her lips were sweet and soft, like the petals of a rose. He moved his mouth back and forth over hers several times. This was Julia's first kiss and Devin needed it to be perfect. She trusted him with all of her firsts and he wanted to make them wonderful for her.

Lifting her head slightly, he kissed the tip of her saucy chin.

'I take all of my insults back,' Julia said in a husky voice, her eyes fluttering open to look at him. 'That was marvellous.'

'We are only beginning.'

'Truly?'

Devin decided that action was better than words. He licked the seam of her lips and Julia opened her mouth for him. He tasted her with slow, drugging kisses, before slipping his tongue into her mouth. He felt her lush body stiffen against his for a moment, but then her arms tightened around his neck and Devin felt her tongue brush his. Julia was tentative at first, but not for long. Her demanding personality could not allow him to be in charge the entire time, even for a kiss. Her tongue tangled with his and her hands moved from his neck to his hair. Devin couldn't resist doing the same. Julia's honey-gold hair had seduced him from the start. He deftly removed the hair-pins until her curls fell long and heavy down her back. Devin's fingers ran through her hair and he deepened the kiss—exploring every delicious corner of her mouth.

Then he made a trail of burning kisses from her mouth to her throat. The noises she made were positively inde-cent and Devin relished every single sound. He made a slow burn of kisses from her throat to her ear and sucked on the tip of it.

She moaned and then said his name. Her hands stilled in his hair.

Devin couldn't stop himself. He continued to lick and tease her ear with his tongue. 'What's on your mind, sweetheart?'

'Before you court me, you should know that I am not trustworthy, Devin. I peeked at you while you were changing—more than once.'

'So did I—I could see your reflection in the window.'

Leaning back from him, Julia's mouth fell open in mock surprise and she cuffed his shoulder with one hand. 'I thought you were a gentleman. You odious hornswog-gler!'

'And I thought you were a gentlewoman, my *infamous* lady.'

Julia's face was flushed and her lips swollen and red from his kisses. She'd never looked more beautiful. 'Did—did you see much?'

Devin winked at her. 'Yes.'

Her eyes grew and her mouth widened into a perfect O. 'Scapegrace.'

'Did you like what *you* saw, my little baggage?'

She pursed her lips and shook her head. 'No.'

'What a fibster,' Devin said, tracing her collarbone with gentle fingers.

Julia sucked in a breath and then whimpered when he moved his hand away from her skin. She grabbed his hand and put it back on her collarbone. 'I might have prevaricated a little.'

'It was a complete bouncer.'

She made a noise of assent, for he was caressing the square collar of her gown—which seemed to make her body boneless against his. Devin couldn't resist covering her mouth with his and kissing her one last time. Thoroughly.

The walls of Broadwick Abbey might not have been thick, but if Devin wasn't careful he would well and truly compromise Julia before they had time for the courtship she needed. He forced himself to get to his feet and pulled her up next to him, making his blood boil with need for her.

Attempting to repair her fallen curls, the tips of Julia's ears turned pink. 'Did you like what you saw? I mean, me?'

'I can hardly wait to court you. Does that answer your question?'

'Yes.'

'Would you mind coming to London after the holiday so that we can continue our courtship? I must return to Lincoln's Inn and my clients.'

'Yes, but we must travel to Town together,' Julia said,

surprising Devin by giving him a hot, wet kiss. 'The London road is quite dangerous. There are thieves on the loose and I don't know if you're up on all the rigs.'

'Thanks to you, my love, there are two less thieves on the loose. I placed information with the constable and he arrested them both. The bridle culls are currently locked up tight in the roundhouse and will travel back to London on the next mail coach for their trial.'

'You still might need me.'

Despite wanting nothing more than to kiss her, Devin's lips curled up into a smile. Courting Julia would never be dull. 'I will not go anywhere without you again.'

'Good, because we need to go to Christmas dinner,' she said, rising up on tiptoes and kissing the tip of his nose. 'I believe that our ten minutes have passed and our families are waiting for us. And I should put my horrible father and my poor stepmother out of their misery.'

Devin put his hand in hers. 'Lead the way, Julia.'

* * * * *

Regency Slang

All the rigs: all the tricks.

Baggage: a synonym for woman.

Bailey's Jug: the Old Bailey was a criminal court which had Newgate Prison nearby.

Basket-scrambler: one who lives on charity.

Blunderhead: a stupid, inept person.

Bosky: drunk.

Bouncer: a lie.

Bridle cull: a thief.

Chaw-bacon: a stupid man; a country bumpkin.

Corker: someone that is astonishing or excellent.

Fibster: a liar.

Flash-cove: a thief or a fence.

Foxed: drunk.

Gammon: deceitful nonsense.

Goose-cap: a flighty young girl.

Gudgeon: a person who is easily duped or cheated.

Gull-catcher: a trickster or a cheat.

Havey-cavey: helter-skelter.

Hedge-bird: a vagrant or a vagabond.

Hell-born babe: a lewd, graceless youth, one naturally of a wicked disposition.

Hornswoggler: a swindler or cheat.

Hoyden: a boisterous, carefree girl.

Infamous: having an extremely bad reputation.

Mucked: ruined.

Peagoose: a poor simpleton, a ninny.

Rackety: noisy or rowdy.

Ramshackle: thoughtless or reckless person.

Rudesby: an uncivil, turbulent person.

Saucy: impertinently bold and impudent.

Scapegrace: an incorrigible rascal.

Simpleton: a person lacking common sense.

Termagant: an overbearing or nagging woman.

Totty-headed: silly or frivolous.

Whisker: a falsehood or whopping lie.

MILLS & BOON®

Coming next month

A MARQUESS TO REMEMBER
Jenni Fletcher

Florence's nostrils flared, as if she were restraining her temper with an effort. 'I still think there has to be a way out of this marriage.'

'There isn't.'

'So that's it?' She stared up at Leo with an appalled expression. 'You're just going to give up?'

'Yes.' He sighed, feeling very tired all of a sudden. This whole argument seemed to have been revolving around his head for weeks. Ironically, tonight was the first time he'd involved her in the discussion, but every time, he'd come to the same disheartening conclusion, that there was no way out. The marriage trap had well and truly closed around him. 'Now I think that's enough of a tour for tonight. I suggest that we both retire and get some sleep.'

'Well, that explains it.' She rose slowly to her feet, her gaze still fixed on his. 'That's why you look at me like so coldly, like you despise me. It's because you do.'

'What else did you expect?' He didn't deny it. 'This marriage isn't what I wanted.'

'Me neither, no matter what you think.' She wrenched her shoulders back. 'All I know is that there has to be some reasonable explanation for what happened and I'm going to find out what it is.'

He looked her up and down, impressed despite himself. With her chin in the air and a fierce glare on her face, she looked magnificently, almost regally defiant. If he weren't still so angry, he thought he might have been tempted to reach out and haul her against him, to stop her mouth with his own.

'Then I wish you luck.'

Continue reading

A MARQUESS TO REMEMBER
Jenni Fletcher

Available next month
millsandboon.co.uk

COMING SOON!

We really hope you enjoyed reading this book.
If you're looking for more romance
be sure to head to the shops when
new books are available on

Thursday 18th December

To see which titles are coming soon, please visit

millsandboon.co.uk/nextmonth